SHE IS HIS WITNESS

# SHE IS HIS WITNESS

## BIRTH OF HEAVY METAL™ BOOK 2

MICHAEL TODD

MICHAEL ANDERLE

DISRUPTIVE IMAGINATION

# THE SHE IS HIS WITNESS TEAM

## JIT Readers

Nicole Emens
John Ashmore
Jeff Eaton
Crystal Wren
Peter Manis
James Caplan
Paul Westman
Kelly O'Donnell
Kelly Ethan
Joshua Ahles

## Editor
Skyhunter Editing Team

# DEDICATION

*To Family, Friends and*
*Those Who Love*
*to Read.*
*May We All Enjoy Grace*
*to Live the Life We Are*
*Called.*

# CHAPTER ONE

The ground shook and the air reverberated with the enraged sounds of hostile creatures and gunfire. The odd shout here and there from the humans punctuated the cacophony. Sal gripped his weapon tighter. He raised his free hand to wipe sweat from his face and blinked when his hand tapped against his facemask.

Funny how you forgot basic shit in the middle of a firefight.

"Jacobs, if you can spare the time?" Kennedy shouted from the ground below him. "I know getting your head stuck in your ass is a full-time job, but if you could unstick it, I'd really appreciate the help down here."

*Right.* He nodded and maintained his higher vantage point for a few seconds longer. While he'd determined the lay of the land, Kennedy had dropped down the smaller cliff to hopefully thin the ranks of the animals which massed relentlessly below. Her plan had been to try to keep a path clear in the event that he saw a way out of the massive bowl that they'd found themselves in, but so far, she'd only managed to ensure that the beasts didn't scale the cliff to where he was.

Which was a good thing, since he couldn't see jack shit through the thick tree cover, much less an escape route.

Okay, he was done having his head up his ass.

Sal glanced at the scene below and narrowed his eyes. Kennedy dealt with the locusts for the most part, but more than a few of the panthers and a fair number of other reptiles that he'd never seen before circled like they used the locusts as meat shields.

That was the thing about the Zoo, he thought with a smile. There would always be something out there to surprise you. He took a few steps to the right, and his armor seemed to move before he even formed the thought. Without hesitation, he jumped, cleared the cliff face with room to spare, and dropped the fifteen or so meters down to where Kennedy fought. As he executed a perfect three-point landing a few paces to the right of her, his armored fist struck one of the circling panthers.

"Superhero landing," he said with a grin and raised his gun in the other hand to shoot at a couple of the locusts that had started to flank her. "Hell yeah."

Sal didn't have to see her to know that she had rolled her eyes. He'd come to terms with the fact that she either didn't get his pop culture references or simply didn't care enough about them to comment while they were in the middle of a firefight. That was okay. Nobody was perfect.

"Did you find us a way out of here?" she asked over the comms.

"Nope." He kept his voice even. "The whole place is an

overgrown jungle, so I honestly wouldn't have been able to see anything anyway."

"Is that what all these trees are?" Kennedy growled, her sarcastic side momentarily revealed as she dropped her empty magazine and let the mechanism slip another into her assault rifle. "Hot damn, I knew we should have come with something that can see through the fucking trees."

Sal gritted his teeth to hold back his instinctive retort. Sure, a satellite feed would have been fantastic but was sadly out of their reach. She was merely annoyed that he had done better than she had, and he didn't need to say anything to make it worse.

"Hypocrite," he said and covered with a fake sneeze.

"What was that?" she asked and raised an eyebrow.

"Nothing," he replied innocently and ran a quick check of his equipment before he moved forward again. "Just... allergies. From all the pollen. We are surrounded by a menagerie of alien plants, you know."

"Right, and I'm sure you forgot to add a filter to your new state of the art suit of heavy armor," Kennedy retorted and moved in behind him. As they inched forward, the animals seemed to back away. They probably merely regrouped for another attack since they didn't seem the types to give up on fresh meat made crunchy by new suits of armor.

"Come on, don't be jealous that I got the newer, shinier, and better suit of armor, Kennedy," Sal said with a teasing grin and turned to face her.

"The fact that it's bullshit that a specialist geek like you gets to try out the new gunner combat armor is irrelevant," Kennedy returned with a growl.

"Hey, you made a good run for the test, but you failed," Sal said and turned away once more. "No harm, no foul. You'll do better once they restructure the Interface to the average gunner's stats."

"The test was bullshit," she grumbled under her breath.

Sal heard it and gasped. "You take that back. Don't blame the tests."

"You designed the test for people like you to be the only ones who can pass," she said belligerently as they continued their slow progress through the jungle.

"Well, since I was the one who designed it, of course it leans toward my style of operating," he said defensively. "Your style is a lot more reliant on reflex and reaction and less on control. Power armor requires far more control. Of course, they take these tests to the lab and adapt the suit with some sort of movement AI and then it doesn't matter." Sal paused to push a series of vines aside to allow Kennedy to pass. She did but flipped him the armored middle finger of her suit as she pushed through.

"I need to be able to react quickly," she growled. "Control won't help me when something jumps at me and I only have a blink of an eye to aim and shoot it. You're saying that years of training and experience are a bad thing here."

Sal shook his head. "I'm not. I'm saying that when using power armor, if you move too quickly or you force the armor to move faster than your body is able to, you'll break bones and tear muscles until you adjust to it. Control is necessary. At least until they push the AI that would prevent that from happening past the development stage."

Again, he didn't need to see her to know that she rolled

her eyes. She knew he was right. That was the reason why he'd been called in to help with the general development. It wasn't because they didn't want gunners to use these armor UIs, but rather because they needed a benchmark to work from. As long as they paid his hourly rate, he was more than happy to oblige.

Kennedy knew that, and he knew she understood. Despite her blustery exterior, she was smarter than most of the gunners brought to the Zoo, and honestly, a much better fighter than most of them. The fact that all that came with attitude and sass to spare made it the deal of the century, even though he had still barely begun the learning curve on how to handle it. The more he got to know her, the more he discovered vast pools of sass waiting to be discovered along with…other things.

Sal was suddenly very happy that she couldn't read his thoughts through the comm system. Not that mind reading AIs would ever be a thing.

Hopefully.

He came to a halt when she stopped abruptly and raised her hand with her fist closed. His body tensed instinctively as he glanced around and his armor reacted instantaneously. He'd added a design that enabled it to use the sensors to detect if the user was in danger of attack or prepared for combat. A few of the combat programs started up and with the armor bunched, although it made for less efficient movement, it protected the vital areas far better.

They'd probably scrap it in the end product, but it had been a good idea anyway.

"What?" Sal asked when he saw nothing to suggest a

problem. The entire Zoo had gone suspiciously quiet, but other than that, there didn't seem to be any obvious imminent danger for them to deal with.

"Motion sensors," Kennedy said tersely.

He nudged the relevant button with his chin and switched his HUD's view to motion sensor. Carefully, he scanned their surroundings. Immediately beyond the view of the naked eye, he saw the jungle awash with movement from the animals all around them. He turned around slowly and made sure to keep his gun raised and ready.

Yup, they were completely surrounded.

"I've started to feel really iffy about our decision to abandon the cliff face as a defensible position," Kennedy said, and all the sarcasm and amusement had dropped from her voice. She was all business now. Sal had seen her slip from casual to combat in seconds, and it never failed to send a tingle up his spine. He'd never been sure if it was a good or a bad feeling, but it was incredibly real, there was no denying that.

"You have any more of those...smoke grenades?" He asked, his voice edged with a steely note. They were in some serious shit. He'd been in enough engagements like this to know that. It was chilling how easily these different species managed to work together and how they used reciprocal tactics despite not being even remotely similar in type. The goop in their bodies seemed to resonate and rise above the basic animal instincts to create a shared purpose and unity.

Sometimes, anyway. He'd also watched them hunt each other down, as you'd expect from a thriving ecosystem.

Carnivorous predators always hunted omnivorous or herbivorous prey, even when it came to alien animals.

"I have the one that you gave me," Kennedy confirmed in response and retrieved the grenade from her suit. He'd given it to her when they'd split up the first time and hadn't even noticed that she'd used one while he was on the top of the cliff. That annoyed him more than anything she could have said. He held himself to higher standards than anybody else could these days. Gone was the slacker doctoral candidate who had faced the prospect of running into the Zoo for the first time with shaking knees.

The animals reacted like they'd waited for a snap of the fingers from some controlling force, and when that invisible command came, they obeyed with a hungry need. They attacked in a single wave without any reliance on tactics like the last battle. Then, they had used the locusts as shields while the stronger, deadlier animals waited on the fringes for the opportunity to go for the jugular.

Not this time. They rushed forward like a solid wall and closed in from all sides, unified ranks of all kinds of creatures that rushed to overwhelm the two invaders.

Their strategy would work. That much was obvious mere seconds into the attack. Sal found weak spots as he and Kennedy stood back to back and fought the animals off after she dropped the smoke grenade. Despite the smoke cover, they would still be able to locate them.

He maintained his fire with his assault rifle as he drew the sidearm from his hip with his free hand. Driven by pure instinct, he used the smaller weapon to push individual beasts back as they tried to force their way in closer.

"Fuck!" Kennedy shouted, and Sal saw in a rear camera

that one of the panthers had laid hold of her rifle arm as another gripped the other hand which held a knife. One of the reptiles lunged at her face and spat a foul-smelling acid that instantly ate into her facemask. A scream echoed through their comms as she dropped to the ground.

"Madie!" Sal called. He spun and shot the reptile three times with his sidearm as his rifle sprayed lead into the rest in an effort to drive them clear of her body. It worked for a moment until his guns clicked empty.

He made a mental note to add a quicker reload mechanism to the guns as the creatures' deadly claws raked his back. The armor withstood the assault for longer than Kennedy's did, but it wasn't long before he was crushed face down and the armor was torn off.

"Fuck."

# CHAPTER TWO

"Fuck," Sal said again and watched the simulation fade around him. The pain in these sims had never been that convincing, but he assumed that was by design. This wasn't a medical sim, after all. It was meant simply to test the combat software and armor designs in a safe environment, and they couldn't really do that if testers knew they would be traumatized. Aside from the fact that they'd be unlikely to find volunteers, there were likely moral reasons and also some very real legal reasons that kept the odd psychopath in charge from releasing their inner Hannibal Lecter.

Hopefully.

He felt the disconnect from his suit. It opened enough for him to pull himself free on his own, but Kennedy already stood over him and helped him up.

"I still think your whole testing thing is bullshit, by the way," she snarked as he stretched. As real as the simulation felt, once you got out of it, you still felt as if you had been lying down for however long it was that the sim ran. A good stretch was definitely required.

"You only say that because you didn't pass," Sal replied with a grin but held a hand up to stop her reply. "We can do this all day. We've done this all day. It's obvious we won't reach a consensus."

Kennedy shrugged. "Yep, you're pretty damn right on that."

He nodded. "Well, I'll try to be more inclusive of gunners next time I'm asked to help with armor software development in the testing stage."

"Appreciated," she said with a grin as they prepared to move outside. As far as testing facilities went, this was relatively a bare-bones facility considering that millions of dollars went into the suits they currently trialed in the Zoo. It was a good place to test them so that they could be mass-produced and sold in other fighting fronts. As with any animal carcasses in the wild, vultures surrounded the Zoo and found dozens of especially creative ways to turn a profit from the disaster that the place had become.

*Does that make me one of those vultures?* Sal wondered as he studied the EKG results from their time in the sim. His were fairly standard. It wasn't particularly important for the test apart from the fact that it enabled the control units to monitor the stability of the subjects, but he liked reports on his mental acuity while in a combat situation. There would obviously always be a small part of his mind that told him he wasn't really in combat and it was all a simulation. The monkey brain in him would inevitably keep him from going full fight or flight, but this was as close as he would ever get to being able to evaluate himself in a stressful environment, and he simply couldn't pass up the opportunity.

He forwarded the results to his work email for a more in-depth study when he arrived home and turned to join Kennedy as she made her way out of the tent where they ran the sim. Again, the bare bones operation prevailed with only a tent erected as a barrier to keep the test subjects isolated from the other people in the building. The conditions weren't as sterile as he liked his testing facilities to be, but he'd already raised the situation a couple of times with those in control and each time, they told him they were working on improvements. He'd now simply stopped talking about it.

They moved out of the tent together, where a team of scientists waited for them. They already had the technical data, but they needed the personal opinions of the people who took part in the tests. That was why they'd brought the whole operation to the Staging Area since they wanted the input from the men and women who were actually in the middle of it all to obtain a better view of what they needed to improve.

"The armor's still shit," Kennedy stated first and rolled her shoulder. Sal remembered that it was where one of the panthers had bitten through her suit. Phantom pain was a common effect of simulations. It had people up in arms all across the world regarding the psychological problems that came with it, but when the people in the simulations had endured far worse situations in actual combat, it no longer seemed to be a significant problem.

"Noted," the scientist said and tapped away at a pad. "Was the performance unsatisfactory?"

"The performance was fine," she said and tilted her head. "But I think that some bugs need to be worked out. It still moves too slowly. Power armor should increase speed, not bog it down."

"She's merely jealous that I rocked it with the new power armor," Sal said and interrupted her complaint with a grin. The scientist didn't look up, but Kennedy did with a smirk.

"That armor is too heavy to be used properly in the Zoo, and you know it, Jacobs," she said with a chuckle. "Unless they scale it up to be basically a tank on two legs, it'll be way too big and too unwieldy in actual combat."

"They can't scale it up," he explained yet again. "The laws of physics would have some things to say about it as it crunched to the ground under its own weight."

"We operate outside the laws of physics out here, Jacobs," she said and emphasized his last name. "Or haven't you noticed?"

She had a point on two levels. He knew he'd made a mistake when he'd called her by her first name in the simulation. They'd had talks about him never calling her Madie, and certainly not calling her anything other than Kennedy while they were out in the field. It was a matter of professionalism. And the fact that she hated to have her first name shortened under any circumstances.

The scientist nodded and ignored their banter for the most part. "Do you feel any side effects from the run?"

She shook her head. "Only a little phantom pain in the shoulder. It should be gone in a few minutes."

"Okay, good," the man said and passed the pad to Kennedy. "If the effects last longer than half an hour, please consult a doctor. Lay out your review of the simulation here and let the biometric scan sign it for you."

"Will do." She smiled and took the pad from him as he moved to her partner. He followed the same checkup procedure, but Sal noted that the man conducted it much quicker and with far more professionalism than hers had been run with.

Sal chuckled as he sat down beside Kennedy.

"I think the good doc has a bit of a crush on you," he said with a grin as the man moved out of earshot. He hoped, anyway.

"Can you blame him?" she answered absently and tilted her head as she tapped out a quick review of the simulation. "And speaking of crushes, what's with shouting 'Madie' in the middle of the sim, hmm?"

Sal shrugged. "Yeah, I know, I know. Rules haven't changed, and to everyone else, our relationship is supposed to look platonic—merely friends with no suggestion of anything more. Still, I'd do the same if we were only friends, so I don't know what you're complaining about."

"Don't think I don't think it's cute, because I do," Madigan said although she didn't look up from the screen in her hands. "But it's hard enough to maintain my reputation as a badass around here without you undermining it by coming to my rescue like the world's most inept knight in power armor."

He nodded and sighed. "Yeah, I get that. Sorry. And also for using your first name. Always Kennedy while in the field. It's...reflex, I guess."

She smiled as she finished her review and let the machine capture her data for the biometric signature as she glanced at him. "I appreciate your understanding, Jacobs. Believe me, I do. It's why I agreed to work with you in the first place."

Sal finished his own review, complete with a few notes about the armor that he'd worn since it was his first time in the simulator with that particular suit. Kennedy was right. The armor was too big to be viable as anything but a shield against more agile combatants. He added a few notes that they could possibly fit it with an actual metal shield to help with that, but he doubted it would be put into action. They'd need to run much larger teams into the Zoo than they had thus far for something like that to even be a factor.

Besides, there were lizards out there that could spit metal-melting acid, so a shield was less than useless unless they came up with a reinforcement material that would be strong enough to fend off physical attacks as well as the acid.

He sighed and set the pad down once he had finished. Kennedy waited at the door of the building. She smiled when he moved toward her, and they stepped out into the blazing Sahara sunlight.

"The money's already in our accounts," she said with a chuckle. "That's one of the best things about working for corporations. They may be bastards, but they paid their money out on time. All the military stuff takes hours of red tape before they make payment. I'm surprised that they haven't already had some congressional hearings about what is spent here."

"They have..." Sal answered and checked his phone quickly for confirmation that the money was already in their accounts. Five grand for a couple hours' work in the morning wasn't too bad, he thought, and it was also a good way to keep one's reflexes honed between trips into the Zoo.

"Huh?" Kennedy grunted, and Sal realized that he'd trailed off in the middle of his explanation. He blinked against the glare and shrugged as he made a face.

"Oh," he said with a chuckle. "Yeah, two congressional hearings and one in the Senate, even though those guys have nothing to do with the budget. There's a lot of press and politics around the Zoo, and there are many people asking questions that they could get answers to with a quick internet search. Anyway, all three hearings ended with the same basic conclusion. This whole operation is run on corporate money, and military spending is kept to a minimum. That added to the amount of money that actually comes out of here made everyone agree that it would be best for their reelection campaigns to keep their paws off the Zoo. If something goes wrong, they can simply blame the corporations, fine them, and sigh in relief that this is happening on the other side of the planet and a long way from American soil."

Kennedy gave him an odd look as she hopped into the vehicle that they'd rented for the day. "You've put a lot of thought into this, haven't you?"

Sal shrugged and clambered up beside her. "I have to, don't I? Considering that we're technically one of these independent corporations?"

"I guess," she conceded and started the engine. He knew from some of their talks that most soldiers around there hated the kind of red tape that went with the US military, and many of them had joined this operation for the simple reason that there was little to no actual oversight and things happened without any real repercussions.

That plus the massive amount of money they could make if they survived multiple trips into the Zoo.

"I'm in need of a drink," Kennedy said. She put the JLTV into drive and moved across the road as the desert wind blew flurries of sand over it. He looked into the distance and mentally measured the stretch of desert before it faded into the massive green swathe that began to take over more of the horizon each day. He didn't like that. It was spreading faster than they'd anticipated.

"It's barely twelve-thirty PM," Sal said but leaned back and put on a pair of sunglasses. "But I could go for a drink too. They're serving meals at the bar now, right?"

# CHAPTER THREE

I wasn't made for this.

She'd been called in to do the regular specialist job, but each successive visit seemed to demand more and more from her on every level. The Zoo grew faster than anybody could have imagined or calculated. That truth made all the news channels and received the attention, but nobody wanted to talk about the shit that actually happened inside.

The plants and animals presented a real problem to the teams that made the runs into the Zoo for the Pita flowers. The animals grew more and more dangerous with each mission, and lately, the squads even had to deal with plants that were not only carnivorous but also far more aggressive. The vegetation clearly viewed the humans as a food source and showed little concern about where their meat came from and what it was wrapped in. Teams had often found old suits of armor that had been cracked open from the outside with the user gone.

Seeing shit like that wasn't good for morale any way

you cut it. It was even worse that the bodies very clearly hadn't been recovered for the purpose of identifying the dead. Were they unregulated bounty hunters or troops sent in from the Staging Area? Did they have family who needed to be notified? What had done the nasty and would the same thing happen to anybody on their squad?

These weren't questions that you wanted to be asked if you ran a team into the Zoo. Courtney had done what she could to identify the dead. This mostly meant she would identify the pin numbers on the suits and radio them to the Staging Area with her sat phone when they had a strong enough connection. Aside from that, there wasn't much else that she could do.

And that didn't help morale either. They needed a specialist, but the gunners did the brunt of the work—or so they thought. Since they didn't divide the teams into squads and instead, ran as a full unit, they now wondered why it was necessary to bring two specialists when only one would do.

It was a fair question and one that had been answered by the Zoo itself when the other specialist in their squad went down. She was the only one left, but somehow the rest of her team also expected her to be so much more than merely a specialist. When another member of their team— a gunner—went down, the leader handed her his assault rifle, and from that point forward, she had been expected to fulfill the role of a gunner to the best of her ability.

Nobody had been particularly surprised when her doctorate failed to transfer the skills of carrying loads with inferior armor or skills with the firearm.

She gripped the gun tighter. While she knew she wasn't

much good, her team relied on her to do her job anyway. She was a part of the line, and they needed her to hold it. On an earlier run—it felt like centuries ago, now— she'd gained experience under fire. After that first time, she'd begun to take a variety of guns to the Staging Area's range and practiced firing them there, but that didn't make her an expert out in the field.

Conway, one of the gunners that she'd worked with before, stood beside her to hold the line and helped to cover her line of fire when it was needed. The animals were a lot more aggressive than they'd been a few months before, but they still hadn't had to deal with anything like the waves and waves of creatures that she remembered from that life-changing trip.

There were other reasons to remember that run, she mused. It had been her first time to actually have to handle a gun as a specialist, and that wasn't the kind of thing someone forgot. But it had also been the first time she'd met Salinger Jacobs.

Youthful and inexperienced as he had been, he'd still left an impression on her that she'd tried to shake ever since. He'd stepped up when his squad needed him and earned respect that way, even though—as she'd discovered when they'd talked later—he'd been tricked into being there.

She remembered thinking at the time that if anything like that had happened to her, she would have been on the first flight out of there and talked to a reparations lawyer as soon as she set foot on American soil. She could probably have retired with the money that came from that. Or more realistically, set herself up in some high-end university with a cushy tenure job where she could pick and choose her projects while occasionally giving lectures.

Sal had stayed. He stuck it out for another job. And another. He was now a very familiar face around the Staging Area, and he and Sergeant Madigan Kennedy had broken away and started their own company. What had they called it again? Heavy Metal? Either way, they had expanded their work and were paid a lot better than she remembered being paid. That showed that despite his age and lack of experience, he had a good eye for business as well as being a kid genius and a much better specialist-gunner than she could ever hope to be.

Courtney had been attracted to him. She even came on to him in the bar once they'd gotten back from that first mission, but he'd rebuffed her, and when he teamed up with Kennedy, she understood why. Some guys simply liked the warrior woman type.

She felt her foot catch on a root, stumbled forward, and almost fell on her face before an arm caught her around the chest.

"Stay focused," Conway admonished and kept his eyes forward. He had used his free arm to prevent her fall, but his weapon remained aimed into the foliage.

"There's nothing I'd like to see more than her face on the ground," one of the other members of the squad said with a laugh. "That way, her more valuable assets are easier to access. What's the point of having a female scientist anyways?"

"Shut it, Wayne," Conway growled. The other man chuckled and proceeded without apparent concern at the rebuke. "Misogynistic bastard."

"I have no idea what 'misogynistic' means," Wayne retorted with a grin. "How the hell can I be something if I don't know what it is?"

Conway flipped the man off as they continued to move forward.

"Where do they grow these assholes?" Courtney asked as she shook her head and gripped her rifle with both hands.

"On some tree somewhere," he answered with a chuckle. "Ignore them. You're doing more than what you're actually paid for, so that's definitely a win in my book."

"Actually, they restructured my contract," Courtney responded. It was hard to talk while on the move, since walking under this much weight meant that she would struggle to catch her breath without the added challenge of speech. "This kind of thing is apparently what I'm supposed to do out here. Well, technically, run support in any capacity as required by the squad leader. So, yeah."

"Any capacity?" Wayne shouted from the front of the line. "Hey, I think I may need a couple of—"

"If you finish that sentence, I will feed you the butt of your rifle, I swear to God, Wayne," Conway snapped at the man, who merely chuckled and pressed on.

"You don't need to stand up for me, you know," Courtney muttered and tried to focus on her breathing. "And it's probably better if you don't. I don't want to be seen as a fragile female to guys like that, someone who needs a man to protect her. It only makes it worse when you have to be somewhere else to protect the rest of the squad, you know?"

He nodded. "I can't help it. I hate bullies, and Wayne is

the worst of the bunch. I'm not sure where they grew him, but he's definitely a bad apple. I know he's a crack shot, but I guess God had to balance out the bad with some good."

She laughed but chose not to reply since she had already begun to lag behind the rest of the group and didn't need any more evidence that she was out of her depth. Her inadequacies irked her because she put a lot of work into staying healthy and put in as much cardio as she could while not in the Zoo. But at the same time, she wasn't used to this much exercise. She could do it, but probably not as well as the guys who did it all the time, and certainly not as well as some of the others could.

Despite everything, she disliked the fact that her lack of abilities only seemed to spur her detractors on. Even though Wayne was merely another meathead special-forces goon with delusions of grandeur thanks to his newly padded bank account, she couldn't help but let his comments get to her.

It was the way she was. She couldn't help it, and she shouldn't have to.

Courtney stopped suddenly, and her eyes widened. Conway took a few steps ahead before he turned back to peer at her and tilted his head. He left the question unasked for a few long moments before he felt it too. The rest of the squad took a few seconds longer to register the distur-bance, and by the time the rest of them realized what it was, Courtney already had her weapon hot and ready.

The ground shook with a decidedly familiar two-step quake. She knew it better than most and had been on the first team to document the massive creatures. Unfortu-nately, theirs hadn't been the first team to realize what a gold mine they could be if you could take them down and survive the onslaught that came afterward and extract the goods located beside the medulla at the same time.

"Fuck, yes," Wayne enthused as he made the stereotypical move and loaded a round into his assault rifle, even though there was already one loaded and all that achieved was to waste the round already in the chamber. Courtney gritted her teeth in an effort to bolster her courage. She didn't want to have to deal with either the massive monster or the host of creatures that would inevitably come afterward.

But it looked like she would have to. She followed Wayne's lead and chambered a round into her already chambered rifle. As she watched the perfectly usable round eject from the chamber, she wondered if, like her, he did it to fill the moment of waiting that seemed to stretch on forever.

*Well, what do you know? That did feel good.*

# CHAPTER FOUR

The heavy footsteps drew relentlessly closer like the massive creature had homed in on them and began to increase its pace.

If she hadn't been so utterly terrified for her life, she would have been fascinated. Well, she was fascinated despite the fear. The creature's size defied physics in ways that she couldn't really comprehend but which intrigued the scientist part of her brain. More than a few educated guesses floated around, but most of them revolved around the possibility that the alien goop somehow allowed the creature to walk around, eat, and breathe without the issues that would come with lower air pressure and heavier gravity than creatures that size would normally have had to live with.

The indisputable reality, in scientific terms, was that this monster should live underwater or be crushed by its own weight. But it existed there, larger than life and with an ear-splitting roar that sent all the other monsters that lived in the Zoo running for cover. Along with any sane human being as well, of course.

So yes, fascinated and terrified at the same time sounded about right.

"Keep your aim at the lower neck area," the squad leader, a man named Roberts, said over the comms. "That's where the critter's armor is weakest, but the slugs miss the good stuff. Once it goes down, form a defensive perimeter and let the doc do her work, okay?"

A selection of affirmative pings showed up on her heads-up display as the monster finally appeared. Predictably, Wayne was the first to open fire, and his massive assault rifle spewed a lethal spray of lead. The creature roared angrily and charged the group as they formed into a pair of V's that drew it into the center. Courtney wasn't sure how they seemed to be able to do this without any obvious previous coordination, but she followed Conway's lead as he drove her to the side. The monster charged into the center, which allowed the eight members of the team to part around it and maintain fire as the beast moved forward and crashed into one of the trees.

Its massive tail flicked to the side and caught Roberts across the chest. She didn't need to hear the crunch to know that it was a fatal blow. It didn't seem fair. They fired unceasingly at the animal from point blank range. The shots ripped into the weaker spots in its gray armor, and it still didn't go down.

But with a single strike of its tail, one of their best was dead.

*Fuck this place*, she thought, not for the first time and definitely not for the last.

She gripped her gun more firmly and shot as best she could. Realistically, though, without any real frame of reference and with multiple shots striking home where she tried to aim and shoot, she couldn't be sure if she actually connected with her target. Her arms slowly grew numb from the sustained action, and soon, she felt lucky to even still manage to hold her weapon as the creature hurtled past them. Conway was the team's medic, and he rushed to where Roberts had been flung.

Courtney wished she could have gone to help too, but as her assault rifle went dead, she saw the massive reptile's eyes flicker as it swept around. It was in pain and very angry at the sustained attack, and she could see the rage. Massive green eyes picked her out as a target as if it sensed that she was the weakest. Then, she looked around and realized that the rest of the squad, except for Conway, had taken cover behind trees. Again, this all seemed rehearsed, although perhaps years of combat training was the real reason.

They were all in cover while she was out in the open with an empty gun. She moved toward one of the trees and tried to keep the massive beast in her sight and reload her weapon at the same time. Pushing back the panic, she reminded herself that she was used to multitasking and had learned to operate a gun. It wasn't too difficult, considering that these were weapons designed to function and go wrong as seldom as possible. Even so, her hands shook uncontrollably, and all she could hear over the enraged roar of the monster was her own heartbeat. The empty mag dropped, but she fumbled the new one and it fell. Somehow, she managed to sweep it up again and stumbled to the nearest tree. She slipped behind it as the creature swung into the attack again.

More gunshots resounded. Courtney heard little over her thudding heart as she slapped the mag into the rifle and caught the bolt on the second try to draw it back and insert a round in the chamber.

The monster rushed past her and the massive tail whipped around the tree that she now hid behind. A flood of wood chips struck her face mask and she recoiled instinctively as the tree groaned, tipped, and slowly keeled over.

Away from her, thankfully, and off to the right.

The ground shuddered as the tree finally impacted. Given the size of the trunk, Courtney wasn't surprised that a blow from the monster's tail had killed Roberts, even with his armor. Anything that had the power to fell a tree of that size would be both painful and lethal to an unfortunate human in its path.

Conway seemed to come to the same conclusion. Roberts wasn't responsive, and there was nothing he could do. To linger there would simply increase the danger that he would meet the same tragic end. He snatched his rifle up and fired without bothering to move into cover. There was something almost hypnotic in the rhythmic thud of the rounds into the surprisingly tough skin of the massive creature, but the assault seemed to only enrage it, not do any real damage.

She gritted her teeth and aimed at the creature's head and specifically for the massive eyes. They moved independently of each other, almost like a chameleon's, as the beast tried to find a target. It seemed undecided like it couldn't determine which of the squad members to attack now that they had all spread out.

Courtney raised the rifle slowly until she could look down the iron sights. That was how she had been taught by the man who ran the shooting range.

Before she could pull the trigger, someone else had obviously had the same idea that she had and acted on it much faster and more efficiently. Blue blood gushed from the wound as the monster emitted one last, blood-curdling roar before it dropped with a massive thud that brought two trees down with it.

Courtney turned to see who'd delivered the killing shot. Her heart sank to her stomach when she saw Wayne on his feet, his rifle posed in a cocky stance as he made a finger-gun gesture at the creature and mock-shot it again.

"Am I good?" he asked nobody in particular. "I'm good."

She rolled her eyes as she pushed to her feet. It seemed Conway felt the same way as he jogged away from Roberts' body.

"What are you, twelve?" he growled and made a quick visual inspection of his gun. "Quit gloating and form a defensive perimeter around the asset. Doc…" He turned to Courtney, who was on her feet by then. "It's up to you to get what we need out of that body."

"Who died and made you queen of the world?" Wayne snarled.

"Roberts died, moron," Conway said and deliberately kept his voice even. "And unless you want to take a picture with your kill, I suggest you get a move on—unless you want your paycheck to be sent to your next of kin."

It wasn't a threat, but it wasn't empty either. Courtney

could already hear the cries from the jungle all around them. It seemed that the whole Zoo had suddenly gone from wild to savage in a split second. They had minutes before the monsters hurtled in to try to kill them. Maybe less.

"Get a move on, Doc," Conway said. Courtney snapped out of her train of thought and let her rifle hang from the strap as she pulled some of the vacuum bags and a scalpel from her kit. She climbed quickly up the corpse of the monster.

It felt wrong. The gargantuan beast still twitched beneath her. It had been alive and full of all kinds of rage minutes before, and she felt she was desecrating a holy place. Maybe she should say some words and hope that it went somewhere where it could exist without the bother of men with guns. Maybe it did, and in that place, wherever it was, it would stand victorious.

She threw the thought aside and cringed as the creature's forepaws and tail spasmed. This was the first time she'd been called upon to do something like this, but as bad as she felt about it, she knew that she needed to move fast.

"Sorry," she whispered and pressed her scalpel to the soft, armor-less flesh where the neck met the head. She made the incision slowly and precisely and penetrated only the skin, careful not to cut anything that was underneath.

She knew it had to smell bad and thanked whatever deity was up there that she had turned her air filters on. Blue blood drenched her suit as she found the sacs that glowed even in the indirect sunlight.

With studied care, she drew them out and sealed them into the first bag. Still working as quickly as she could, she drew out a couple more. It would be more than enough to guarantee that the whole of the team got a fat payday. Assuming they all survived, of course.

"You done, Doc?" Conway asked. The sounds of the animals around them grew louder. She had the impression that they waited to gather in greater numbers before they launched an attack, although she didn't remember them doing that before. Maybe with the Zoo spreading so quickly, the animals had all drifted farther and farther apart.

She hopped down from the carcass and nodded. "All done here," she said and tried to ignore the blood on her gloves as she stored the sealed sacs carefully in her kit.

"Wayne, drop the grenades," Conway ordered. The rest of the squad seemed to accept the medic's taking charge of the situation, and the other man did as he was told without complaint.

"Switch to motion sensors," Wayne said as he dropped a couple of the grenades. A second ticked by before they released the odorless smoke. After months of testing, they'd finally found a way to make the smoke mask the pheromones that filled the air when the big monsters died, making it easier to get in and out with valuable sacs of blue goop. It didn't help much when they tried to get the Pita plants out, though, since the animals seemed to react with a lot more violence and intensity when those were plucked. In addition, the plants gave the pheromones off constantly, while the monsters only discharged them once.

They cleared the area, and the animals seemed to have no interest in pursuing. Even so, Wayne dropped another one of the smoke bombs to cover their trail as they made a beeline back to the Hammerheads. It was a rapid march, but their spirits were higher now that the prospect of a decent paycheck was in sight. A few creatures crossed their paths, but they quickly moved away into the jungle before the team could open fire.

Not everyone's spirits were high, though.

Once they reached the vehicles after hours of moving quickly through the Zoo, Conway looked in the direction from which they'd come.

"It's shitty that we left Roberts out there," he lamented as the teams mounted up. Courtney saw Wayne open his mouth to say something, and from the small grin on his face, she could tell that it would be less than tasteful.

To her surprise, though, the man shut his mouth again. She would have thought he was unable to keep his mouth shut, even in honor of the dead, but then again, as much as these guys had their jokes about the specialists on their teams—and women in general—they had to respect the men who had been given command over their own squads. Usually non-commissioned officers, or NCOs, these were men and women who led by example and knew how to kick ass and take names and still keep a full squad under control.

People like Sergeant Madigan Kennedy, Courtney thought with a small twist of her mouth as she scrambled into the Hammerhead. Once everyone was in, they began the slow return journey to the Staging Area.

"Look," Conway said once they were moving, "you need to adjust your situation. Whatever contract you were pressured into signing clearly isn't working for you and has obviously been structured to totally screw you. Since you're a freelancer, there's not much I can do, but if I were, you, I'd find someone you trust to go over your contract and initiate some changes. No offense."

She laughed. "None taken. I'm not sure I have anyone in the whole of the Staging Area that I'd really trust, though."

Well, that wasn't true. There was one person she knew she could trust. Despite everything about him, she knew that he was honest enough. More so than anybody else she could talk to anyway, although she wondered if she allowed her personal feelings to cloud her judgment.

She did, but that didn't mean that she wasn't right. Whether he liked her or not, she wanted him for his body. Maybe he would want her for her mind. The thought made her smile as she massaged her sore muscles absently, relieved that the run was finally over.

## CHAPTER FIVE

It had been an exceptionally long day, but thankfully, it had almost drawn to a successful conclusion.

He hated being out there. Born and raised in Arizona, he'd always managed to convince himself while growing up that he'd gotten used to the dry heat of the place. But once he'd left and enjoyed the cooler climates of the Northwest, he simply couldn't adjust to it again. The heat stuck to you like a wet blanket and wouldn't let go. It made him feel sick and exhausted.

But there he was, out in the middle of the second largest desert in the fucking world. Well, not anymore. A jungle had begun to cover it now, but that fact hadn't changed the weather very much. It was still hot, and it was still dry—like blow-drying your entire body at the same time.

The men guarding the helicopter caught sight of him. At first glance, he didn't make an impressive figure at barely a hair above five feet, eleven inches, and while he put a lot of work into keeping himself fit, he was always lean rather than bulky. His red hair was cut short to the standard two inches and fully covered by the black beret he wore that adhered to the color code of his combat uniform. The black eagle on his chest did catch their eye, though, and they saluted sharply.

It wasn't often that they had a colonel straight from the Pentagon to oversee this place and he could see why. It was a hellhole—military discipline combined with the worst of capitalism.

They had a commandant to handle that shit, thankfully. He was there to oversee the Pentagon's projects and honestly couldn't give a damn about the management of the place. For all he cared, it wasn't even a military base.

An assistant in dress uniform waited for him at the helicopter. The woman kept her head down as the rotors spun loudly enough to make speech impossible. She indicated for him to step inside.

Colonel James Anderson was no stranger to helicopters, although the ones he'd boarded while in the Recon Division had been considerably larger and more suited for flying in hostile territory.

Well, this wasn't exactly hostile territory, he supposed, but there was still more than enough shit out there that wanted him dead to dissuade him from considering it friendly territory.

He sat down and strapped himself in before he pulled the headset on. The whine of the rotors was pleasantly deafened by the sound-canceling headphones and replaced instead with the drone of the pilots performing the preflight checks. The assistant took a seat across from him and put her headset on too.

"Colonel Anderson, Team Six is ready for action on your command," she said quickly. She'd introduced herself on his first visit there, but he'd forgotten her name already. There were far too many non-essential personnel in the place for him to keep track of.

"Give them the green light. I want them to engage the hostiles before we arrive at the construction site," he stated over the mic and leaned back in his seat as the helicopter began to ascend. Too many bad memories had been scorched into his mind to make the sensation of take-off a pleasant experience. He ran his fingers over the burn scars on his arm and hands. The assistant, who had a lieutenant's bars on her collar, forced herself not to stare.

The colonel was used to it. He could have had surgery to remove the ugly scars and so avoid the stares and unasked questions. It was all bullshit, and more than once, he'd caught himself wondering if it wouldn't save time and effort to simply do it and get it out of the way.

But the scars were memorials of men and women who wouldn't be remembered any other way. He'd rather die than give the assholes in the Senate the satisfaction. Let them stare. Let them remember. This was their fault. He felt the guilt and damned if he wouldn't make sure that they felt it too.

"Comm check," a voice said through his headset. "This is Team Six Red Squad Leader. Do you read me, Falcon, over."

"Roger that, Red Team Leader," Anderson said and entered the usual groove of the pre-mission rituals. "This is Falcon, reading you loud and clear. All team leaders, please respond, over."

"Red Leader, comm check."

"Blue Leader, comm check."

"Green Leader, comm check."

Each of the team leaders would take control of a four-man fire team. This wasn't a real operation—or rather, Anderson didn't want to justify it with that name. It was a lobbyist's wet dream. With the companies making these new suits of armor, they wanted the best of the best to try them out before they sold them to whatever market they found the most profitable. So not only would his boys run into a camp full of illegal bounty hunters in armor that they'd only trained in for a few weeks, but they would have to give the suits up once the test was over.

So much bullshit.

"Comms confirmed, Team Six, you have a green light—repeat, green light—to engage the hostiles, over," Anderson said and tried his best not to sound bored though he failed miserably.

Twelve of the best special forces operatives that he'd ever had the pleasure of meeting would be decked out in the finest and the latest of field suits easily worth what each of these guys made in two years. And they'd use them against a bunch of underfunded, underfed black market bounty hunters decked out in old, cheap knockoffs that had been patched together from what the second-hand retailers couldn't use.

This whole thing was a travesty.

They would take about three hours to arrive at the hostiles' location. Anderson sighed softly and rubbed his eyes as the sensation of the rotors spinning faster than the naked eye could see vibrated through the cabin that he rode in.

The half-hour ride felt like it would go on forever, but they finally lost altitude and dropped over the sand dunes to what was the tail end of the construction of the massive walls meant to keep the Zoo contained.

He returned every salute offered to him by the men waiting near the helicopter. One of them shouted details about the situation. Team Six had checked in when they left their vehicles and now approached the enemy camp on foot. They could have made it there without much hassle, and considering how outgunned the bounty hunters were, it only seemed fair to give them fair warning of the amount of shit that headed their way.

But no. The bigwigs back in Washington wanted to test the suits' capabilities while used in a stealth operation too, and since all the other tests would involve killing the Zoo's animals like fucking trophy hunters, this was the only chance that they would get.

*Let's get this over with.* Amanda, his wife, had a nice roast waiting for him back home, which he could eat while he watched the game. Amanda was a bigger Eagles fan than he was, and she'd made sure to instill the fervor in their two sons too. That was something to look forward to. Run the op, make it look good so that the lobbyists had something to sell come next quarter, and get all his boys back home safely.

He could focus. For them, he could do this.

The colonel stepped out of the temporary landing platform and the soldiers led him through the site, the lieutenant assistant close behind him. Anderson's keen eyes studied the area's defenses. They weren't set up to fend off a real attack by a coordinated team—heavy on the artillery, with a couple of what he could only describe as anti-aircraft guns aimed in the direction of the Zoo along with five machine gun nests. It was crowd control intended to deal with the masses of animals that he was told threw themselves at the fences on a daily basis.

The soldier in him protested and he shook his head. By comparison, the side facing away from the Zoo only had a guard tower which housed a single man with a sniper rifle. Granted, another wall was being built in that direction, but if anyone had a mind to sabotage the construction, it wouldn't be difficult to infiltrate the sites. Maybe some explosives, a few mines set up near the actual construction, and that would stop the building for months.

He smirked. It wasn't like anybody was stupid enough to actually do that. From what he'd been told, the whole world needed the Zoo to be contained within the Sahara, so maybe the crowd-centric defenses were the right way to go.

But old habits died hard, and his years conducting and operating in black sites had ingrained the need to study any fortified position and immediately identify weak spots. He couldn't help it. It was almost a part of his DNA by this point.

The colonel entered one of the buildings near the wall itself, where the men who escorted him snapped salutes before they returned to their posts. He half-heartedly offered one of his own before he stepped into the building and closed the door behind him.

The darkness inside was almost as stark as the brightness outside. Anderson had to blink a few times to adjust to the situation. This was all off the books, of course, hence the cloak and dagger behavior, and it had to look like this place was merely another part of the construction site.

A handful of scientists were already inside with their eyes focused on over a dozen screens. There was one for each operative's HUD, as well as a couple that monitored the status of each man and the power armor he wore. Anderson rubbed the bridge of his nose and already regretted the decision to wear his contacts today instead of glasses.

"Colonel Anderson," the lead scientist said with a small, professional smile as he offered a pudgy hand. "I'm so glad you could join us."

"The pleasure's all mine, Dr. Bial," Anderson lied and his gaze flickered over the screens. The scientist offered him a headset. He took it without a word and listened to the status checks that were required for this mission.

So much bullshit.

"Okay, Team Six," he commanded over his comms as he folded his arms in front of his chest. "Let's give these suits a stress test. Get a jog going and try to cut the arrival time down, over."

"Roger that, Falcon," came the voice of Red Leader. "Beginning stress tests, over."

# CHAPTER SIX

His gaze remained fixed on the screens. The brightness of the desert glared in the shared HUDs in stark contrast to the clear darkness of the room. Little was said during the time it took for the men to trek through the desert. There were a couple of false alarms, but as Anderson neither heard nor saw anything himself, he wasn't surprised when they kept moving.

Ever since he'd been given his wings, he'd been expected to run these operations rather than take part in them, and that felt wrong. He knew that he wasn't psychologically cleared for active duty, which was why his superior had put him on the bench, as it were. The US government had put the better part of three million dollars into transforming him into an efficient killing machine, and even though he couldn't perform in the same function, he knew that they wouldn't allow his talent to go to waste.

Anderson smirked and watched the team's progress. One of the screens showed the various GPS markers over a topographical map of the area. His specialty had always been colder climes involving mountains and snow for the most part, but from what he remembered from a conference over a decade ago that he'd attended on the subject, maps of deserts like the Sahara changed from day to day. That added to the fact that their intel on the location of this bounty hunter camp was three days old meant that they had sent out a group of highly trained men in top-of-the-line armor on intelligence that could be twelve hours out of date, for all he knew.

Fucking bullshit. What did these million-dollar-a-year CEOs know about running a real op? Didn't they know that properly acquired intel was almost ninety percent of the job?

No, of course they didn't. They'd played video games that told them that wherever a good guy showed up, bad guys would automatically spawn to stop them. Or try to, anyway.

He shook his head again.

Less than an hour into the operation, Red Leader raised his hand and closed it slowly into a fist. Anderson narrowed his eyes and made a note to ask if there was a problem with coordination while wearing the suits. Power armor was reactionary and acted in a split second to augment any movement made by the wearer. No matter how advanced—until some egghead figured out how to make an AI that could read minds or predict the future—there would always be lag. Sure, it had been shaved down to milliseconds, but when bullets flew at over a thousand meters per second, milliseconds counted.

Besides, you had to train your body to coordinate with

half-ton armor that moved a fraction of a second after you wanted it to.

Anderson made a note to bring up the coordination issue with the developers. He wasn't sure if it was a software or hardware problem, but it was a problem, even if the boys out there handled it admirably. That was what they were trained for, above all else. Adapt to adverse situations and constantly push forward.

The colonel scratched his chin as the troop split into the three four-man teams. Each would conduct the three stages of the operation, and for it to go right, they'd need to run those stages within seconds of each other. Otherwise, they would handle almost a hundred occupants of the bounty hunter camp without back-up.

Green Team stayed behind, and their long-range programs picked up and connected to their specialized rifles. No conversation issued over the comms. None was needed. The men with the long-range scopes highlighted the men in the watchtowers that surrounded the camp. There were crowd-control measures in place that told Anderson that they had problems with the animals from the Zoo, but they were a lot more careful with their security.

Apparently, a place that dealt with most of the lowlifes and bottom-feeders that seemed to gravitate to Africa had left them paranoid. There were at least a dozen guard towers and all sported snipers and machine gun nests. Anderson scratched his chin again as the snipers marked off the various guardsmen.

His gaze traced the members of Blue Team as they headed toward the encampment. They moved smoothly and the camouflage programs worked well enough, but these new suits were too big and too heavy to be effective covert tools. They were…heavy armor, at best.

"Green Team in position," came the call.

"Blue Team in position," came the second call.

"Roger that," came the call from Red Team leader. "Awaiting your countdown, Green Team."

"Roger that. Countdown commencing," Green Team leader said and kept his voice soft even though the helmets they wore were supposed to isolate their voices from the outside world. Three targets were highlighted, the pair of snipers and the machine gunner on the southernmost tower. A fourth guard who patrolled the area was also picked up.

"Clear to engage, Green Team," Anderson confirmed.

"Roger that, Falcon," Green Team leader responded. Four pops sounded in succession. They followed one another so quickly that they might have been the same shot but, like puppets who'd had their strings cut, all four men dropped.

Anderson knew that CEOs would try to claim that there was a coordination system in the suits, but that was stone-cold training and nothing in the world would convince him otherwise.

The other two teams didn't need his word to follow up. They breached the barbed-wire fence in seconds and quickly infiltrated the camp.

He smirked. This was bullshit but when he watched the work of men he trusted to do what they did best, it brought a smile to his face every damn time.

The bar was open at all hours and it was business as usual when they arrived there mid-morning on the following day. Sal wondered how they managed that. He'd never worked in a service job before, all things considered. Still, he knew people who did, and they were adamant that twenty-four-hour places were the worst to work in. No closing hours meant having to deal with customers at all hours and at all times.

He shook his head, sure that these people had figured the schedule out. It wasn't like this was a seven-eleven outside a campus. This was a bar in the middle of a military base. They had to be better at people and time management than those places.

That simple assumption made sense. He knew that enough money was dropped on this place to allow the owner to hire enough staff for all hours of the day or night.

It was good business management. Men and women who put their lives on the line on a daily basis did need liquid courage to go out there and face it again. It was the cost when the cutting edge of science was this sharp.

"Or rather, when the cutting edge of science is on you," Sal remembered saying to Kennedy one time when they'd been alone at his apartment. It hadn't been a popular joke, especially when he did it with a Russian accent. It had been even less popular when he tried explaining the joke to her and she told him that she got it. She'd rolled her eyes and he'd simply stopped and moved on. Take the loss, learn, and don't repeat.

It wasn't a great joke. He had a weird sense of humor so

47

he'd liked it, and each time his mind went back to it, he always ended up with a private chuckle.

Which was exactly what happened this time, and Kennedy narrowed her eyes at him as she took a sip from her lager.

"Are you thinking about that joke again?" she asked.

"You know it," Sal said with a grin and toyed with his own pint glass. He still wasn't that much of a drinker. His mind worked at odd hours, and he was always careful not to hinder that. He had good ideas all the time and was usually smart enough to put them down with pen and paper. If he was drunk, he was more likely to forget. And since his income was essentially based on what his brain was capable of, he had to take good care of it.

"I know, I know," he said as she fixed him with an unrelenting stare. "It's a stupid joke. I think it's funny, okay?"

Kennedy chuckled. "It's not stupid. Well, it is, but that doesn't make you stupid for liking it. You have a special kind of brain is all." Sal opened his mouth with a retort but she stopped him when she raised her hand. "The good kind of special. Like…think of it as a higher kind of funny that requires someone with a higher understanding to get?"

Sal chuckled and shook his head before he sipped his drink. "Look at you, making up bullshit to make me feel better. Nah, I'll concede. It's a bad joke. Like bad puns. They still make me chuckle. It's like there's a little kid inside me—the one that still laughs when a stuffy professor talks about the gasses in Uranus."

Kennedy grinned, and when he narrowed his eyes, she laughed and covered her mouth since she'd just taken a sip from her beer.

"Oh, my God," he said with a smirk. "Did you think that was funny? Did I say something stupid that you thought was funny?"

She shook her head but still laughed and tried to keep the beer in her mouth.

"Aw, you have that little kid who likes silly jokes too," Sal said and brushed some of her brown hair behind her ear. "I'll be sure to exploit that later."

Kennedy finally recovered her composure and drew in a deep breath. Even in the darker lighting of the bar, Sal could see that her face was flushed.

"Oh, God," she gasped, still trying to contain herself. "Please don't do that to me again."

"Deal," he said. "So long as I get to make you say, 'Oh God,' for other reasons later."

She grinned and tilted her head with a challenge in her eyes. They had been at the bar for the past couple of hours, but Sal had spent most of it getting connected with the teams that would head out into the Zoo in the near future. Over the past couple of months since they'd broken away and started to work on their own, they'd had to rely on running the jobs with others. It meant a profit split with them too, but when the alternative was to go in with only the two of them, it wasn't much of a choice at all. The Zoo grew more and more dangerous the larger it became.

Sal realized that the flush in Kennedy's cheeks wasn't only from her attempt not to snort beer out her nose. She'd actually been drinking all this time.

He didn't blame her. Despite all his personal rules, he wished he'd been drinking too.

"Look," he said finally and glanced at his own beer,

which was only half empty despite the fact that he'd nursed it over the past few hours. "I need to get back to my place. There is paperwork to do, and I think I need a nap. So... unless you call me earlier, I'll meet up with you at three, okay?"

Kennedy nodded. "Sweet dreams. And...paperwork, I guess."

Sal chuckled and moved to the bar where he indicated for the bartender not to serve her anything else. The man nodded and tapped his nose as Sal made his way outside.

# CHAPTER SEVEN

Madigan tilted her head as she watched Sal leave. He was...different. She'd had other boyfriends before. There had been a couple of military guys, but she found that they got really defensive with her very quickly. Either that or they felt slightly emasculated by a girlfriend who was in the special forces. Actually, when she thought about it, there were a couple who hadn't even been in the military who had felt that way. Men either reacted like that or had some sort of fetish that involved domination by a warrior woman or something along those lines.

It creeped her out. None of them saw her as Madigan. She always meant something else to them.

Sal was different. And she thought that in the best way possible. He was wrapped up in that quick-working little mind of his, and while there was sexual chemistry between them, he seemed more willing than most to let that be an isolated part of their relationship. When the sex came up, it was fun and it was good, but it never invaded the rest of what she'd come to regard as a really great friendship.

Until now. She tilted her head and stared at her glass. He'd made a sexual innuendo, and she hadn't given him any shit for it. Maybe she had drunk too much. It was barely a quarter past midday, and she had already downed three beers. No, it took a lot more than that to get her drunk.

Maybe she had merely adjusted to that side of their relationship. Nope, it couldn't be that. It might be that the beers had landed in an empty stomach. She chuckled and took another long sip from the glass. Whatever the reason, she was comfortable around Sal—and more importantly, he seemed to be comfortable around her. Now that she'd come to know him and all his little oddities, that was probably the most impressive thing she'd seen all year.

Considering the year that she'd had, that was saying something. Between her visits into the Zoo and... No, that was pretty much it, but that still set the bar high. Madigan smiled as she leaned back in her seat. He was comfortable being his weird, odd self with her. For some reason, thinking that made her feel a gentle tingle in her body. Not necessarily sexual, but not necessarily...not.

She finished her drink and turned toward the bar. As she raised her hand to ask for another one, she noticed someone she recognized on one of the stools. The woman sat alone, and her short blonde hair was pulled into a tight bun. She had the look of someone just out of the Zoo, too. Madigan wasn't sure what it was—relief mixed with exhaustion, maybe.

"Dr. Monroe?" she asked and leaned closer to her. The woman looked around, seemingly uncertain as to who might be talking to her as she nursed what Kennedy assumed was a Jack and Diet Coke. It took a few attempts before Monroe realized who was speaking and turned to look at her.

"Sergeant Kennedy," she said with a smile and pushed off her stool. "So nice to see you again. It's been a while."

"It's just Kennedy now," Madigan said and gestured for Monroe to join her at her table. "Well, Madigan Kennedy."

"Oh, right," the specialist said with a chuckle as she took the seat Sal had vacated. "I heard that you had struck out solo. And doing a pretty good job of it too, if the rumors around the base are to be believed."

"Well," Madigan said with a shrug, "not 'solo.' I've worked a lot with Salinger Jacobs. He's actually the brains behind this whole thing. I'm the muscle. I don't think I would have been able to figure it out by myself, although I'm certain that it's the same for him."

Monroe's laugh sounded odd and almost forced. "Oh, right, I remember. Jacobs—not doctor, just Jacobs."

Madigan pointed at her and laughed. "I'd completely forgotten that. It's hilarious."

The specialist chuckled softly. "Has he actually managed to get his doctorate yet? Personal experience in a place like this is almost certainly a shoo-in for any doctorate committee out there. Just saying."

Kennedy nodded. "I mean, I know that he's finished his thesis—"

"Dissertation," Monroe corrected.

"Right, what did I say?" she asked as the bartender brought another pint for her. He looked at Monroe's almost empty glass and she nodded at the unasked question.

"Thesis is usually for BS or master's degrees," the specialist said and watched the bartender whip her up another drink and bring it to the table in under thirty seconds. "A dissertation is usually longer and is required when applying for a doctorate."

Madigan nodded. "I'll keep that in mind. Anyway, I think he has already finished his, but he said something about having to go back to the States for some sort of discussion and he wasn't ready to leave yet."

"Yeah, I can understand that." Monroe sipped from her straw. "I mean, it's not every day that they bring anything other than fully-fledged doctors out here. And since he's not tied down to some doctorate commission or anything like that, he's essentially free to turn his dissertation in whenever he pleases. You know, within reason. Besides, he's young. He has time before people ask what he's doing with his life."

"Well, he's doing pretty great for himself, I'd say," Madigan said. "I'm not going to lie. When I was his age, I'd probably have been willing to kill to make as much money as he makes now."

Courtney chuckled. "No shit? What kind of money, if you don't mind my asking?"

Kennedy inclined her head as she contemplated her answer. Her brain felt a little fuzzy, but when she thought about it hard, the details came back to her. She couldn't imagine that it would be a bad idea to lay out the details of their situation to someone like Monroe. While she didn't necessarily trust the woman, it wasn't like she would give away state secrets or anything like that.

"Well, we do the usual trips into the Zoo," Madigan

said. "You know, collect the flowers and stuff, and a couple of companies offer bounties for his depiction of the flora and the fauna in there. It's not that much money, I suppose, but it's not much more work than he would do otherwise. It's his field of study anyway. I'm basically his gunner and make sure that he doesn't get eaten while he hunts down science or whatever."

Monroe smirked, and the ex-sergeant chuckled. She knew that it was a lot more complicated than that for Sal, and she was sure that they would have many conversations about how much more complicated it was. And for her part, she liked to let him talk. He was passionate about that sort of stuff, and while she had a decent understanding of what he was talking about, having him talk about what he was good at was miles better than the stupid jokes he tried to come up with when his mind was idle.

"Anyway," Madigan said as she returned to the track of the conversation." Yeah, that's the bread and butter, but we've had a lot of outside contracts from people to test weapons and armor and software for suits and armor. They need people who've actually been in the Zoo. Not only gunners, since they need some specialists' input there too."

Courtney nodded and leaned back. "So, since you guys already have a specialist, I don't suppose you'd need any more on your team? Do you need someone else to join your little start-up?"

Kennedy set her pint down on the table. She traced her finger thoughtfully around the lip of the glass. "What do you mean? Do you mean you?"

"It's been on my mind," Monroe said with a shrug. "I've

never actually worked here on a government contract, so it's never been secure. They want me to stay since I'm one of the people who's been here the longest, but they continually change my contract. And if I want to work here for the company, I have to accept the changes that they make, even when they put in some clauses that aren't...well, they aren't made with my well-being in mind."

"Your company's screwing you over," Madigan said and put her own honest opinion forward to simplify the situation. "Got it."

The specialist laughed. "Yeah, pretty much." She took another long sip from her drink and winced as the alcohol hit her system. "You'd think with all the screwing over that I've had during the past few years that I'd be the most satisfied gal on base, but lately it's been...all screw, no orgasm, you know what I mean?"

Courtney made a face, a little surprised at herself because she didn't usually talk this way. She was generally much more civilized with her language, but there was something about Kennedy that made her feel comfortable. While she'd never been particularly foul-mouthed, she wasn't exactly a nun either. The more the expectations of her increased in the workplace, the more she adjusted her language to fit what she'd always thought a doctor should sound like.

But as she sat there and talked with someone whom she knew had no preconceived expectations of her, and with a fairly substantial serving of alcohol in her system, she felt comfortable to release her sailor mouth without any inhibitions.

It seemed like Kennedy was shocked by her language

too. The woman leaned back in her seat and laughed out loud as she nodded.

"That's actually a very fair assessment of the situation," Madigan said with another chuckle. "I hope you don't mind, but I'll steal that line for later use. I'll make sure to put you down as a source."

Courtney shrugged. "It's not like I'll trademark it or anything. Steal away."

"You might want to consider trademarking it," Madigan said with a laugh. "I mean, if your company screws you over like this, you should probably look out for yourself as much as possible, you know what I mean?"

Courtney smiled. "Yeah, I guess. It's not like I want something for nothing, you know? I've put a lot of work into this place, and I have done so for a while now. Recognition isn't my style, but I'd still like to be paid fairly for my efforts."

"You know what?" Madigan said forcefully and leaned forward in her seat. "Screw those guys. Not literally, of course. They don't deserve your assets." She grinned and put emphasis on the first half of the word. "You should drop them and come work for us."

"Yeah," Courtney said with a laugh. "Simply drop my contract, rip it up in front of those motherfuckers, and strike out on my own like you and Jacobs."

"Hey, you could come work with us," Madigan said and held her hand up before Courtney laughed it off. "I'm serious. You're one of the best in the business. Anybody would be lucky to have you, and I think Heavy Metal deserves some of that kind of luck."

"Heavy Metal?" Courtney asked and raised an eyebrow.

"Oh, yeah, that's what Sal called the company," Madigan explained. "I'm still not sure why, but hey, we can always change it later. Nothing's written in stone here."

Courtney nodded. "Are you serious? It seems like you guys already have a specialist on your squad, so if you need any new additions, it makes more sense that you should bring in a couple of gunners, not another specialist."

Madigan shrugged. "Sure, Sal's a pretty good specialist. He's also a really good gunner too, so it's more half and half. Since I'm dedicated to the gunner side of the business, we could always afford to have someone balance it out on the specialist side. Besides, it would be really cool to have an actual doctor on the team and not some wannabe."

"Hey, come on," Monroe said and took a moment to finish her drink off. "Jacobs is one of the best in the business too, PhD or no PhD."

"That's fair," Kennedy agreed with a nod. She finished her own drink and placed the empty glass on the table. "Although his ego doesn't need any further inflation, so I will deny ever having said that."

"You won't hear a word from me about it," Courtney said. She wanted to make a joke about something else of his that might need inflating, but all things said, no matter how drunk she was, she simply wasn't that kind of person.

"In all seriousness, though," Madigan said as their empty glasses were replaced with full ones. "It's always worth a shot. Since we're still a start-up, you'd be one of the founding members, and if Sal can pick up some more of the gunner-ing, maybe we'll have a place for you to take up the full-on specialist role, you know?"

"I'll think about it," Monroe said with a smile. "I really will. So far, all I've done here is sell my mind. It's time to move into something that I actually care about." She took a sip of her drink and nodded. She'd been drinking for a little while and the alcohol had moved past the initial impact toward steady inebriation. That was how she knew it was working.

"Besides," Madigan continued, "there are many other benefits to working with Salinger Jacobs other than his brains, you know?"

Courtney leaned forward and tried to pretend that this wasn't a topic that had been on her mind since the conversation started. "Oh, yeah, I wondered about that," she said and kept her voice deliberately casual. "I've heard here and there that you and Salinger are an item."

Kennedy shrugged. "It's nothing serious. We work together and we like each other. Since we spend a lot of time together, it made sense, you know?"

It didn't make sense to her, but she nodded anyway. "So, you two didn't start anything until after you started working together?"

"No, it was a little before that, actually," her companion said and shook her head slowly.

"I mean," Courtney pushed, "I kind of threw myself at him after that first mission, but he wasn't interested. Honestly, he blew me off that first time."

"Really?" Madigan asked. "I went to his place later that night, and he seemed plenty eager to join in."

She raised an eyebrow. "Is that so?"

"Oh, yeah." Kennedy nodded. "I'm certain he thought that I was a wet dream that first time, though. He'd already gone to sleep and was on pain pills. He was in a bad way after that first mission."

"I remember that."

"Yeah, I thought that he wouldn't believe I'd gone there, especially if he wasn't all there." Courtney leaned in closer, not wanting to miss a detail. "Anyway, I left him a pair of my panties to let him know that it actually happened. Even then, it seemed like he was afraid to talk to me after that— like he didn't want to bring it up. It took another visit to his place to get him comfortable with the fact."

She laughed. For some reason, this fit with her mental image of the man. "Leaving your panties behind, huh? That's a neat trick. So how was he?" she asked.

"I was pleasantly surprised," Madigan said. "Most younger guys have some…well-documented problems, but he managed to steer clear of those while still being very… young and energetic. Ten out of ten would fuck again."

Courtney laughed, and Kennedy smirked as they raised their glasses and clinked them together.

# CHAPTER EIGHT

Anderson watched the captured video of the mission. He still wasn't happy with it. The boys had fulfilled their objective as well as could be expected from them, but the armor hadn't performed as advertised.

It was top-of-the-line, no disputing that. It was also groundbreaking in that these suits were touted as the first power armor in which the power covered the entirety of the armor. It was honestly rather impressive considering the advantages this could have in the field. Anderson would have liked a good look at the suits before they were tested out there, out of professional curiosity more than anything else. Folks in the field relied on IT geeks to operate effectively. It wasn't that he didn't trust those guys, but they weren't the ones who were out there and who risked their lives.

Despite all that, Anderson couldn't shake the feeling that his boys used unfinished products. They were the guinea pigs required for the people in high rises in New York to satisfy their investors enough to put these things in production. He'd been told that the software and hardware had been put through extensive testing before the mission, but if this was the first real field test and it involved live fire, there were a lot of questions that he would raise with his superiors when he got back.

He knew what they would say. All's well that ended well, and so far, the field tests had gone spectacularly. The new software proved incredibly useful, even if it needed a few tweaks here or there. He thought specifically of the long-distance software that had a couple of bugs that involved the distance reader. It wasn't something that couldn't be worked around. In fact, it had been, because a couple of the longer shots had required the members of Green Team to make some calculations of their own before taking their shots.

That particular scenario had involved shooting bounty hunters on some dirt bikes, so it would have been difficult to call one way or another. Survivors had not been a part of the mission, and so they'd taken their shots and made the kills required.

He was proud of the men. His opinion of what this whole thing was hadn't changed, though.

Red Leader, Sergeant Addison, a trained Navy SEAL, approached him in the center of operations. He was out of the armor now and dressed in his fatigues. Addison was the de-facto leader of the squads, even though Anderson had the nominal title. The colonel trusted the man with power armor boots on the ground better than himself, and he'd asked him to join him once they'd returned from the attack on the bounty hunter base.

Addison saluted sharply. "Colonel Anderson. It's great to have you here to oversee these operations."

He returned the salute and patted the man on the shoulder. "The pleasure is mine, believe me. That was some impressive work out there, sergeant."

"Thank you, sir."

He indicated for the sergeant to join him in the center of operations and they moved into the relative cool of the small building.

"I looked at your preliminary report," Anderson said as he sat in front of some of the screens.

"The power armor makes shooting relatively simple," Addison said and pointed to one of the videos. With the partially powered armor of the past, the massive rifles made it difficult for the users to maintain both their balance and their aim intact. Now, however, the operatives in full power armor seemed unaffected by the rounds they fired despite the bullets being large enough to take aircraft down.

They had to be, all things considered. Anderson had seen videos of what teams had to face and fight inside the Zoo.

"Guns weren't the problem," Addison continued. "Plus, the software was designed to help with kick so that there wasn't any adjustment needed or anything like that. It took a few attempts to get used to it, but we figured it out in the training phase."

The colonel nodded and made a note on a pad in his hand.

"These suits aren't much good for covert operations,

though," the team leader continued. "It's just… Imagine if you had to walk around in the tin man outfit from *The Wizard of Oz*. Sand in the joints doesn't change mobility, at least not so far as we were able to see, but it's rather like walking around in APCs. They're loud, that's my point, and no matter what kind of camo software you have on the outside, anybody we try to sneak up on will hear us from a mile away."

"They can probably fix that by isolating the joints," Anderson remarked while he continued to make notes on his pad.

"I'd like to see them do that without ruining the mobility," Addison said with a smirk. "That's already as limited as fuck. Seriously. You're stuck in a constant goose-step, whether you walk or run. Any movement along the spine area is limited to the point where it's a very good thing that they put in rear-view cameras."

The colonel nodded. "That all seems like something they could put into a training regimen."

"Well, yeah, but what's the point?" the team leader asked with a shrug. "They will come up with something more workable in six months. The only reason someone would try to specialize in armor that's already antiquated is to show off how badass you are, and bragging rights only get you so far in the world."

Anderson smirked and typed mobility and agility on his pad. He had the individual reports from the men, but they were all 'on a scale of one to ten' questions, which limited the actual viability of the answers. Perhaps that was intentional. Anderson didn't give a fuck whether it was or wasn't. If they wanted to waste his time with this shit, he would do it right, goddammit.

"Did you encounter any problems with the software, though?" he asked.

"It needs some fine tuning," Addison said and sounded reasonable rather than concerned. "But I'm fairly sure that they'll leave that to the individual user's preference. I assume that those individual users will be—"

"Guys who want personalized security for their private islands, yeah," Anderson finished for him. He'd seen the report that detailed how much it cost to build these things.

Base models would be sold in the mid-six-figures, easy. The ones that the operatives used now, with the software upgrades plus whatever it was that they could do to fix the problems that the operatives had identified...he could see each model going for a million dollars without breaking a sweat. And while it would be a good decade before the US military saw any of these in action on their side, there were more than a few billionaires out there who wouldn't mind paying that much money to have a couple of walking tanks in control of their security.

"How's Blue Team's progress?" Addison asked as the questions stopped.

"They're still moving toward the satellite marker. They should check in within a couple of minutes," Anderson said and completed his notes on Addison's thoughts on the armor's performance. If nothing else, it would give his superiors enough reading material to make them think twice before they sent him on bullshit assignments like these for the near future.

"Falcon, this is Blue Leader, over," Michaels said over the commlink.

"Roger that, Blue Leader. What is your ETA?" Anderson

asked. He followed the GPS markers that moved toward the massive heat spot about three miles into the Zoo. Normally, it would have taken them a mere few minutes to reach that spot, but the jungle wasn't an easy place to navigate, especially in the heavy suits of armor.

"ETA is roughly five minutes, over."

"Roger that. Any updates on the armor?" Anderson asked. He could see Addison roll his eyes and look away out of the corner of his eye but he didn't react.

"Nothing to report," Blue Leader responded. "Suits are operating at peak capacity."

"Roger that, Blue Leader." The colonel leaned back in his seat. "Let me know once you've engaged the target."

"Will do, Falcon."

---

It was barely past midday. Courtney almost never got drunk and certainly never before dinner, so having to deal with wobbly legs during the daytime was a foreign experience for her. Not a bad experience, on the whole. It was something she could get used to.

Besides, she wasn't really drunk. She still had some coordination and could probably pass the visual test that many of the cops ran in her hometown. That said, she would not pass the breathalyzer, though.

*Imagine that*, she mused. Daddy's precious little girl— the one who hadn't even been allowed to go out for a party until she moved out of her parents' house and into a college dorm—now working on her daytime drinking.

If that wasn't a massive middle finger to the status quo

of her life, she didn't know what was. She'd probably want to figure out what the hell it was that she didn't know and do that too at this point. She grinned and managed to keep herself from stumbling as she moved toward the houses. It was difficult to set up apartment buildings in a military complex, so they had merely grabbed the prefab that had been left over from the rest of the buildings and used as little as possible to make up some livable little houses for the various non-military personnel on base. The actual men and women in the armed forces had to share a barracks on the other side of the base.

It was a decent enough arrangement, even if it did mean that all her neighbors were doctors and engineers like she was. It wasn't a terrible situation, but it could definitely be improved.

Courtney realized that she'd walked past her own house. She'd been lost in her thoughts of personal rebellion and completely missed the right turn that would lead her to the tiny little quasi-house that she'd called home for the past...holy shit, two years.

That was some depressing shit right there.

She was about to turn back when she realized that she knew where she was. Sal Jacobs lived in the tiny prefab house at the end of the street. She'd seen him exit the bar a few moments before she'd started talking to Kennedy. It had been hard to hear, but he'd said something about paperwork and a nap. She'd talked long enough for him to be finished with his paperwork by now.

And if he was finished, maybe she could help him with that nap that he'd mentioned?

Courtney giggled uncharacteristically at the odd yet not

entirely unbidden thought. She'd carried a torch for the man for a while. He'd probably rebuff her again, but there was no harm in seeing if he needed some company, right?

She made her way to the house and was about to knock on the door when she saw that it was cracked open. Before she could have second thoughts, she pushed it all the way and looked around. A desk stood to one side with a closed laptop on it opposite a small TV and a comfortable couch —standard in all the houses, she knew. The blinds were drawn but there was no sign of Jacobs.

With a wonderfully giddy feeling at the excitement of exploring the unknown, she stepped inside. She moved toward the door at the back of the living room-kitchen, which was open as well. Sal laid on his bed, his eyes closed. He was asleep, though he hadn't bothered to change out of his fatigues or get under the covers of the single bed.

It seemed wrong for her to leave him like that, and she slipped inside his bedroom and closed the door behind her. Her heart pounded like it had when the massive monster had rushed at her the day before, but this was a different kind of excitement. The forbidden kind. She smiled and knelt beside the bed.

He was young. That surprised her a little. He didn't act it while he was awake, but asleep, she couldn't help but realize it.

Sal groaned softly, his eyes still closed. She froze in place, her eyes wide, and waited for him to wake up and see her there.

He didn't.

She grinned and licked her lips as she leaned in close to his ear.

"Hey, baby," she whispered in a sultry tone. He groaned softly again and a small smile touched his lips.

"Hey," he murmured back, still fast asleep. She smiled and leaned forward again.

"I want you so bad, Sal," she whispered. "I need you so bad."

The smile lingered as he groaned again. Courtney was about to stand and leave, but as she turned, she saw that her words had definitely had a very visible effect on him.

His fatigue pants were baggy but prone as he was, she could see his erection had already tented the fabric.

She couldn't resist the urge and ran her hand lightly down his stomach. It seemed perfectly natural to push his pants down, along with the boxers he wore underneath. She gasped softly as she freed his cock and her fingers wrapped instinctively around the quickly hardening shaft. Licking her lips, she rubbed her thumb over the thick head and gave it a few strokes.

"Fuck," Sal whispered in his sleep and Courtney smiled. She was there. He was ready for some action. What the hell, right?

She pulled her shirt off, pushed her pants down, and kicked them away. Once she was fully undressed, she slipped onto the bed with him. Her fingers found his cock again and stroked it with more purpose this time as she leaned in to whisper in his ear when he moaned again.

"I want you to fuck me."

# CHAPTER NINE

Madigan checked her watch. She knew that their days were all skewed the longer that they stayed on base. As it turned out, without some real military discipline in effect, she found it hard to keep to a regimen. She technically wasn't a part of the military anymore and with Sal working the odd hours that he did, it was difficult to keep to a decent schedule.

She'd never been much of a night owl. He was and could work all night, but once he fell asleep, she couldn't have woken him before midday even with a howitzer.

That all changed while they were in the Zoo. It was odd how having one's life on the line could motivate one to change one's personal schedule.

Sal had told her that he'd meet her at three unless she called him first. She checked her watch again. He'd also said that he would finish his paperwork and take a nap. She knew that paperwork had a tendency to pile up when he didn't feel like doing it but considering that they'd been required to wake up comparatively early to get in on the simulator tests, she doubted that it would be given any kind of priority. He'd be napping, and she didn't want to interrupt that. He got grumpy when he didn't get his sleep. She'd had an example the morning before when it had taken more than a regular quantity of coffee to stop him from charging through that sim as quickly as he could.

Madigan tapped lightly at her phone but shook her head. The reality was that she was in no condition to drive, even if it was a damn long way to where she was still living. The thought occurred to her to head over to Sal's place. It was a lot closer, and maybe she could nap with him.

She shook her head. Best to get to her own place. The coffeemaker in his little house was the worst. She needed the good stuff, and she needed it bad. Sal would have to get through his "paperwork" on his own.

Her mind returned to Courtney. The woman was sweet and a little lost. She wasn't trusting, but she'd had her mind so focused on what she was involved in that it never occurred to her that someone would want to take advantage of her work for their own gains. It made her sad, but Madigan felt good for having been able to at least offer some help. She'd obviously need Sal's okay too before she brought in any new members into Heavy Metal, but she doubted he'd have anything against it.

He'd talked to her about Courtney before and had only had good stuff to say. She doubted that would have changed.

She still felt bad for sending the poor girl off on her own, though. It occurred to her now that she could have walked Courtney home, at least. She seemed to have had trouble handling her drink.

Kennedy shook her head. Aside from walking into the Zoo—which honestly was highly improbable—there wasn't much trouble that Courtney could get into in the Staging Area. The girl would be fine, and once she sobered up, they could talk about her joining their little start-up in earnest.

That was assuming that Madigan remembered what they had talked about. She chuckled and shook her head. No, that wouldn't be a problem.

---

Courtney pushed herself up from the bed. She tingled all over in the best way as she ran her fingers down her naked body. The light sheen of sweat had begun to evaporate and cool her off. It hadn't been too engaging, but since she'd had to do most of the work, she had felt a delicious burn in her muscles toward the end to complement all the other sensations that had rushed through her body at the time.

As her feet hit the ground, she staggered a little and registered a faint soreness between her thighs. That was normal, right? Plus, there was still plenty of alcohol in her system. Both would fade after she'd had some good sleep and coffee.

She turned when she heard a gentle snore from Sal as he rolled over. While she'd put his clothes back on, she'd wondered if she could pull off the same wet dream trick as Madigan had. She smiled and bit her lip as she resisted the urge to go at him again. Maybe some other time.

Courtney slipped into the bathroom, closed the door behind her, and put her clothes on. After a quick moment of thought, she undressed again, pulled her panties off, and hung them over the shower curtain. She smirked as she pulled her pants on again.

Well, it was some evidence that whatever had happened wasn't a wet dream. What he made of finding a strange pair of panties in his room was up to him, of course. She had a few fantasies of how it might play out, but she didn't want to push her luck.

She slipped out of the bathroom. He still slept and snored softly, and she slipped out of the bedroom. She staggered a little on her way to the front door and pulled it shut behind her as she turned to the right to walk toward her house.

With a grimace of irritation, she shielded her eyes from the sun as she looked at a massive expanse of sand that stretched out in front of her instead of road.

"Left," she growled under her breath, turned, and headed back up the road. "Fucking...I live to the left."

---

Anderson focused on the screens when he saw the HUD cameras flicker on to give him and Addison a real-time view of what the soldiers saw. It was odd how even in the middle of the day, the thick foliage inside the Zoo made it seem like the sun was setting. Visibility was low, so the men had activated the selection of sensors that allowed them to see without a full switch to complete night vision.

The colonel gritted his teeth. The Zoo definitely wasn't the nicest of places to be in under any circumstances, but the fact that they now headed directly into the belly of the beast—a metaphor that he really wished was less literal at this point—made it all that much worse.

He gripped the arms of his office chair. He hated to have to sit on the sidelines of these missions. While he'd specialized in mountainous terrain, he also had extensive experience in jungle terrains and could be an asset out in the field on this mission.

No, Anderson thought and shook his head gently. He hadn't been cleared for combat duty for a reason, and he wasn't stupid enough to think that he was in any way better equipped to make that call than a trained therapist. The man was a veteran himself and had served in the army during Desert Storm. He'd handled a lot of the PTSD cases in the military for decades. It was safe to say that he knew what he was talking about.

Even so, the colonel hated his place on the sidelines like this.

"Falcon, do you read?" One of the comms initiated contact. It wasn't Blue Leader.

"I read, what's your status…Blue Three?" Anderson responded once he'd identified the man by his suit's call signal.

"We have some trouble with the comm on our end," Blue Three said and sounded annoyed. "Do you pick up any signal issues?"

He shifted his gaze to the real-time diagnostics and realized a few seconds later how much of a mistake that was. It was all a bunch of gibberish that showed all kinds of errors, for all he knew. He turned to one of the scientists in charge, but the man shook his head.

"No issues on this end," Anderson said over the comm.

"I've been read into reports that indicate that the Zoo can interfere with radio signals. Try to keep the comm as clear as possible."

"Roger that, Falcon, we'll keep you updated on our progress."

"I appreciate that, Blue Three," he responded. It seemed like an intentional design flaw to not account for the signal problems that were supposed to emanate from inside the Zoo. Then again, considering that this would be the only time that these suits would be used there, it might be that the folks in charge of design didn't want to add a new and expensive way of working around something that it wouldn't have to handle ordinarily. If there was some rich bastard who wanted to play cowboy around there, he was sure that the man could design that feature himself.

But that was talking too far into the future for Anderson to worry about. He would probably be retired by the time these suits became available to the general public.

"ETA fifteen seconds," Blue Three growled over the comm. No, the colonel realized, it wasn't a growl. It was a warble, which indicated that something now definitely interfered with the transmission.

The heat signal had begun to move, Anderson realized. He keyed his microphone.

"Blue Team be advised, the target is on the move westbound toward your location," he said. He keyed his mic again. "Blue Team, do you copy?"

A cough of warbled static was interspersed by indecipherable snatches of speech. He could hear that the men attempted to say something but only odd syllables and a warped word made it through here and there. Frustratingly, he couldn't make out anything of real value.

The tone didn't sound good, the colonel decided, and turned to the man in charge of the damned suits.

"Is there anything you guys can do about this?" he asked, his tone more hostile by the second due to the irritation of being unable to hear what his team had tried to communicate. The video footage was now scrambled too, he realized.

"The problem isn't on our end," the lead scientist said and shrugged.

"I don't give a rat's ass," Anderson retorted. "You get me a stable connection with my team if you have to walk out into the Zoo with a damn TV antenna, you hear me?"

He hadn't heard himself speak in that tone in a while, and the results were fairly gratifying. But this wasn't the time to congratulate himself on still having the ability to motivate people into action, he realized as he turned to the screens once more. Despite the flurry of activity around him, the comms were still dead and there was no damn live feed from the HUDs either.

The words still broke through in disjointed snatches, and the overall tone sounded less and less like the operation would even remotely qualify as a success.

Anderson turned to the scientists, who still scrambled to avoid another verbal reprimand. Or maybe they thought that he would actually send them into the Zoo with nothing but comm equipment.

Again, he reminded himself to keep the damned congratulations for another time—preferably one when his people weren't about to die out there.

Suddenly, one of the HUDs activated, and while the comms were still warbled and disjointed, he could make out a reasonable picture of the action through the feed.

Enough, at least, to see it wasn't good. The bright flashes as the massive assault rifle fired repeatedly weren't encouraging, and the blue and red blood that poured from large wounds in the animals that were cut down was vividly graphic.

The worst was that he saw no sign of the rest of the squad, and the man seemed to make no attempt to try to find them again. The single soldier responsible for the barrage of firepower was clearly in a fight for his life.

"Give me the motherfucking comms back now!" Anderson roared and fixed a scowl on the scientists. They already worked at full capacity, so he saw no change in their pace. He had thought that yelling at them would make him feel better, but he was wrong.

"Fuck!" Anderson snarled as he turned and paced the room.

"Falcon, goddamn it, do you copy?" The desperate voice of Blue Leader drew him back to his place at the screens.

"Give me a fucking update!" the colonel snapped as a wave of relief washed over him at the knowledge that there was at least one of the four men still alive.

"Blue Three is down," the voice said. The connection was sound, but the voice sounded loud and jittery. It was still Blue Leader, but the man sounded…different.

"What about the rest of your team?" Anderson asked. He leaned closer to the screen when he realized that the single HUD that had come through was now absent. Had that man been Blue Three? Anderson gritted his teeth and gripped the back of the chair that he'd previously sat in.

There was no response, but the three remaining HUDs came back online with the sound of gunfire over the comms. Shouted orders for the three men to regroup could be heard before the HUD from Blue Leader suddenly flipped on. The image of a massive monster came into view. It was blurred since the movement was so quick, and the footage vanished as quickly as it had appeared.

"Shit," he growled and turned to Addison as the two remaining members of Blue Team began to run. He could see Blue Leader being dragged through the underbrush, but he couldn't tell if the man was alive.

"Calm down, Colonel," Addison said. Anderson looked at his hands. They gripped the chair so tightly that they shook with the strain and the muscles bulged on his forearms.

"I'm not—" he started, then stopped and closed his eyes as he paused to take a quick breath. The comms went dead again, and so did the feeds. He doubted that he'd get them back again.

"Colonel?" the sergeant asked.

He shook his head. "Fuck. This was a fucking mistake," he said and shook his head in an attempt to clear it. "We need to send Red and Green Teams in after them. Recover them. Make sure—"

"Colonel, with all due respect," Addison interrupted, "this is what my men are trained for. They are trained for covert operations. I was on board with them acting as guinea pigs as long as everything was under control and all the problems with these fucking suits were fixed." He raised his voice at the scientists, who still worked furiously to fix the bugs even though the lives were already lost.

Anderson shook his head. "I understand that. Addison, believe me, I understand that."

The sergeant nodded and folded his arms across his chest.

"Fuck," the colonel said again. "This is fucking terrible. This is all on me. I should have realized that going in there without backup was a mistake. I'm so sorry."

"It's not your fault," Addison said with a scowl. "Besides, the chances are that if we'd sent the other two teams in with them, they'd be dead too. So really, it's a good thing that they didn't go."

He shook his head. The adrenaline rushed through his body and made his hands shake as odd flashes of memories that he wanted to be repressed forced their way through. He didn't need this. His assistant would have his pills, but he didn't want to show weakness by taking them in front of his people. He took a deep breath.

"Okay, Sergeant, call up the teams. Tell them to stand down and prepare for an evac," he finally said after a long pause. "Pack up the fucking suits and tell the developers that they need a whole truckload of work." He turned to the scientists. "You got that? Are you working on the bugs?"

The lead scientist turned. He looked more upset than Anderson did, clearly not used to listening in as people died. "We can't—" he started but cleared his throat as he shook his head. "All the problems that we experienced were on their end. Until we get the suits that they used, we won't be able to do anything."

"What *can* you do?" Anderson snapped as Addison exited the building.

"We can request a recovery operation with the Staging Area," the man said, and he obviously struggled to stay calm. "They'll have people trained to deal with the mons… animals in the Zoo, and they stand the best chance of recovering the suits."

He nodded. Better those underwhelming mercenaries than to waste more spec-ops men.

"We've recovered all the footage that they sent out," one of the other men said, his voice shaking. "Much of it is corrupted, but that plus the location data should give whatever team is sent out there a chance."

Anderson nodded. Well, they were human beings too. They deserved the best chance that they could get if they would risk their lives to help fix his mistake.

It was his mistake. There was no denying that. Anderson shook his head.

"Look, I'm sorry for yelling," he finally said with a sigh. "Thank you for all your hard work. I need…I need a moment."

He stepped out of the room and made sure to close the door behind him before he dropped to his haunches and covered his face with his hands.

He needed to write a report about this, he realized. Not only a report, but it had to be on the armor's performance, not…not the death of four men.

Fucking bullshit.

# CHAPTER TEN

Sal opened his eyes and groaned softly. His vision adjusted slowly to the light that glared behind the shades that he'd pulled. It was bright enough in the room to make him groan once again and turn away to pull the pillow over his head.

"Too bright," he growled. "Make the bad yellow face in the sky go away, please."

Reluctantly, he realized that he was too awake to be able to fall asleep again although he longed for a couple more hours of rest, at least. His eyes opened once more and he scowled at the damn window.

He hadn't slept very well. As tired as he'd been, he'd dropped off quickly but into the restless kind of sleep in which he constantly tossed and turned and had some intense dreams.

The dreams hadn't necessarily been bad, though. He pushed himself from the bed with a jaw-splitting yawn that made him close his eyes as he stood and stretched. His body was tender in places that he hadn't realized he'd used, and even then, some of the painful places weren't even muscles. He groaned and rubbed his groin tenderly as he shuffled to the bathroom and grumbled about "crazy sex dreams" as he propped the toilet seat up.

His eyes widened when he saw a pair of panties hanging from the shower curtain rod. His brain was still foggy, so it took him a few seconds to put the pieces together. They had definitely not been there when he'd taken a shower before his nap, which meant that they'd been put there afterward. Ergo—

Sal frowned and glanced around. He moved to the door of the bathroom and peered out to make sure there wasn't anyone on his bed.

There wasn't, and he blinked. It hadn't been the first time Madigan had pulled something like this, he knew that, but he thought that she'd given up on the sneaking around. They didn't exactly advertise their relationship, but neither did they hide it anymore.

So it hadn't been a dream. He plucked the underwear from the rail and inspected it closely. There was nothing to indicate who owned it, but who else could belong it to? The panties had to be Madigan's.

He shrugged and hung them up again before he concluded his business in the bathroom. After washing his hands, he picked them up again and studied the pink lace as he returned the bedroom. Madigan didn't usually wear pink lace. Sal had enjoyed a fairly wide selection of her underwear over the past few months. She usually wore black, and…well, lacy, but more often than not, she varied between hot and racy to utilitarian and comfortable. It was odd how both made her look fantastic, although maybe that was more about what they encased than the actual fabric or design.

Pink and cute simply didn't seem her style, though, Sal thought as he sat down on his bed. And it wasn't like she had a lot of opportunities to invest in new clothes out there.

Then again, what the hell did he know about women's underwear? Sal nodded and conceded the point as he opened his closet to reveal the safe that had come with his room. He wondered if they expected people to have something that they needed to put in a safe. Then again, there were some fairly high-profile folks who lived there, and since they were assigned random living situations, maybe it was a good idea to put a safe in every house.

Sal sure was thankful for it. He punched in his twelve-digit code and waited for the device to catch up with his quick dialing. Finally, it beeped, and green light glowed across the buttons before it unlocked. He put the panties beside the ones that Madigan had left behind and reached in deeper. His hands closed around the sealed container and pulled it out.

It had once been one of the environment containers, but after a few months of caring for a plant that was probably worth somewhere over four million dollars, he had devised a few interesting methods to keep the plant alive during the frequent trips he took. It needed indirect light, so he fitted a small grow lamp that he'd "borrowed" from one of the labs on base to turn on and off in time with the sun outside. After a few different attempts, he'd also managed to find a way to pump the water in through a small device at the bottom that infused the soil rather than dripping over the Pita plant.

It wasn't the best solution, which was why it took a little while to grow, but two flowers had already bloomed on it, and he could see a third take shape among the leaves. Everything was clear and green, and the flowers gave off a gentle glow that was consistent with what they were observed to do in the wild.

"Nice to see you happy and healthy, Madie," Sal said with a smile and moved the container out in the sunlight she'd been deprived of while being hidden inside the safe. He refilled the water pump, which had enough water to last for almost a full month. This was something he always did diligently at regular intervals, but it was easier to do it whenever he took her out of the safe since he did that regularly to run his tests.

He donned his gloves and opened the container. A quick scan made sure that none of the horror pheromones had been released. He ran a quick check on the artificial soil to make sure that it still had all the nutrients needed and also tested the acidity level. There was nothing out of the ordinary, thankfully. It had taken a fair amount of testing to find the perfect combination that would keep Madie happy and healthy.

Was it odd that he considered this plant more and more like a child or beloved pet? Well, he didn't have either, but he assumed that this was how he would treat any future children or pets he might have.

"Getting waaaay ahead of yourself there, Salinger Jacobs," he said to himself as he found a syringe in his pouch and pressed the tip into the bud of the flower. That had taken a lot of testing too, but eventually, he had eventually identified where the flowers had the heaviest concentration of the goop he wanted. It was different when they were picked since the goop was flushed out into the petals and therefore diluted.

He stopped at three milligrams when the area that he thought of as the goop sac under the flower began to lose some of its glow. He needed to run more tests to see how much could be withdrawn and still leave the blossom unaffected. With the first that had bloomed, he'd gone too far. After he'd drawn every last drop of goop, the flower had wilted the next day. He'd proceeded with a lot more caution after that.

Sal left Madie to soak in some sunlight through the shades, moved to the kitchen with the syringe, and opened a package of water crackers that he'd otherwise ignored until now. Depressing the syringe plunger, he coated a cracker with the blue, glowing goop. Well, not all of it. There wasn't enough of the stuff to cover the entire surface of the snack, but it was enough for a trial run. He inhaled. The goop had an odd smell. It wasn't a bad smell—fresh and light, the way blueish-green might smell if it were an odor and not a color. But at the same time, it wasn't appetizing, in much the same way that the smell of soap was nice, but you didn't want to eat it.

The scientist grinned when remembered the one time his grandmother had washed his mouth out with coconut soap after he'd said a few choice words about not being able to spend the night at the house of a friend who had received a PlayStation for his birthday. He hadn't been able to taste anything else for a week afterward.

"Well, down the hatch," he said and winced as he realized that he had started to talk to himself more and more over the past couple of months. If he kept this up, he would become an evil, demented scientist within the next year or so if poorly-thought-up backstories in bad action flicks were to be believed. That or he would invent something that would be evil.

Either way, the end of the world by this time next year wasn't an impossibility.

He bit down on the cracker and managed to take the entire thing in one bite. There wasn't enough of the stuff on there to taste much. Hints of freshness much like a breath mint immediately released, and as the stuff made contact with the skin inside his mouth, it burned like a hot pepper and made him chew and swallow quickly. He filled a glass of water and gulped it down.

"Every time," he complained and shook his head. He always forgot that it tasted like the world's strongest jalapeño.

Sal moved back to his room and added the syringe to the used pile in his pouch before he zipped it up and placed it with the rest of his equipment. He sealed Madie's container and once again made sure that none of the anger pheromones were released before he slipped it back into the safe.

"There's nothing like an experiment you're willing to test on yourself, right, Madie?" he asked before he closed the safe once more and made sure to wait until it secured. That done, he pulled fresh clothes on and, with another stretch to try to ease his sore muscles, made his way to the door. It was almost three, and Madigan would already be waiting for him. He wondered if meeting at the bar was a good idea. It seemed like he did nothing more than help her along with her drinking problem, all because it was a convenient place to find work.

He needed money, so she needed to get this under control. He was in a bar all day and didn't get drunk on a regular basis, after all.

# CHAPTER ELEVEN

As it turned out, she wasn't early. He looked for her at the entrance and wondered if she had gone inside. The possibility that she was still in there, drinking or sleeping it off, also crossed his mind, but he put it aside. He already knew that she had taken a detour, at least.

After a few minutes of waiting, he was about to turn back when an JLTV pulled up outside. The driver weaved from one side to the other, which would have been spectacularly dangerous if there had been anyone else on the road. Thankfully, there wasn't, and Sal had only a handful of nail-biting moments before Kennedy jerked to a stop in front of him. She wore sunglasses and looked a little flushed. He raised a brow and grinned.

"Well…look what the cat dragged in," he said with a soft chuckle as she pulled herself out of the vehicle.

"Not…not so loud," she said and raised a hand.

"I'd ask if you had a rough night," he said as he checked his watch, "but considering that it's actually three-oh-four in the afternoon, should I ask how your morning went instead?"

"There was drinking," Kennedy muttered. "And there was talking to a blonde. And then there was…" She paused and shook her head.

"That's okay," he responded with a small smile and patted her on the shoulder. "I think I have a good idea of what you did."

Kennedy lowered her glasses to glare at him. "What did I tell you?"

"Not…so loud?" Sal asked and raised a brow. He was usually allowed to make lewd references to their meet-ups provided that he kept it properly veiled. It seemed like she wasn't in the mood for that either. Was only a couple of hours of sleep enough to create a hangover?

"Exactly," she said and patted his cheek lightly. "Anyway, what do you have for us?"

"I just got here myself," Sal explained as they headed to the door. "I was looking for you since I said that we would meet here at three unless you called me. Since you didn't, I wasn't sure if you were still sleeping it off."

She looked at him again. "You're acting weird. Why are you acting weird?"

He tilted his head as he pushed the door open for her. "I have no idea what you mean. I'm always weird, remember."

"No, you're weirder than usual." She walked in and waited for him to follow before she continued in a low voice. "If you want to have sex, you'll have to wait. I'm still a little buzzed."

He nodded. "Fair enough, but that'll probably have to wait too." He went to the board inside the bar. It was used by most the people on base who wanted jobs or had jobs and needed people. Since everyone stationed there essentially haunted the bar at some point or another during the day, it was the only way to facilitate work arrangements without having to use the base's server—which, like most things, came with a horde of fees.

There were more than a few excuses that he used to escape his sense of guilt over facilitating Kennedy's problem. He really needed to talk to her about it.

Before he studied the board, he turned to her and tapped her shoulder. "Get us a table, would you? And do me a favor, try not to get too drunk before I get there."

"No worries on that end, friend of mine," she whispered, tugged her sunglasses off, and tucked them into her shirt. "What I need is some serious hydration."

"I think I'm there with you. Could you get me something to drink too?"

Sal held his phone up to the board, took pictures of the various postings, and noted those that would take place within the next few days. One in particular caught his interest—a research trip sponsored by a lab back in the US that would pay top dollar for registration and qualification of the different animal and plant species that had appeared in the last six months.

He guessed that they would probably still search for the Pita plants, but it wouldn't be the focus of their work. The study and research were what he liked doing most while in the Zoo, and honestly, the necessity to kill things while they gathered the flowers for money seemed like a necessary evil that he had to tolerate to be able to go out there and get data. The job was perfect.

When he walked to the table, Kennedy was already deep in conversation with a couple of men prepping for their trip into the Zoo the next day. A quick look told him that this was the team that would do the research run. Not because they had any physical traits that gave them away, but because he'd worked with them before.

"Jacobs!" one of them said. Because of his short stature and bright orange hair, everyone called him the Leprechaun, even though he had actually been born in southern Michigan and, according to him, had no trace of Irish blood.

"Sergeant Young," he said and gripped the man's extended hand. Despite being almost a full head shorter than Sal was himself, the man's strength was more than prodigious, and he pulled the specialist in for a hug tight enough to leave him gasping at the end of it.

"How the hell are you doing?" Young asked as he ruffled Sal's hair. "Last I heard, you was in business for yourself."

"Yeah, I opened my own company," he said with a laugh as he fumbled to restore order to his hair with his fingers. "If you're not a gunner, they merely milk you dry when you work for the military. I got out of my contract and started running jobs for myself. It's mostly research stuff like testing out the new armor, but Kennedy and I have ached for a Zoo run for a while."

"Yep, yep, the former Sergeant Kennedy filled us in on that," the sergeant replied and winked at Kennedy, who grinned and shook her head. "After that very profitable trip that the five of us had together last month…" He indicated three other members of his team, whom Sal remembered were called Sousa, Ito, and Carson. "We've ached to take another trip with the two of you. Although now you work for yourself, we were worried that you wouldn't take any more trips into the Zoo."

"Well, that's not true." Kennedy patted a seat that she'd saved for Sal. "But it's a little more difficult for us to find jobs that need personnel. Are you guys playing that research trip that starts tomorrow?"

"Yeah," Young replied as he followed Sal's example and took a seat. "Big money is backing an excursion for the lab geeks to look around. We're actually in need of a couple more specialists and wouldn't mind a couple more gunners too. Despite the amount of money funding this, most of it's going into R&D instead of boots on the ground, so we're actually short on staff."

"Hey, no need to ask us twice," Sal said and raised a hand in mock-surrender as he looked at the glass that Kennedy had put in front of him. She'd gotten Diet Cokes for both of them, he thought with a twist of his mouth. He supported the idea, but not the choice of drink. He took a sip anyway.

"I can't promise a full wage for freelancers, but that's not why most folks have joined this field trip anyway," Young continued. "There are a lot of incentives. Bringing in new specimens gets a bonus. The more details involved, the bigger the bonus, of course. Plus, we'll head into Pita-rich territory, and there's always money in that."

Sal nodded. "No one pays freelancers full-wage, sadly, but we don't mind. We're in it for the incentives. Plus, we can use our specialized company tech to find the Pitas easier, which means more incentives. Also, the small matter of the bounties on the flowers—that will be split evenly across the whole team, right?"

"Bullshit," Kennedy interjected. It was a back-and-forth that they'd worked on to help the teams see what they would gain by letting the freelancers come with them without actually putting it out there.

"Come on, it's only fair," he explained and tried not to be too theatrical about it. "I mean, it's their mission to begin with. We're simply along for the ride."

"Well, we appreciate the gesture, believe me," Young said. "I have a little one who'll start college in a few years that I'd like to be fully paid for with my time here."

"Who are you to call anyone little?" Ito asked, grinned, and yelped as Young's hand flashed across the small table to smack her across the head.

"I'll call you little if I please it, Ito," Young retorted good-naturedly.

Sal and Kennedy laughed and clinked glasses before taking a celebratory sip of their non-alcoholic beverages.

"So what time do you guys plan to take off tomorrow?" Kennedy asked once the tussle between Ito and Young had died down.

"Well, the idea is to start at sunrise, close to around oh-five-thirty, but with the amount of non-military personnel involved, I'd say that we probably won't leave before oh-six hundred." Young drank deeply from his beer.

"We'll be there at sunrise, then," Sal said. "If only to keep your opinion on specialists from dropping too low."

Young chuckled. "We all know you're no specialist, Jacobs. Sure, maybe you are, technically, but with a shooting arm like that, I'd say that you're more of a gunner.

Besides, after the fighting that we forced you to put up with the last time, you've earned the right to be a little late, specialist or no."

"Please," Sal said. "That little skirmish with the bounty hunters was nothing compared to the shit we ran into on my first trip into the Zoo. I think I told you that story when we got back, right?"

Young nodded. "That was one hell of a hazing stunt Kennedy and her people pulled on your first time, no lying. Still, I'm glad they did, elsewise you would have simply been another soft geek when we met up, and we would have never come to know the badass that lay underneath."

"No need to butter his ego up any more than it is already," Kennedy protested and shook her head.

Sal grinned in response. "I don't think my ego has ever needed that kind of lubrication anyway." The team laughed, and she groaned.

"Let's change the subject," Young said. "Please. I really didn't need that mental image. I wanted to talk to you anyway, Jacobs, before we left. We had a couple of run-ins with some new and interesting wildlife on our last run into the Zoo. Sadly, though, our specialist died in the field before he could punch all the shit into the server. Unfortunately, that means our team lost out on the bounty that usually goes into that. It's not much in the way of cash, but if you'd like some quick spending money, you'd get the full specialist cut on it."

Sal nodded. "If you send it over to me, I can have it turned in before we take off tomorrow."

"You're the best, Jacobs," Young said with a laugh.

"Come on, Young." Kennedy shook her head. "Sure, it

makes you feel good, but I'm the one who has to work with him when he's riding the compliments like a fucking sugar high."

"Hey," Sal said. "I can take a compliment without getting all uppity about it."

"You might want to try it once in a while," she said, almost under her breath but not quite.

Young laughed. "So, why are the two of you only drinking the virgin stuff?"

Kennedy shrugged. "I don't know about him, but I'm coming off a rough bout from earlier today. I need something to take the edge off, and something without alcohol seemed like the right thing."

Sal looked at her oddly. Now she simply laid it out for everyone else to see? It seemed odd, considering how much she protected her image in front of these guys. Or wanted him to protect her image, anyway.

He shook his head. He would probably bring it up when they were alone, but it was something that could wait.

"Well, considering that I still need a couple of active brain cells for when I spend most of the night putting all this data into the local server, I think that not drinking is the way to go for me," Sal said with a small smile.

Young shrugged. "I've got to say, I admire your resilience. While I'm fairly sure I don't share it, if you do plan to put a real drink in you, the first round is on me. For the both of you," he added and winked at Kennedy again. She chuckled and patted his cheek.

"I might take you up on that, Young," she said with a grin, "but I have some work I need to get done. You ladies can walk into the armory and walk out with some subpar equipment. Us freelancers need to pay for our subpar shit."

"Hey," Ito interjected as she flicked her hair back. "I take offense to that. They're the only ladies on this squad." She indicated the rest of the men on her team.

They laughed at the joke but instinctively straightened their postures and puffed their chests out at the comment.

"Well, now that the testosterone is suitably pumped up in the room," Kennedy said with a raised eyebrow, "I think I need to go and make sure that we're all stocked up for tomorrow." She patted Sal's shoulder. "I'll meet up with you tonight for an inventory check."

He nodded. "I'll get started on those specimen reports too."

"Well, I didn't mean to bring the mood down," Young said, not happy that they were leaving. Sal suspected it was because the man had something of a crush on Kennedy. He could see why, of course. He chuckled and pushed from his seat.

"You didn't," Sal replied as Kennedy had already headed toward the door. "Us freelancers need to work odd hours. It comes with the territory." He patted the man on the shoulder, and after a moment of hesitation, mussed his hair up too.

"Revenge is a dish best served cold." He laughed as Young slapped his hand away. "I'll see you guys tomorrow morning."

The team raised their glasses in response, and Sal broke into a jog to catch up with Kennedy.

"You're going to see Boulos then?" he asked when they reached the parking lot.

"Yeah, he's still working on my armor," she said. "Don't worry about it. I'll bring all the equipment to the take-off point at o-dark-thir—"

Sal raised his eyebrows, and she shook her head.

"Sunrise," she explained. "I'll bring the equipment at sunrise."

Sal nodded as she turned and walked to the JLTV, but after a moment, he called her back.

He needed to talk to her. Ground rules needed to be put in place during a real talk. This was fun and all, but he felt like some things were spiraling, and he wasn't sure that he had it in him to check the fall on his own.

"What's up, Jacobs?" Kennedy asked as she retrieved her sunglasses and slid them on.

It didn't need to be now, though.

"I'll see you later." He shook his head. Kennedy knew there was something on his mind, but she was almost as bad at approaching stuff as he was. They both needed to get better at it. Later.

"Yeah," she said with a smile. "I'll come around to your place after I'm finished at Boulos'."

"I look forward to it." Sal forced a smile in response.

# CHAPTER TWELVE

She knew there was something bothering him. He'd also grown more and more protective of her. It wasn't that she didn't approve. For once, she didn't mind that there was someone out there who cared about her, mostly because he didn't force his care on her. He showed it, kept his distance, and made sure that she wanted it first.

Sal was weird in all the right ways. She'd never thought that brainy would be her type. Then again, there were a couple of things that she had learned about herself that had been a surprise. Not all of them were pleasant, but they weren't necessarily unpleasant, either.

She smiled, maintained a firmer grip on the wheel than she usually did, and eased her foot off the gas pedal. It wasn't like these damn vehicles could move that fast anyway. She'd grown up driving cars that her father had "improved" and tried them out with her brothers. They always broke down after a couple of miles, but they could rush those miles faster than most cars could.

There was probably some sort of gem of wisdom that

she could glean from that little nugget of information from her past. She might even be able to figure it out later. For now, though, she kept her mind focused on the tasks at hand. Maybe after a couple of beers and some time relaxing with Sal.

Provided that their relaxing didn't take the rest of the night.

She smiled at the thought as she pulled to a stop outside the armory, yanked the parking brake on, and hopped out. It was only a quarter past four, so the place would still be fairly busy considering that there were a couple of patrols heading out the next day as well as the field trip, as Young had put it.

If she was honest, she felt cooped up when she simply hung around the base, even if it was the safer option. They made decent money for their part in testing the new suits and new weapons. Since companies now used the Zoo as a test and display ground for their new popular products, that was a cash cow that would pay indefinitely if they wanted it.

Still, she wanted to be out in the Zoo. It wasn't the easiest work, but it did have a sense of realization that came with it. Like she did something for the betterment of mankind. Well, protecting folk that were doing something for the betterment of mankind by shooting hostile creatures in their very exotic faces.

It was the best job in the world, Madigan thought with a grin.

She moved through the aisles of armor and noted the inventory officers who rushed around and checked off the various items that they needed. Their needs kept the folks working in the store busy. If she knew Boulos, though, he would hang out in the back and pretend to be busy. Folks with budgets were assholes, she knew that all too well.

Oh, to have a budget paid for by somebody else. She paused to think about how nice that would be for a few seconds before she moved to the back of the armory. Her gaze swept the store in search of where Boulos might hide his massive bulk behind a tiny laptop to pretend that he was too busy "filling orders" to help those who needed orders filled out in person.

She found him where she'd expected to. He was hunched over a small pad that was propped up against a couple of RPGs in the very far corner.

"Boulos?" Madigan asked.

"I'm filling some orders," he said without looking up. "I think Albie can help you. He's at the front desk."

"Right," she said with a grin and leaned against a shelf. "I think you've used that a few too many times since there's nobody at the front desk anymore. You do know that it's a prime sales day for you today, right?"

He looked up from his pad and blinked. "Oh, Kennedy. I didn't realize you were coming today."

"Well, some shit came up," she explained, moved in closer, and peeked at the display on the pad. She made a face when she finally saw it. "You know, I hear that the dialogue in these movies is the worst."

"It's not like there's a wide variety of choices out here," Boulos argued but hastily removed the porn from the screen. "I'd kill for a satellite internet connection—and not only for access to decent porn."

Madigan shrugged. "Hey, I'm with you on that.

Although people like you and me are probably the reason why they decided to skimp on the satellite connection and forced us to use the highly regulated base server instead."

Boulos laughed. "Well, I'm glad to know that I'm not alone here. But enough about hypothetical porn access. What can I do for you today, Kennedy?"

"Well," she said, "it looks like Jacobs and I are going into the Zoo again sooner than expected, so I'm really here in the hope that you're done with my armor so we can get it out there."

He nodded. "It's basically finished. I only need to tweak the sensors a little. I saw a couple of problems that came from buggy hardware, so I fixed that. I'll finish it off and have it over to you tonight if that's okay."

"That works," Madigan responded. "I also hoped that you could fix me up with something for Jacobs."

Boulos tilted his head. "I thought he already had a specialist suit?"

"He does," she replied. "But I wondered if you had something that worked more like a hybrid. Folk expect him to take on the responsibilities of a gunner more and more, and while he's shouldered it like a champ, I have to keep his ass alive—at least until I get the big payout that I joined his company for."

The store manager nodded and turned his attention to his pad. "I think I have something for you. It has some power armor functionality, especially an armored gun arm that's fitted for some of the newer, bigger assault rifles that they make, but it's still relatively nimble. It's as close to a hybrid as I have within your budget. How will you pay for this, by the way?"

"Put it on the company's bill," she said. "I'll talk to Jacobs about it, and if he doesn't want it there, I can eat it."

"Really?"

"Yeah." Madigan shrugged. "Again, all the costs that I end up paying myself are considered investments in the company, all of which add up to the percentages that I'll receive when we make it big."

Boulos looked impressed. "It sounds like you have all the business details figured out."

"Well, I have the getting paid part figured, anyway." She grinned at him. "After that, all the decisions get a whole lot easier."

"That's basically it in a nutshell, to be honest. I'll have all the stuff delivered to your place in the mor—" He paused when she raised an eyebrow. "This evening. I'll have it delivered in a few hours."

"That's what I wanted to hear, Boulos." She winked at him. "See you on the flip side."

"You'd best survive this trip, Kennedy," he said as she walked away. "You and Jacobs are my best customers."

"Best?"

"Well, favorite, anyway," he conceded. "Good luck."

"You too."

# CHAPTER THIRTEEN

Sal leaned closer to the screen and studied the display. About six months ago, if he'd been shown a picture like this, he would have immediately called bullshit. Something about that kind of cranial structure had no place on Earth—nor something of that size, either. For a moment, he was forced to wonder what kind of life he would now live if he hadn't come all the way over there to risk his life at the cutting edge of biology.

Well, his sex life had certainly received a jump start since he'd arrived. He also exercised a lot more, so that was a bonus.

But all in all, this was the stuff he lived for. The first picture was incredibly blurry and made defining what he looked at difficult. The eyes were spread like a praying mantis', but the animal had an endoskeleton and bone structure that told him that whatever the goop was, it liked to mix and match various kinds of animals and plants together. It almost seemed like it tried to find an ideal creature—evolution mixed with genetic splicing. In most western countries, this kind of experimental shit was illegal, which in turn explained why so many people were interested in the results.

He leaned back, rubbed his eyes, and shook his head. A couple more pictures were somewhat clearer and revealed a projection of the torso that was segmented like an insect's but also furred like a mammal's. It only had four legs, though. Comparing sizes was a little difficult.

The reason why he stared at the very blurry image was that it was the only shot of the creature from the front and thus gave him an unimpeded if fuzzy view of the thing's head. The specialist had obviously panicked and perhaps thought that the creature had looked directly at him, but with eyes mounted like that on such an odd skull, it had clearly already seen the man and looked around to identify any other threats.

He made another note that the eyes' positioning on the skull indicated an herbivorous diet, although he put a question mark on that. It was clear that this was not the animal that had attacked and killed the specialist in question, but it was still new. Nothing in the database indicated the existence of something like this, which made Sal wonder how much the discovery was worth.

There were sections of the animal that certainly classified it as a "rare species"—the kind that weren't already existing creatures with logical enhancements to size, strength, and agility, but were actually combinations of different creatures as well as additions that weren't even on record for existing animals. Rare animals were those that also brought in the heftiest paydays. It was difficult to really say what these creatures were capable of, but Sal felt that this sort of thing was what he was supposed to be both fascinated and terrified by.

It was his favorite combination.

The whitepaper had begun to take shape. Thankfully, whoever the late specialist was, they had been thorough in their documentation of the animals that they encountered. While the creature that he was looking at was the only one of note, there were also a number of additions he needed to make to some of the animals that were already in the database.

He looked outside, surprised to see that the sun had already set. Time really did seem to fly when he had fun. He leaned back in his seat, and the cheap office chair that had been provided with the apartment squealed under the strain.

Why had Madigan felt the need to come to him when he was asleep? Was she drunk and simply in need of a fuck? Did she not want to wake him? Did she think that if she woke him, he might not be in the mood?

Well, she would have had a point, he realized. To wake him in the middle of a nap was a gamble. He'd either wake up willing and able or angry and sleepy.

He stretched his arms above his head and groaned lazily. His nap hadn't had the intended effect, and he already felt weary. That added to the fact that he would probably not have another good night's sleep for what could be up to a week in the Zoo meant that he might want to simply complete this whitepaper, enter it into the database, and check if the payment came through in the morning. Madigan would understand if he put off their meeting.

Then again, he realized that, too, was something of a lottery. Of the Russian variety.

He put a note on the creature's apparent lack of six limbs in a separate file. He wanted to add enough to the database for him and the squad to get their payday, but he also wanted to retain the more complete store of information about the animals in the Zoo for himself. Nothing that might compromise the lives of the soldiers in there, but definitely the kind that would bring profit once he was able to complete his collection.

Holy shit, he hoped that his selective sharing of information didn't put lives in danger.

---

As she opened her eyes, she dreaded the sensation of light that seared her eyeballs. The darkness that greeted her was an intense relief.

It was the only kind of relief that she would have for a while, she mused. A vague sensation of vertigo filled her body, followed quickly by the very familiar feeling of nausea. Her mouth was dry, and her body ached vaguely all over.

"Damn it," she murmured and pushed herself up from the ground. She'd tried to get to bed, at least, which showed that she'd had some presence of mind. Still, she hadn't been that drunk. Drunker than she'd ever been before—she could concede that much—but nothing like the stories she'd heard from her friends in the sorority that her mother had pressured her to join of how they'd blacked out. Memories of what had happened while she was drunk were unclear, but they were there.

The relief that washed over her was quickly pushed aside when she realized that her thighs were sore as well as what lay between them. She hadn't been a prude in college, despite that she never drank as much as her "sisters" had, and she knew that feeling very well, even though she hadn't experienced it in a while.

The memory of where it had come from rushed in too. The feeling of need as she'd stepped into Sal's apartment. Her lowered inhibitions had overridden her moral compass to allow her to take what she'd wanted, no matter the fact that he hadn't even been conscious enough to know what she'd given, nor by whom it had been given.

The memory of him hardening in her hand brought that need back to her, but there was also a sensation of disgust that pushed it easily to the back of her mind.

"Holy shit," she whispered and rubbed her temples, which now pounded painfully. "What the hell did I do? Although he was happy to be involved and he'd moaned and helped me along."

She stumbled to the kitchen and filled a glass with water, then hunted for aspirin to take with it. It would very likely bring little relief, but it would have to be enough. She needed her mind clear.

"What can you offer a guy to make him forget the fact that you essentially raped him?" she wondered aloud as she gulped the pill and water down. "I mean, I could always not tell him. The fact that I didn't wake up in cuffs tells me that he didn't call the authorities." That said, there was no way to know exactly what and how much he remembered. It could all be a dream to him, or he could remember everything.

It was a risk that she would have to take. She couldn't keep this to herself, especially if she wanted to work with him. Shit. Them. Did she have to tell Kennedy? Well, maybe Sal could do that for her and spare her the trouble.

She needed a shower first, though. Courtney quickly stripped off the clothes that she still wore from the day before and stepped into the shower. She sighed as she felt hot water wash over her bare skin and almost hoped that it would help change her mind about what she had to do, but no such luck.

"Fuck," she whispered and scrunched her eyes tightly closed.

---

Madigan shook her head. The alcohol had begun to clear from her system, and despite her best efforts to rehydrate herself, she still hadn't managed to ward off all the effects of the drinking. Her mouth felt like the desert outside, and she knew the vague pounding that had started in her head would only get worse.

There was only one hope now, and that was that she wouldn't still be hung over come morning. Which meant she had to get some food and water in her system.

She shook her head, dressed again, and headed to the mess hall. The place wasn't as busy as it could have been, she realized. It was already past rush hour. Most folks came to eat around six or seven, and it was already eight-thirty.

Despite the fact that her stomach rebelled against each bite, she forced herself to eat, and thankfully, it seemed to settle a little more with each mouthful.

Her cure had already begun to work.

She complimented the meal of mashed potatoes, steak, and string beans with soda to help ease her sensitive stomach further.

There was still no promise that she would function efficiently in the morning. Then again, if she was hung over, it wouldn't be the first time she went out into the Zoo absolutely wasted. In fact, when she thought about it, there were more than a few of her earlier trips of which she had no memory of the first day or so.

She smirked. Rose-tinted goggles or not, those had been good times. Still, she felt like times were about to get better. She smirked, pushed to her feet, and once she'd punched her use of the mess hall in, she left. Fucking freelancing meant she was charged for everything she used. It was par for the course when it came to government-run facilities, and this place was no different. It still stung given the many years' service she had behind her.

Madigan stepped outside and breathed in the cool desert air.

"What do you know?" she said to herself. "I do feel better." Was it weird that the more time she spent with Sal, the more she talked to herself? She wondered if he realized he did it. There had been a few times when she'd spend the night and woke up to him muttering like he was in the middle of an argument with himself.

Then again, she had seen him argue with other people. She would never tell him to his face, but he was the smartest man she knew. Having an argument with himself was the only way his opponent even stood a chance to get a word in.

She decided not to call for an JLTV. Sure, she did have some quasi-religious objections to walking anywhere she didn't have to, but like everything else in the damned base, she had to pay for that too. Well, she always charged it back to Heavy Metal, but she still felt guilty. She knew that Sal knew what she did, but he never confronted her about it. That was the worst part.

Kennedy gritted her teeth. Maybe she could walk tonight. It was in that twilight hour where the place still absorbed the heat from the sand that had been blasted by the sun all day. Everything in the desert cooled off quickly, though.

It was the perfect temperature for a nice walk through the Staging Area.

"He's making me a better person," she complained. "Or a more conscientious one, anyway."

She set off and paced herself like she did when she was in the Zoo, making sure to maintain a constant speed. Her boots struck the pavement in a neat, almost musical rhythm.

Was this what meditation was like? She'd never been able to do it when she sat cross-legged and chanted inanities. But losing herself in the repetitive movement and rhythm of walking allowed time to pass quicker. While she would have preferred to drive, she certainly could get used to this walking stuff.

Not that she would do it often. Sal had made her more conscientious, not a masochist.

She blinked, and her mind slipped out of the daze that she'd dropped into when someone stepped into her path. Someone who hadn't seen her and yet headed in the same direction.

Madigan narrowed her eyes and focused on the figure now slightly ahead of her. They were between streetlights, which made it difficult to see who it was, but the flicker of light on short blonde hair, plus the distinctive half strutting gait that she'd come to recognize, told her it was Courtney.

The fact that she was there wasn't too hard to explain. The specialist lived in the area and only a few blocks away, in fact. Where she was going made less sense, though. She moved away from her own home toward the houses on the outskirts.

When the woman turned into the street that Sal lived on, Kennedy felt less like they were walking the same path and more like she was a stalker. Like she was some sort of psycho, jealous girlfriend who followed the women that her man hung out with.

It wasn't a pleasant sensation, she realized. She didn't feel jealous, but the thought that Sal might think she was didn't sit well with her.

They moved closer to Sal's home. Madigan wondered if denial was the reason why she had somehow convinced herself that Courtney was going somewhere else, right up to the moment that she went down the path that led to his door. She gritted her teeth as the specialist knocked.

Had Sal called her there? Was this some sort of planned tryst?

It took him longer than anticipated to answer the door, and the blonde knocked again, more insistently this time.

"I'm coming, damn it," Kennedy heard him say, and a few seconds later, light flowed into the darkened street and he stood in the doorway.

"Courtney?" Sal asked, and a confused smile played on his lips. "What are you doing here?"

Well, at least it didn't seem like he had expected her, Madigan thought. Small victories.

"Hey, Sal…Jacobs," his visitor said and shook her head.

"You can call me Sal," he said with a chuckle.

"Sure, Sal," Courtney said and brushed her hair quickly out of her face with a small smile. "I need to talk to you. Can I come in?"

"Uh… Yeah, sure." He stepped aside so she could enter. Madigan scrunched her face with the effort to resist the urge to walk up to the door before he closed it again, announce her arrival, and interrupt whatever it was that the other woman was there to say.

The nice feeling that she'd had before disappeared. She wasn't jealous. Definitely not. But it still felt odd that she wasn't happy about Sal talking to Courtney alone.

Seriously, she reminded herself, she wasn't jealous. She simply didn't like it. It wasn't like he was her husband or anything and she had no real claim on him. They simply worked together and had a little fun on the side. Who was she to claim exclusive rights to his fun?

Okay, maybe she might be a teeny bit jealous.

# CHAPTER FOURTEEN

"So," Sal said and looked expectantly at Courtney, who had taken a seat on his couch. "What brings you here to my neck of the very proverbial woods?" He moved to the kitchen and filled two glasses with water. He would have offered her something else if he had it. He really needed to restock with something that wasn't dry crackers that tasted stale no matter how new the packaging said they were.

She smiled and didn't answer until he moved closer and set the glass of cool water in her hands before he sat on his office chair across from her.

"I needed to talk to you about something," she said.

"So you said," he acknowledged with a nod. "Don't take this the wrong way, but you look rather the worse for wear. If I didn't know better, I'd say that you suffer from a severe case of hung-overitis. I obviously don't know you that well, but you simply never seemed to be the type of person to drink a lot. Socially or otherwise."

Courtney shrugged her shoulders. "I made an exception today. It was a seriously shitty day."

Sal nodded. "I hear that. Is that what you came here to talk about?"

"Well, sort of." She paused to take a sip of the water and winced. For a moment, she thought that the water tasted bad, but then she remembered how bad her mouth tasted, and she swallowed smoothly and took another sip before she continued. "I just got back from a trip to the Zoo. They paired me with a bad team. Not incompetent, but the folks weren't the nicest. It was while I was in there that I realized that the contract that I work under has left far too much to the interpretation of the team leaders I'm sent in with. Long story short, they screwed me out of a big payday over something that I literally had no power over."

Sal nodded and leaned back in his seat. "Well, you know the conditions under which I was brought here, so you know that I mean it when I say that I've been there and done that. It sucks hard. And not in a nice way."

Courtney chuckled, made a face again, and shook her head. "Anyway, I had a chat with one of the cooler members of the squad once we got back, and he basically woke me up to the fact that I would do much better if I had someone to help me to negotiate my contracts—maybe even someone to look at them and help me to figure out what I should do with my time here, you know?"

Sal nodded cautiously. "Um…sure. I always thought you were here to be on the cutting edge of your field and all that. The money merely provided something of an incentive for a job well done."

She shrugged. "Yes, but at this point, with everything I've learned, I can probably make a lot more money if I return to the States and head up some sort of task force hell-bent on recreating the goop's conditions—and with a lot fewer risks involved. Specifically of the 'kill you and eat you' variety. But at the same time, I still feel like I need some guidance on how to handle the whole situation. Someone to keep my focus not on the work I want to do, but what I want to get out of it, you know? And if I'm honest, you and Kennedy are the only ones who really spring to mind when I wonder who I can turn to for help on that."

"That's...interesting." Sal paused to bite the inside of his cheek before he continued. "I'd be happy to help you out there, and I'm sure that Ma—Kennedy would feel the same." *Dammit.* "I can't speak for her, but to me, you're one of the good ones. You were there with me on my first run into that fucking jungle, and you're one of the few who actually helped me out there. So, again, I can't speak for Kennedy, but you're damn right I'll help you in any way I can. And I'm sure that my partner in crime will say the same if-slash-when you ask her."

Courtney smiled and winced. Again. Sal narrowed his eyes and leaned forward to rest his elbows on his knees as he studied her keenly.

"What's the matter?" he asked when he realized that she avoided his gaze.

"There's probably something you should know before you agree to get into any deals with me," she said, clearly uncomfortable now. "And while I really, really appreciate everything you said about me being one of the good ones, you might want to hold off on that kind of judgment as well."

Sal leaned back again and left his glass of water untouched on the coffee table to his right as he looked sternly at Courtney. Well, he tried, anyway. He wasn't sure how to pull off the kind of glare that made people stop beating around the bush and tell the truth, but he did do his absolute best.

"Look, I really don't want you to hate me," she said tentatively, and when he didn't offer any reassurances, she gulped and pushed forward. "But this afternoon, I spoke to Kennedy. We were both drinking, and she mentioned how she and you are…an item or something. Anyway, I was really, really drunk, so instead of going home, I came here while you were napping. I saw you there, and with all my inhibitions gone, I…well, I guess I…raped you. Or at least took advantage." She looked at him, almost on the verge of tears. "I woke up and remembered everything. I felt so guilty that I had to come to tell you. I'm so sorry."

Sal scratched at the side of his jaw and simply looked at her with a blank expression as he thought through what she'd said.

"Huh," he said and realized that she waited for him to say something. "So those were your panties hanging from the curtain rod in the bathroom." He stood, moved into his room, and after a short while, returned with the lace underwear. "These are yours?"

"Oh." Courtney looked down and avoided his gaze. "I almost forgot about that."

"Well, it's a good thing that I know which sexy woman

those belong to," Sal said with a nod. "Before I saw them, I actually thought that it was merely a very intense dream."

She looked up and pushed her blonde hair from her face. "Wait...you think I'm sexy?"

"I'm pretty sure that the only people who wouldn't are blind," he responded with a nod and placed the panties on his work desk. "Although that would quickly change if they could touch...you...no, that's a terrible joke. I can do better."

"So, you're not mad about what I did?" she asked.

"Look, before I got here, I wasn't exactly a stud," he replied and shook his head vehemently. "All things considered, I'm sure that I actually had a fantasy of a very hot, very smart, scientifically-focused woman taking me while I was asleep. Is it in a morally dark area? Sure. But as far as I'm concerned, no harm, no foul, right?" He shrugged.

"Huh." Courtney took another sip of water. "I'll be honest with you. I actually thought that you would be a lot angrier than this."

"What can I say?" Sal said with a small smile. "I'm a pretty chill guy. Although I'd appreciate it if next time, you could wake me up for it. It'll make my nap time a lot more enjoyable, I think."

"Deal," she said with a laugh. "So you want there to be a next time?"

He shrugged. "I guess we'll cross that bridge when we get there, right? So, if we're done with that, and we've established that you are one of the good ones—bad choices while drunk aside..." He made a gesture of pushing the whole conversation away with his hands. "Why don't we get back to our original topic of conversation?"

"Sure," Monroe said, and the abashed look on her face faded to be replaced by something a little more hopeful. "So, what is it that you and Kennedy do for money now that you're freelancing, anyway?"

"Well, we've had a couple of trips into the Zoo," Sal replied. "One was to find some armor that someone left behind. And a research run. Both times, most of our money came from finding the Pita flowers and bringing in intel on the new and improved animals in there. Did you notice how it seems like the goop actually experiments with different animal types? It seems to mix and match as if to force evolution into something like the ultimate... animal, or creature or whatever?"

Courtney nodded. "Yeah. I mean, it seems silly to even think of it, but whatever that stuff is, it makes some interesting changes to the biological makeup of these creatures and plants."

"Plus, it seems to be able to recreate a dinosaur's genetic code," he said.

"We're not sure if those big creatures are dinosaurs, though," she cut in. "There are similarities, but there are also similarities between them and birds and modern reptiles. It could simply be that—turned up to eleven like the rest of the animals."

Sal shrugged. "I guess. Still, I thought it was cool that an alien goop beat us to a Jurassic-Park-type disaster."

"Again, not really," she said with a grin. "Sure, the goop is what makes all the changes, but it was humans who fucked up and tried to do too much too quickly. As usual."

"So long as we don't start charging people to come and visit, I think we'll be good," he responded with a chuckle.

"I'd honestly not put it past some billionaires to pay to have some sort of hunting trip into the Zoo," Courtney said dryly. "You know, trophy hunting. And then I would laugh when karma decreed that the dumbasses end up getting shit out the back end of one of those big non-dinosaurs."

Sal chuckled. "That actually sounds too close to reality to be an action movie directed by Michael Bay."

Monroe laughed and covered her mouth.

He intended to continue his analogy, mainly because he had a long list of bad things to say about that director in particular, but he was cut off by another knock at the door.

"Are you expecting someone?" Courtney asked.

"I don't usually have a lot of visitors around here," he said. "Oh, right. Kennedy said she would come by to run some inventory for the trip we're taking into the Zoo tomorrow. Maybe that's her."

It was true. He didn't have that many visitors. But maybe having Madigan around would stop him from saying something that would make his conversation with Courtney awkward. He was known to do that, and Kennedy was so much better at keeping social situations smooth. She had the kind of wit and social awareness that he'd failed to develop in his younger years.

Sal opened the door. He smiled, and relief washed over him when it was, in fact, Kennedy on the other side. Oddly, she looked surprised to see him and studied him quickly.

"Hey," he said. "Come on in."

"Thanks," Kennedy replied, although her gaze swept the room. Courtney sat on the couch and sipped her water.

*Well, they're both dressed,* she thought to herself. *That's a good sign, right?*

"I was talking to Courtney about helping with her job… situation," Sal said. "Can I get you something to drink? I guess I should say some water. That's all I have."

"I'm good, thanks." She seated herself on the office chair where Sal had sat and turned to face Courtney. "I do remember talking to you about some of your business troubles. You asked if we needed any new faces on our crew, and I said…something about needing someone who's a full-time specialist since Sal is half and half? I think? My memory's a bit vague on the details, though."

Courtney nodded. "Yeah, I do remember something like that. But Sal works well as both a gunner and a specialist. I don't see why you'd need me."

"Like Kennedy said, I tend to get, uh…excitable about the gunner part of my duties," Sal said. "Plus, the only way we can expand is to bring in more personnel. I mean, we're doing that Zoo run tomorrow, but most of our money has come from research jobs. We could definitely have more bodies on that."

"Besides," Kennedy said and refused to give up Sal's seat even though he hovered uncertainly nearby. "Sal is a good enough gunner that he could take that job over entirely while leaving the job of being a specialist to you."

"I'm not sure we can pay you a specialist's salary yet, though," Sal mused. "We barely get those ourselves. Salaries, that is. Most of our money comes in from incentives and bounties. We've put together a good amount of seed money, but we're still a start-up."

Courtney nodded. "I'm sure it'll pay dividends if I get in on the ground floor, as the saying goes."

"You're damn right," Kennedy replied with a grin. "Damn, I wish we had something to drink to celebrate."

"I have—"

"Not water," Kennedy growled and rolled her eyes. "How many times have I told you that you need to get some actual booze in this place?"

"It's not like I drink all that much on my own," Sal said.

Courtney looked away. For some reason, she felt like she was an intruder in this conversation.

"Well, you should have some anyway," Kennedy said with a smile and pointed at Courtney. "For when we have company."

"I think you're wildly overestimating how much company I have," he retorted with a laugh. "I mean, three people in my place is more than I've had in...well, it's the most people who have been in this place since I moved in."

Madigan chuckled. "And that's fucking sad. Look, I'll email you the inventory details. I got you a new suit." She paused and looked at Monroe. "I don't think we'll be able to inventory something for you this quickly—that's if you want to come with us. I can square it with the team, though, if you feel like coming, Doc."

Courtney nodded. "I do want to come. And I've rented from the warehouse for a while now. I have no problem doing it again."

Sal nodded. "I'll work on your contract. They get those processed quickly. You can't make money if you don't have your T's crossed and your I's dotted, right? So...I'll see you all in the morning?"

The specialist nodded and grinned. "Thanks again. Both of you. You have no idea how much I appreciate your help on this."

Kennedy smiled. "You can never have too many good people to watch your back. And you're one of the best, Doc." She stood and headed for the door, with Courtney following. A few steps away from the entrance, she caught sight of the panties on Sal's desk. Pink and lacy, and definitely not hers.

The icky feeling in her stomach hadn't gone away. Madigan wanted to feel happy that they would now work with someone like Courtney, but she'd seen how the doc looked at Sal. She wasn't sure when the woman could have left those behind, but she knew that they hadn't been around when she'd last visited.

It wasn't like she was Sal's wife, she reminded herself yet again. They had fun and worked well together, but when you lived and worked in a place like this when you could die the next time you went to work, it wasn't like the usual combination of societal bonds between two people who had sex applied. Or if they did, she certainly hadn't abided by them.

There was no reason why she should expect that Sal would.

Madigan decided that she simply needed some time to get her feelings in order. She was good at that and had done it all her damned life.

Why hadn't she brought an JLTV, anyway? She fucking hated walking.

"Fucking doc needs to learn some manners, though," she grumbled under her breath as her annoyance fueled her pace. Then again, with the lack of rules in this place, it wasn't like she was the one who could teach manners. But the least the woman could do was not leave her underwear lying all over the place.

Sal watched the two women leave his place and exhaled a long sigh of relief. He didn't know how Madigan would react to what had happened earlier that day, and while he was perfectly fine with it, she might have a thing or two to say.

Knowing her, there was also a good possibility that the conversation wouldn't be verbal. Not entirely, anyway.

He shook his head, retrieved the panties from his desk, and walked to his room. It wasn't like Kennedy to not notice the small things. She had a good eye for detail. Then again, Courtney's business troubles had been the focus of the conversation.

Still, it was best to keep these out of view. He folded the underwear neatly. The fabric was smooth and easy to work with, he thought with a small smile as he opened the safe again and replaced it where he'd left it earlier. He gave Madie's container a light, appreciative pat before he shut the safe again.

There were much more dangerous things to be found in his place than underwear, he thought with a grin as he entered the code to lock the safe.

# CHAPTER FIFTEEN

Anderson looked up from his dinner—a far cry from the roast he'd hoped to return home to—a moment before someone knocked on his door. He couldn't say how he knew to expect the visitor. He hadn't really paid attention, and honestly, after he'd taken his meds, he didn't even want to pay attention. After the day he'd had, all he wanted to do was finish his meal of quickly heated rations of rice and diced chicken and get some sleep. He'd address the fuck-ups—his own and everyone else's—in the morning.

He sighed, took a sip of water, and wiped his mouth with a paper napkin as whoever it was knocked again, more insistently this time. The colonel pushed his chair back and went to the door. He'd been given a small prefab building to claim as his own. They'd even set up a small workstation and a cot for him to use. It wasn't the Ritz, but it was miles from the worst place he'd had to sleep in.

He opened the door, surprised to see Dr. Bial standing outside.

"Colonel," the man said, out of breath, "there's been a development."

"Can't it wait until the morning?" Anderson asked and rubbed his eyes. His anti-anxiety medication had the side effect of making him sleepy.

"Sir, our instruments picked up the team's cameras again," the scientist snapped before Anderson had even finished his question. "They're alive. Well, three of them are. They made it out of the Zoo. We've sent some vehicles to bring them back here."

"What?" Anderson demanded, and his sleepy demeanor dropped like a mask. "Are you serious?"

Bial nodded as a smile touched his normally dour features. "We haven't been able to make contact with them, but we at least have three survivors of the mission."

The colonel couldn't resist a relieved chuckle as he leaned forward and placed his hand on the man's shoulder. He knew that he had been harsh with him and the whole scientific team. They weren't military, so that made it easier, but they were there on orders like he was. And he knew for a fact that they had worked tirelessly through the whole day to try to fix what had gone wrong. What had he done?

He'd motivated them to do better, he thought.

"What's their ETA?" Anderson asked as they both headed to the command center. He strode at a swift pace, and the scientist barely managed to keep up.

"The JLTVs just picked them up," Bial answered, a little out of breath although he still matched him stride for stride. "They should be back in fifteen minutes, with a few variables."

The colonel nodded. "But we lost contact with them inside the Zoo. How did we get it back?"

"We had suffered interference," the man explained. "When their comms went down, we assumed that the squad members had too but, as it turns out, they merely had some technical difficulties."

Anderson nodded. "I'm sorry for my tone earlier, Bial. I...I have bad memories of losing squad mates."

"I've worked out here in the Zoo for fifteen months, Colonel," his companion assured him, "so believe me when I say that I know that your heart was in the right place. You might want to share your feelings with some other members of my engineering team, though."

"I'll buy them all some top-shelf whiskey," he responded with a chuckle. "Only one bottle, though, for them to share. I work in Washington, but I don't make that much money."

Bial laughed, and Anderson realized that he hadn't made the best joke. The man was simply as relieved as he was himself.

They reached the compound's gate, which was dragged open to reveal the blinding headlights of the JLTVs that waited outside. The vehicles rumbled in, and the gates were shut and locked quickly behind them. Guards and all other personnel who could peered out into the desert to make sure that nobody and nothing had followed the arrivals.

Thankfully, no one raised the alarm, and Anderson strode to where his men swung out of the vehicles. The team was no doubt relieved to be able to disembark. The JLTVs were still personnel carriers, and the suits that the men wore were too large to sit comfortably. They made it work, of course, but after their nightmare trip into the zoo, it must have felt like the last straw on the proverbial camel's back.

There were four suits, but only three of them moved. The colonel's initial relief was instantly tempered by regret when he saw that the fourth suit was missing the whole of the right leg. It was Blue Team Leader, he realized.

The scientists rapidly removed the armor from the weary survivors. They didn't look too badly wounded—nothing life-threatening or that would require them to be rushed to the base hospital for emergency surgery. One had a broken leg, but the armor had hardened around it and kept it from further damage.

"Status report," Anderson said and attempted to keep his tone professional as he squatted beside Blue Two.

"We were swarmed," the man said as he examined his own body with a practiced eye. "Hundreds of the critters came from all sides. It was like they were protecting some-thing. Blue Leader went down, but we managed to get him back. He…he was dead when we found him, and they'd torn the leg off, armor and all. I swear to God, they piled on us at one point, but they couldn't get through the armor. We managed to push our way out and drag him… drag him out."

"You did some good work out there, son," his commanding officer said.

"What kind of mission report will you send back, sir?" he asked.

"Well, I'll give commendations to all members involved," Anderson said and patted the side of the young sergeant's head. "Some serious medals will come your way.

I'll also give this armor some scathing reviews. Software issues aside, simple animals shouldn't be able to make a crack in this stuff, much less detach a full leg."

The man nodded. "Thank you, Colonel."

He nodded and gazed at the rest of his men. The priority was to get them medical attention now that they were out of their suits. The man with the broken leg would probably be stabilized and shipped back to the Staging Area, where he could recover under proper medical care, while the rest would either be sent Stateside or back to their original deployments. This whole operation was an absolute disaster from the beginning. That was what you got when military men and women didn't plan the missions. Priorities got skewed, and men's lives were put in danger.

Anderson shook his head and made his way back to Mission Control. Bial fell quickly into formation behind him.

"You know what I'm going to say, right?" the man said, his voice terse. He sounded like he braced himself for another dress-down from the colonel.

But he'd taken his meds. Even with the relief of seeing at least most of the men back and alive when he was sure that they hadn't made it, he didn't have the energy to go through the paces of being argumentative.

"We need to head back in to get that leg," he said with a nod. "Even only the leg has too much for us to allow it to fall into the wrong hands. For reasons of national security as well as for those who made them, we need to send someone back in to get it."

Bial nodded and narrowed his eyes. He was surprised

that Anderson hadn't yelled at him for suggesting that vital personnel be sent in to recover what was essentially a broken piece of equipment.

The colonel didn't like it and it was an incredible waste for something that would, in all probability, be lost in the Zoo for the rest of time, but his experiences in Washington had taught him about how things were run there. He could refuse, but his higher-ups would be yelled at by some CEO in a thousand-dollar suit and Anderson, in turn, would receive firm orders to assemble a team to get that piece of shit back.

It was just the way things were done, and right now, he was too dazed to put up a fight. At least this way, he could stay on top of it and make sure that while the orders were corporate in nature, he could keep the planning and execution as military as possible.

"What kind of options do we have for tracking that leg?" he asked one of the younger men who sat in front of the screens.

The researcher turned in his office chair, and his expression suggested that he expected an outburst. "It doesn't look good, sir. There aren't any tracking devices in the legs of the suits. The arms have the comm units, and the headsets and torsos are tracked via GPS implants."

"That's something you'll probably want to write up as a design flaw, then?" Anderson asked. What the hell did he know about these things? Only how to use them, apparently.

"Sure." The youth nodded. "But we didn't anticipate someone losing a leg during these test runs, sir."

Anderson nodded. "Well, write it up anyway. To the

task at hand...we can have teams scour the Zoo for pieces that might or might not be chewed up and shit out by the wildlife. Is there any way to track them?"

"Well, the software connections in the suits give off a unique low-frequency RFID signal." He turned to the screen. "It's not powerful enough to be detected with satellites, but if you had a scanner that was set to search for that exact signal, you could probably track it within a certain range and follow it back to the source."

"What's the range?" Anderson asked.

"About ten klicks."

"Crap," Anderson said. "How large an area does the Zoo cover at this point?"

"Most recent pictures mark it down as just over seven hundred square kilometers."

"So we essentially need to get within ten klicks of something in an area the size of fucking Texas," the colonel muttered, more to himself than anyone else in the room. "I don't need to be a mathematician to know how sucky those odds are."

"I could...run the numbers for you," the younger man said and looked openly confused.

"That's okay," he replied and shook his head. "I think it's well quantified as looking for a needle in a haystack. All it lacks is to throw some venomous snakes in the mix to liven things up."

Bial looked oddly at him, and Anderson shook his head once more.

"I just took my anti-anxiety meds," he admitted. "I'm not really myself right now."

"We can start work on a tracker, Colonel," Bial said and

patted him lightly on the shoulder. "You should get some rest."

He nodded. "I'll probably not be any good to you guys if I wait around here, anyway. I'm more likely to get in the way than not, right?"

An awkward exchange of glances between the men in lab coats told Anderson unequivocally that he was correct, but nobody wanted to tell him outright. He could understand that.

The colonel waved a hand vaguely and quickly exited the operation command. He could always yell at them for something in the morning simply to keep up appearances. For now, he would head to bed with the knowledge that things weren't as bad as they could have been.

He reached his little corner of the complex and stripped to his civvies. After he hung his uniform over his desk chair, he dropped onto the cot and closed his eyes. It was cool in the evenings out there in the jungle, but he didn't need a blanket. Between exhaustion and his meds, he dozed off without difficulty.

# CHAPTER SIXTEEN

Sal growled as his alarm went off and he dragged himself out of bed. A trick that someone had taught him was to never leave his alarm within reach. That successfully avoided the temptation to wake only enough to turn it off and go back to sleep again.

His bare feet touched the cool floor and he was shocked awake before he reached the ringing and vibrating phone. He turned it off and snarled a wide barrage of curses at it as he stretched and yawned. He had acquired a little of Kennedy's skill for foul language even while he yawned. He smirked. Still tired, he rubbed his eyes but registered the first smile of the day. At least he got that out of his system.

He shrugged into the clothes he'd left out for himself the night before—a tank-top and a pair of combat pants over boots. He'd originally started to wear gear like this because it helped him to fit in with the other folks around there. As he gained some muscle mass, he realized that clothes like this were actually comfortable. People around the world would be a lot nicer if they could go into work wearing stuff that breathed as much as these did.

By the time someone knocked at the door, he'd made coffee and finished a lightweight breakfast. The sun wasn't even up yet. Who the hell could be visiting now?

He opened the door and narrowed his eyes at Kennedy who stood with her hand raised and obviously about to knock again.

"You'll piss the neighbors off with that racket," Sal said, and she grinned. "It's not even five yet. What the hell are you doing here?"

"Courtney and I thought it would be a good idea to get a head start on the day," she said cheerfully. He looked over her shoulder. The specialist already sat in the JLTV with a cup of coffee in her hands.

"So," Madigan asked, "ready to go?"

"Yeah." Sal shrugged and decided to go with the flow. "Let me get my bag."

He left the door open and hurried to where he'd set his bag the night before. It was designed to be easily carried or latched like a backpack to his suit. He pulled it over his shoulder and locked the door behind him as Kennedy hopped into the driver's seat.

"Since we'll be a little early," she said once they were on their way, "it means we'll be able to try out some new equipment that I bought. Funny how that worked out, right?"

He rolled his eyes and tried to ignore a slight shiver. With the sun still absent from the sky, it was too fucking cold to be outside. He'd picked California as a place to do his dissertation for a reason, after all. He wasn't made for the cold.

"I managed to rent one of the new E Mark-Twenties from storage," Courtney said. "They should deliver it to the launching area right now, actually. I've never tried any of those."

"I'm still rocking the fifteens," Sal said with a laugh. "With decades-old software. I might as well be using Windows Vista."

"Well, you were," Kennedy said without moving her gaze from the road. "I took the liberty of getting you something a little more dedicated for combat but which also has the specialist software you might need out there. I thought it would be a nice surprise."

"That...is a nice surprise. Thanks," Sal said. "How did you afford it?"

"Well, I put it on Heavy Metal's tab," she said quickly, her gaze still focused intently on the road. "I put all this in the inventory report that I emailed you."

"The inventory report that I told myself I would get up a little earlier than usual to read since I spent most of the night working on the white paper that the squad wanted to have finished before we started off this morning?" Sal raised an eyebrow. "Yeah, I...haven't gotten to that yet."

"No shit," Kennedy said with a laugh. "I mean, I can totally eat the expense myself. I merely thought that you might want to have it on the company in case you didn't like it and wanted to turn it in."

He nodded. "That sounds reasonable. Leave it on the company's account. We can afford it. But...which one did you pick up?"

"It's a C-Class Hybrid," she replied. "It has a power-armor arm fitted with one of those new assault rifles, but it also works with most of the specialist software. All top-of-the-line software too, courtesy of Boulos."

"That old fox," Sal said with a chuckle. "Remind me to write him a Christmas card."

"He's a Muslim," Kennedy said.

"Kwanza, then?" Sal tilted his head. "Do they even have Kwanza cards?"

"I'm fairly certain he'd prefer a huge stack of porn," she said as she pulled up where the teams had already started to assemble. "He complained to me about how the server's restrictions pissed him off to no end."

"I'll…keep that in mind," he said with a nod. He pulled himself out of the JLTV and walked to the section designated for them. Boulos had left their deliveries of weapons and suits already marked off with a drawing of an electric guitar. As usual, he'd extended the deadline for delivery although he had called her to let her know.

"Heavy Metal," Sal said with a chuckle as he unpacked his new suit. "I like it."

"Well, it's an idea for a company logo," Kennedy said and immediately slipped into the boots of her armor. "If we survive long enough to need a company logo, that is."

"Hey now," he protested and followed her example. "With three of us, that's one-third of a higher chance that at least one of us will survive to make sure Heavy Metal goes the distance."

"Hey, that's nice," Courtney said. She strolled up to them, already in her suit and with her helmet tucked under her arm. "You guys already think of me as a part of the group."

He made a face as he adjusted his arm in the heavy grip for his assault rifle. "I'll really miss how easy it is to get into the specialist-only suits."

"You won't miss it when you let the power armor do most of the heavy lifting of your equipment," Kennedy retorted as she tugged the armor over her waist and wiggled it around to position it comfortably.

"Yep, you're right on that," Sal said. "I would appreciate some help to carry all the shit since you gunners always leave me to carry an equal portion anyways."

"Well, we only give you what we know you can handle," Madigan said with a sweet smile as she finished fitting her shoulder pads.

"Aw, I'm so flattered," Sal said, and sarcasm dripped from his tone. "What do you know? Have power armor, still faster at putting it on than you are."

Courtney looked away as Kennedy flipped him off. Even out there, something as ordinary as putting on armor and prepping for a Zoo run still seemed like she somehow intruded on a private moment between the two. It might simply have been a chemistry thing, but the funny banter between them might also be a way that they mentally prepared themselves to put their lives in danger. The interchange seemed like mutual reassurance that what they did was something that they could handle.

She'd never had someone to do that with and always had to process this stuff on her own. It would be nice if she could get in on the whole banter thing.

But not today. She could figure it out with Sal and

Madigan later. Maybe it would come naturally the more they all worked together.

Courtney put her helmet on and fitted her pack to her suit as she turned to see the sun arc its way over the horizon.

"It's like you said when we got back from my first trip," Sal said as he moved to stand beside her. "Something that beautiful has to come with a little bit of crazy to keep it balanced."

He stared out at the Zoo with his helmet cradled in one arm.

She smiled as the particularly vivid memory of that trip resurfaced. The fact that it was the run on which she'd met and worked with Salinger Jacobs for the first time was only a part of it. It had been downright traumatic as well as profitable. They had shared a tough experience, and things had only become more and more difficult since then.

They might be looking up now, though, she reminded herself. It was only a day since her last trip in there, but she felt refreshed and ready for it. Which was odd, considering that she had never felt ready for it before. Maybe this new feeling was somehow related to her having gotten laid the day before? She shrugged mentally and filed that thought away for deeper study later.

"How's that C-Class working out for you?" she asked.

Sal made a face. "I've tried out hybrids and worked with full specialist suits. I thought that there would be overlap in a hybrid, but some spots that I'm used to being powered aren't, and ones that I'm used to being specialist aren't. It will take time to adjust."

"Well, at least you have a team you trust working with

you," she said with a small smile. "It's safer that way. If you screw up, you have someone to fall back on."

He narrowed his eyes at her. "What makes you think I'll screw up?"

She shrugged and grinned. "I'm working with the odds. Your first time was lively, but there's always room for improvement."

He opened his mouth to ask what she was talking about and shut it again as she winked and turned away as the rest of the teams arrived. Kennedy kept an eye on Courtney as she walked away too.

Madigan grumbled something under her breath, but Sal didn't catch it. He still tried to figure out what Courtney was talking about. Besides, if Kennedy had something to say to him, she could speak up. It wasn't like her to hold back if she had something on her mind. She was outspoken all the way.

The other teams assembled quickly now that the sun climbed above the horizon. The sky was still the vibrant mixture of deep reds and yellows of the desert dawn, but the slow rise in temperature told Sal that the last stray vestiges of cool air would soon vanish.

He pulled his helmet on. Young had said that they were understaffed for this mission, but it certainly didn't look that way. Over four dozen people had already assembled and prepared to head out into the Zoo with enough vehicles to take them all already gassed up and ready to move. Whoever funded this run had some deep pockets. Even so, he was sure that the objectives behind the mission were widely overestimated, which was why there were petitions for extra people to join in at a lower hiring rate.

And there he was, bringing more people into the game already.

"Okay, folks, listen up," a voice intoned over the comm line that they shared with the others heading out. Almost fifty expectant people had now gathered. Young had been right, though. It was past oh-six hundred and the sun was already fully exposed and working hard to reach the top of the sky by the time everyone had completed their preparations.

"The mission parameters will have been entered into all your suit databases," the voice continued, and Sal now recognized it as Young's. "This is a research-heavy run, so stick close to your specialists and follow their lead. Specialists, it's on you not to lead your gunners into sticky situations. The same bounty for the Pita flowers applies, but they aren't the main objective or money-maker for this run."

"Another thing," the leader called out before they turned toward the vehicles. "All research bounties will be distributed evenly. So the harder you work, the more all of us get paid. If anyone lags behind and tries to profit on everyone else's work, I'll beat you to death myself so we don't have to share our bounty with you, is that clear? We'll meet back at the JLTVs in five days. Anyone who isn't there in time walks home."

A horde of affirmatives issued over the comms.

"Good," Young replied once it had all died down. "Your squads should show up on your screens now. Good luck."

Sal checked his team. Predictably, it was made up of Kennedy and Courtney...Dr. Monroe, rather. But the surprise came when Young, Ito, Sousa, and Carson showed up there too.

"Hey, Sergeant Kennedy," Young said. He joined them with the other three as they moved toward the vehicles. "I'm glad to see your face on my squad's roster sheet."

"Yeah," she drawled and patted the man on the shoulder. "I'm sure that was simply a lucky coincidence."

Her armor was of superior quality and make than Young's government-issued suit, which meant that he stumbled a few steps from her tap before the inner gyros of his suit regained their balance.

"And you must be Dr. Monroe." Young chuckled and moved quickly out of Kennedy's reach. "It's a pleasure to have you on board. You come highly recommended by both Jacobs and Kennedy, so I'm sure you'll fit right in."

"I appreciate it, Sergeant Young," Monroe said as she shook the man's offered hand. "I look forward to working with all of you ."

"All right, boys," the leader said and thickened his drawl intentionally as they mounted up. "Let's go make us some money."

"Sure thing, Leprechaun," Ito said with a grin.

"We sure are...estrogen-packed here today, aren't we?" Sousa asked as he looked around and noted that three of the members of his seven-man squad were female.

"Yeah, consider yourself lucky," Kennedy growled. She sat awkwardly, still not fully adjusted to her new suit. "I've been in testosterone-heavy squads before, and all the penis-measuring was pathetic."

Young laughed and nudged his teammate on the shoulder. Sousa mumbled some inanity that was lost in the rumble as the engines started up.

# CHAPTER SEVENTEEN

Sal examined the power-armored arm on his suit. It still felt contradictory that he could actually grip without using his hand to do so. It looked pretty damn cool and all, but it would take time to adjust to it. That plus the need to focus to gain control of his arm again when it was time to shoot things was discouraging at the beginning of what would inevitably be a dangerous enterprise.

That said, the ability to disengage his arm from the power armor to be able to work as a specialist was impressive. It looked like he was shedding skin like a snake.

"I call it 'specialist mode,'" he said to Kennedy after he'd tried it a couple of times. "So when I actually do it, I'll 'engage specialist mode.' And when I pull the arm back on, it's 'gunner mode.'"

"You'll have to promise me that you won't shout that nonsense when we're actually in the field," Kennedy growled.

"I second that motion," Young said with a grin.

"Thirded," Monroe said with a shrug. "Sorry, Jacobs."

"Whatever," he responded cheerfully and shook his head. "You're all simply jealous of how cool my new hybrid armor is."

"That or wonder why you focus on how cool it is instead of doing your job as a specialist and collecting data," Madigan retorted. "We're in the Zoo for a reason, you know, and it's not to come third in a cool contest."

"Hey, I...wouldn't come in third," Sal said. "Besides, that's why we brought Monroe with us, right? To be the specialist so I could be a gunner?"

"No, we brought Monroe along so you could have help with the specialist-ing while you were being a gunner," Kennedy said with a chuckle. "Besides, there's two of you, which means double the people to make money for us on this trip. So get cracking and make me some money. I'm not here for the pleasant and aesthetic views, you know."

"Are they always like this?" Monroe asked Young as they dropped back in the squad. The vehicles were well out of sight now, and the familiar sights and sounds of the jungle surrounded them and cut them off from anything but the Zoo itself.

"I've only been out here with them once," Young said. "But that one time was enough to tell me that...well, yes, they are always like this. They keep the banter up almost non-stop. It's actually good for morale and keeps people distracted from all the different kinds of death that we might find out here. Although I did promise death by beating to those who don't pull their weight in this run so..."

"Right." Monroe saw where he was going with that. "I'll get to...specialist-ing, I guess?"

"Don't...don't do that," Young muttered. "Don't encourage him. It makes all this worse." He turned to face where Kennedy and Sal still walked. "Hey, Jacobs, get to work. Make us some bounties. None of us are out here for free."

"You're jealous!" Sal called and shook his head. "Fine, I'll go into...specialist mode!"

"Just fucking don't," Kennedy warned.

"Too late, already love it," he said and switched his face-mask's HUD to the specialist software. It removed the targeting reticle that followed the assault rifle in his arm and allowed him to look around as he made adjustments to the different programs to figure out which he'd need at which time.

"You have the Pita tracker working on your phone now, right?" Sal asked in a private comms channel and glanced at Kennedy.

"Roger that," she responded and kept her voice low even though her suit blocked anyone whom she didn't want to listen in.

"Good. Keep our heading toward the nearest cluster large enough to warrant a visit," he said. "Since we took a different direction from the rest of the squads, we should be able to keep clear of the money that they make while we make some of our own."

Kennedy nodded and they clicked out before anyone noticed the communication. People tended to be suspicious of private channels, so Sal had learned to keep their conversations brief when it came to their own trademark method of tracking the money-making plants and their flowers. It was best to keep some things exclusive to Heavy Metal, right?

Sal peered into the heavy growth and made sure his motion detector was on. As they got deeper into the jungle, the lack of direct sunlight should have meant that smaller plants wouldn't grow as much, which in turn would make it much easier to navigate the area.

He really needed to lose the natural assumption that the Zoo would behave like a regular jungle. The underbrush was as thick deeper in as it had been outside. And since it was much darker there, navigation was more difficult.

But then again, not as difficult as it could have been.

It took almost complete darkness to see the phenomenon with the naked eye. He'd noticed it on their last run while they set up camp. It had been later than anticipated, which meant that they had started off in the dead of night and so he'd seen it. Tiny blue lights glimmered like pinpricks in the trees and glowed through cracks in the bark. These were the minute indicators of the presence of the goop inside the plants.

Except that they were more noticeable now and easier to see. It was as if the bigger the jungle became, the more goop the plants had in them, which in turn made the forest grow faster…a perfect, balanced circle. Sal supposed that it went on ad infinitum too. The goop had created a jungle that was meant to grow, and that was exactly what it did despite all the efforts of the men and women at the Staging Area. He wasn't even sure that the wall could stop it.

That was both terrifying and awesome at the same time, he thought with a chuckle.

Either way, he could tune the night vision in his HUD

to detect the very particular kind of light that the goop in the trees emanated, which made navigation so much easier.

He'd given Kennedy the specs to put into her suit, as well as Courtney, with a stern warning to restrict it to Heavy Metal personnel only. He needed as much as he could to sell back to these people once he had finished there.

The altered night vision gave him an almost daytime view of the area, and when he engaged the motion detectors, there wasn't much in range that he couldn't see.

Satisfied that everything now worked optimally, he glanced around, and his eyes were immediately drawn to movement on the trees. He'd already noted the presence of advanced, tree-dwelling simians, but as he stepped closer, he noticed that something much smaller moved over the surface of the massive trunks.

"What is it?" Kennedy asked.

"Insects," Sal said, almost amazed. "Well, make that arachnids, since they have eight legs but they act like insects."

They shuffled along in a line in much the same way that ants did. He turned the viewer in his HUD up to give him a better view of them. They didn't seem to notice that he approached.

"That's weird," Monroe said as she joined him. "I don't think I've seen insects around here at all. Except the...you know, giant ones. Never anything scaled down to proper insect size."

"Arachnids," Sal corrected and spoke softly as he usually did when he focused. He didn't want to interrupt the line, so he had to follow one of the tiny creatures climbing up the tree to get some decent, up-close shots. He made sure that they were all in the real lighting so that the perception wasn't altered by his night-vision addition.

"What?"

"Eight legs, that makes them arachnids," he said impatiently as he snapped as many shots as he could, both of the individual arachnid and all of them working together.

"They have a thorax as well," Monroe pointed out. "That makes them insects."

Sal shook his head. They could quibble over the exact species of the little bugs that they looked at later. For now, he was curious as to why they all carried small globules of bright blue matter in their jaws. Obviously, they carried the goop around. Had they taken it out of the tree? Or had they brought it to the tree? Both were valid options. Various species of insect had nests and hives in trees, but he'd never seen any of the animals actually interact with the goop in an outward fashion like this before.

He chuckled. They acted like insects, despite their eight legs. He didn't know of any arachnids that worked in a hive-mind like this.

The two specialists took more pictures and added them all to the databases in their suits before they moved on.

"These are probably the first insect-arachnids we've seen out here," Sal said with a nod. "Add that to the bounty. Do you think we're not carrying our own weight now, Sergeant Young?"

"Shut up and get back to work," Young responded. Ito made the sound of a whip.

Sal looked up suddenly, and his eyes flickered to their left. He could see Kennedy glance around too. He nudged a button with his chin, minimized all the specialist software, and reactivated the gunner capability of his suit. It was a nifty and well-designed piece of technology, he admitted as he focused and gripped his gun tighter when he raised it cautiously.

His improved view revealed a full pack of the hyena creatures, at least twenty of them. They chipped and yelped to catch the attention of the rest of the pack as they circled and moved closer to the squad.

"Heads up," Sal said. The suit chambered a round in his rifle as he raised it level with the approaching pack.

"Make a circle, back to back. We have hostiles on our six too," Young growled, his own weapon hot and ready. The squad complied and surrounded the more vulnerable member of their group. Sal was used to it being him, and he remembered how annoyed he had been by the concept. He could only imagine that Monroe felt the same right now.

Tough. If she wanted to live, she had to let her gunners protect her.

Sal opened fire. He remembered what these weapons felt like to shoot without the aid of power armor. They kicked hard and kicked high, which made it difficult to aim at anything when he wrestled with his own weapon to keep it down and relatively stable. He suddenly realized that his approach was all wrong. These assault rifles were designed to shoot like this. He allowed himself to work with the weapon and in a few minutes, didn't even feel it kick as the shots were quickly filtered out by the suit to protect his hearing.

The effects were dramatically visible, Sal realized as the

hyenas yelped and tried to evade the bullets. It was hard to feel sympathy for them, though. Memories of how they had tried to clamp down on his skull on his first trip were hard to forget. These attacked, but he'd noticed that they weren't the bravest or most persistent of creatures. As soon as the fusillade began, they backed away quickly. He stopped firing when they turned tail and disappeared into the jungle. He didn't like them, but there was no reason to kill if they didn't attack.

He turned to see what the rest of the squad had to deal with. Five of the massive, venom-fanged panthers lay on the ground around the squad and a couple more now retreated. Sal narrowed his eyes. Unlike the hyenas, the panthers weren't the type to run as soon as potential prey showed aggression.

Still, five out of seven made a heavy loss for the pack. He made a note of the change in their usual behavior.

"There's nothing new here for us to pick up, right?" Young said as soon as they were clear of any animal attacks.

"I don't think so." Sal glanced at Monroe, both for her opinion and to make sure she was all right. She nodded in the affirmative, and he took it on both counts.

"We should still collect some samples, though. Just in case," she said.

"Agreed," Young said. "We'll stick around for five, and then we move out."

# CHAPTER EIGHTEEN

They didn't need five minutes to collect samples. The most time-consuming project was when Sal collected venom from the panther's fangs, and that was only because he needed to disengage from his power arm to do it. They set off again in no time.

His mood dropped slightly. He'd killed these animals before, and it had never been a problem. For some reason, and only for a short while, he had forgotten that killing was something that he actually had to do. That was why his spirits had been higher at the beginning than they were now once reality set in.

It wasn't like his mood influenced the group or anything. He was sure that they would be perfectly happy if he became a bit quieter.

"Hey," Kennedy said. She stepped beside him and nudged his unarmored shoulder. "Is everything okay? You're quiet now, and I don't think the jungle can take that."

Sal smirked and shook his head. "Yeah, I'm fine. I

remembered how much fun there is to be had here in the Zoo."

She smiled and nudged him again, gentler this time. "Yeah, I get that. Keep your chin up, though. You don't want the rest of our team to come and have this same conversation with you."

"Well, maybe I like the attention," he said.

"Yeah, that's you," she muttered and rolled her eyes. "Attention whore. Drama queen. Egomaniac."

"I get the point." Sal nudged her in the shoulder this time. "Stop...describing me."

"Hey, do you pick that up?" Young called from the back.

"Pick what up?" Monroe asked and looked around a little fearfully.

"I have interference on my comm chat," Young said and tapped at the console on his hip. "I can hear something, but I'm not sure what it is."

Sal checked his comms locator. It was a useful device that let him know if there was comms chatter near him without the necessity to actually listen in. Something definitely pinged the signal above zero, but there wasn't much signal.

"The Zoo causes all kinds of interference," he said and linked the comms to the speakers in his helmet. He listened intently for a few seconds and could hear something other than the regular interference static, but he couldn't make it out. "Kennedy, do you think you can clean this signal up a bit?"

"Sure, let me break out my quantum generator to reverse the polarity of the neutron flow," she rumbled and waved a dismissive hand. "How the hell am I supposed to clean the signal up a bit?"

"I installed trademark equipment on the suit when I used it," Sal explained quietly.

"You what now?" Young asked.

"Nothing," he said and turned to Madigan. "Remember, I showed it to you—"

"Oh…right." She shook her head and loaded the software. Sal claimed credit, but it was actually something that Boulos had helped him work on. The man was an engineering genius, and with a little scientific help from Sal's end, they were able to develop software that could clean up the communications while inside the Zoo by counteracting the very unique radio signals that the goop gave off.

It was a rather obvious solution, but sometimes, you needed geniuses to see what stared you in the face.

The signal cleared slowly, and a voice stuttered through. The man spoke in a raspy, pained voice in a foreign language.

"He's speaking Russian," Ito interjected quickly. "I didn't know we had any Russian operatives in the area."

"We don't," Young said. "They set up another base to the north and have run missions like ours from there. We haven't run into them yet because…well, the Zoo is huge and growing."

"He doesn't sound like he's doing too well," Sal said and hastily inserted himself into the transmission. "We read you on this end. Please respond, over."

"I can speak Russian," Ito said, almost offended.

"Well, would you really want to translate everything this guy says?" Kennedy asked.

Ito nodded. "Good point."

"Hello?" the man said in a heavy accent. "This is Lieutenant Gregor Popov, Fifth Battalion. Do you read me?"

"We read you loud and clear," Sal said. "Well, loud, anyway. Are you in need of assistance?"

"Suit is damaged. Can't move from here. Rest of squad was attacked." The signal grew clearer the more Sal and Boulos' program worked on it. "In desperate need of help."

"Roger that, Lieutenant." Young cut in. "This is Sergeant Lionel Young from the UN Staging Area. Can you send us your coordinates?"

"Roger…roger that," Gregor said, and after a moment of muffled static on the mic, a series of numbers and letters appeared in Sal's HUD. He assumed that it had done the same thing with everyone else's.

"That's only five klicks from here," Young said.

"Are we really going to rescue a Russian?" Sousa asked. "Aren't they the bad guys?"

"I'm…still here," Gregor said.

Sal killed the comm connection for the moment. "In this particular situation, I think the fact that he's a human makes him…well, maybe not one of the good guys, but definitely not one of the bad guys," he said. "Maybe something along the lines of a lawful neutral?"

"What?"

"Nothing." Sal shook his head. "I say we go in after him."

"We need to keep working," Young growled. "Since there are seven of us, we can split up. A team can help the Russian while the rest maintain the heading."

He nodded. "Sounds like a plan. Kennedy and I can help the man while you guys follow this heading."

Monroe made a face, and Sal talked quickly when he saw that. "The idea is that if we're to split up, we should have at least one specialist per crew. That way, we cover more ground over less time. And since I can work as a gunner and a specialist, it makes sense for me to be on the team with fewer people. That's my logic anyway. But I'll shut up now, okay."

Young nodded. "That actually makes sense. Jacobs and Kennedy, head off to help our Russian friend. The rest of us—"

"Maintain a northwest trajectory," Kennedy interjected. "Keep walking for ten klicks or so and you'll find a big collection of Pita flowers. We'll circle around and meet you there."

"That's a plan," Young responded. "Good luck, you two." They'd been over this on their last mission with Young. He knew that they had a way to track the plants without having to wander all over the place, and he was perfectly content to leave it in their hands as long as Sal and Kennedy divided up the bounty.

"Stay safe," Monroe said with a small smile and punched Sal in the arm. Hard.

"Owww...will do," he transitioned smoothly but rubbed where she'd struck him. "And you too. Keep your eyes open."

She smiled and moved forward to follow the other squad members.

Sal connected to the comm channel that Gregor was still on. "Hold on there, Lieutenant. We're on our way to your location."

"Much appreciated," he replied, the relief very evident in his voice even through the tenuous connection.

"So," Kennedy said as the two of them headed off. "You seemed pretty anxious not to hurt Dr. Monroe's feelings back there. That was really sweet of you."

"It made sense, and I blurted it out before I even considered that she might think that I had excluded her or something," Sal said and shook his head. "With a brain as big as mine, there's not much distance between it and my mouth."

"She's a sweet girl." She looked sideways at Sal. "It's nice that you stick up for her like that. She seems the type that's smart enough to jump too easily to conclusions. It's nice of you to make sure that she knew that she wasn't being excluded from this little Heavy Metal excursion from the group."

"Yeah, I don't think she liked it, anyways," he grumbled and didn't notice Kennedy's inquisitive tone or sidelong glances. His eyes and attention were already on a new kind of tree that he hadn't seen before. It simply…grew right in the middle of the jungle, lower than the massive trees over it. Despite that, it still towered over the bushes and under-brush that covered most of the ground and made it hard to navigate. Like it didn't need the sunlight.

The new species was noticeably slender. Most of the trees were large enough to necessitate a short walk to circumnavigate them, but this was thin enough that Sal could hug it and make his fingers touch. It would be a stretch, but still.

"Look at this," he said and shuffled closer. The trunk curled upward like a vine on an invisible post and sprouted leaves all along toward the top, where a cluster of flowers grew. Kennedy seemed annoyed at the change in the topic of conversation, but she kept moving.

Sal ran his fingers over the diamond-shaped leaves. They were blue instead of green, and as he looked closer, he realized that the veins in the leaves glowed and even pulsated a little.

"Ten bucks says that those flowers at the top have a higher concentration of goop than any of the Pita flowers," Madigan said and zoomed in for a better look.

"No bet," he replied. "Ten bucks says that if we try to cut the tree down to get to them, we'll be swarmed by angry Zoo animals."

"No bet," Kennedy said with a small smile.

Sal took a moment to collect a small sample from the leaves and the bark as well as to snap a few pictures with his HUD before they moved on.

There were no visible indicators to show the passage of time as they pushed deeper into the Zoo. Barely any sunlight filtered through the leaf cover above them, and even with the goop-powered night vision, it was difficult to tell what time it was without checking the clocks in their suits. A couple of hours passed before they neared the coordinates Gregor had given them.

Sal connected to the comm line again. "Hey, Gregor? We're approaching your location now. Can you give us a little ping to lead us to where you are? We need to connect with our team again and would rather not have to scour the area in search for you."

There was no response, but a soft ping glimmered on their HUDs that turned them slightly to the left of their current heading. It wasn't long before they reached the man.

"You…have no idea how good it is to see human face again," Gregor said and sighed loudly with relief. "And I hated most humans this morning, so you should feel flattered."

The man looked to be in his thirties with a scruffy beard and a handful of scars on his face. Not much else could be seen since the rest of him was covered in full power armor that had been chewed at relentlessly by what was most probably the hyena creatures, if the shape of the bite marks was any indication. The wiring was exposed all over, and from the looks of things, would be a pain to fix.

"That armor won't go anywhere," Kennedy muttered and voiced the obvious for her and her teammate.

"No shit," the Russian said with a laugh.

# CHAPTER NINETEEN

Sal kept a wary eye on their surroundings. As he was the specialist there, he felt he should do something. But as it turned out, Madigan was the one who knew about the technical side of the armor, so she ran the diagnostics on Gregor's suit.

From the look on her face, things did not look good. Not a huge surprise, he supposed. More like a disappointment even though he'd seen scrapped suits that looked better than that.

For the moment, he watched the shadows for whatever creatures had caused that degree of damage. He gripped his rifle firmly and took a moment to glance at the oddity of his new suit before he shook his head and resumed his watchman responsibilities.

"Well," Kennedy said and removed the wires that had communicated the diagnostic from the Russian's suit her to hers. "Most of the sensors have shorted and the power armor functions have been disabled. On the bright side, most of the hardware was isolated so the inner computers were shut down before they were damaged by the short, so the suit hasn't been completely trashed. It'll still need a lot of work, though, and you won't be able to move in it until you get it back to a shop."

"Wait—they isolated the hardware but not the sensors or the power functions?" Sal asked and scowled. "And they let people walk around in it outside a testing room?"

"That's Russian engineering for you," Kennedy said, her face all scrunched up as she thought hard. "I read about this somewhere. They decided against isolating their power functions since it reduces the movement lag by thirty percent...or something like that. I guess they applied the same thinking when they designed their sensor systems."

"Well, sure," the specialist said with an annoyed laugh. "It'll reduce the lag, so you move faster with the power armor right up to the point where something goes wrong and you get electrocuted. Speaking of—"

"His vitals look fine," she said. "Life support is one of those isolated systems, and it indicates that everything is okay. You have a couple of bruises and a twisted ankle, but you should be fine. Still, you might want to get yourself looked at. The air filters in your suit are fucked up. We haven't registered a lot of these new plants and the pollen may be toxic."

"Let me guess..." Sal said and shrugged meaningfully.

"Air filters were brought in by cheap company," Gregor confirmed with a small chuckle.

"I sense a pattern with all this Russian engineering." Sal shook his head.

"Much functionality, not much for safety," the Russian confirmed with a nod of his head.

"We need to get you out of that suit," Kennedy said.

"But what about what you just said?" Gregor asked. "About the poisonous pollen or something?"

"Well, if there was any around here, you would already be dead," she pointed out. "Your filters are shot, so it won't make any difference. It's best to get you out of here as quickly as possible because I'm not carrying your ass."

The man uttered something in Russian and shook his head as he pulled slowly at the locked levers that held his armor together. Sal disengaged from the powered part of his suit to help Gregor, and it was now Kennedy's turn to keep watch. As advanced as her suit was, it still wasn't nimble enough to handle the small manipulation of the various screws that were utilized to keep the armor in place. The idea behind them was that the software implanted could do the work for you when you wanted to get out, but the fact remained that there was the chance that something would go wrong. Sometimes, you would need to get yourself out of it without the power assistance or have someone do it for you.

It still took a few minutes and a fair amount of pulling and tugging before they created a hole large enough for Gregor to step out.

He pulled himself free, and suddenly, Sal realized why he hadn't wanted to be stripped of his armor. He was dressed in a pair of boxers, a pair of combat boots, and a tank top.

And that was it.

"Do your commanders not allow their men to wear

their suits fully clothed?" Kennedy asked after she gave the man a moment to compose himself.

"No," he replied. "There is little ventilation inside. Gets quite hot when in use."

"Huh," Sal said and managed to bite off a chuckle. "Is that something that you might want to bring up with them when you get back?"

"Probably," the man said. "Although I do not think that there will be any changes. Budget problems, you see."

"We could probably get you hooked up with our armorer, and he could fit a custom add-on in there to help you," Sal said with a smile.

"That is impossible, I'm afraid," Gregor said, still visibly uncomfortable at being this naked in front of two strangers. "The designs in that suit are proprietary to Russian government, and nobody can inspect that without being thoroughly vetted."

"I got a pretty good look on the inside," Kennedy said with a grin. "Does that mean that I'm vetted by your government?"

"Well, you were trying to save my life," Gregor explained. "Is different."

"Sure," Sal growled. He slid himself back into his power suit and hefted his gun. "In other news, we've probably hung around here long enough. I would prefer not to wait here for whatever did that to your suit."

Kennedy nodded. She drew her sidearm from her hip and handed it to Gregor. "Try not to copy the design of that, would you? I'm sure that there's some company that owns the patent to it."

"Very funny," the man said with a forced chuckle. "That

said, I can't leave this armor here for the same reason. Is there any chance that one of you could carry it back? It's only fifty kilograms, easy weight for someone with full power armor."

"Are you serious?" she asked and glared at him.

Sal shrugged. "Can your suit carry that kind of weight?"

"Well, yeah, but it'll be a pain to maneuver with," Kennedy explained. "And dangerous if we get into a sticky situation."

"I can't leave it behind," Gregor said.

"Would your government be willing to pay to get it back?" the specialist asked.

"I doubt it," the man replied.

"Well then, will you be willing to pay her for the extra trouble of carrying your suit out?" Sal asked and for the first time, truly understood the expression about pulling teeth.

"I can do," Gregor nodded. "It would be preferable if my government could foot the bill, as Americans say."

"Do...Russians not say that?" Sal asked.

"Well, we have our own saying, but is better if we start to move again?" Gregor said.

"Just to confirm, though," Kennedy said as she moved to the suit which still lay on the ground, "if your government won't pay, you'll pay. Let's say...five hundred dollars?"

"Deal," Gregor said with a nod. She shrugged and looked annoyed at how easily the man had agreed to the price, which told her that she could have asked for a lot more. Either way, verbal agreements were binding in this abandoned section of the world, so she closed the suit again and strapped it to hers. The power armor picked up the extra weight smoothly.

"More to the point," Sal said as they set out into the jungle again. "What was it exactly that attacked you?"

"It was a group of the panthers that worked with a pack of those hyenas," Gregor replied. He looked uncomfortable again, but for very different reasons, the specialist suspected.

"They were working together?" Kennedy asked.

"Yeah, like they were willing to make team to bring us down," he replied. "And they got damned close, too. They came from behind and dragged a couple of our men away before we even realized that we were under attack. After we turned to fight the hyenas, the panthers jumped down from the trees. There wasn't much we could do. I was separated and those who survived from my team were pushed back by sheer numbers. The fact that they didn't try to return for me says the worst. Either they didn't survive, or they assumed that I hadn't and left me out here to die."

"Which do you think is more likely?" Sal asked.

"If I had been with my proper team, I would say the former," Gregor said. "But this time they teamed me up with new men—some mercs brought in from South Africa. I didn't know them that well, so I literally had no idea what to expect. They could be loyal and dead, or alive and cowardly bastards. I'm not really sure which I'd prefer."

"Maybe they're loyal and alive, and haven't been able to find you yet?" Sal asked and tilted his head in query.

"That is surprisingly optimistic view of the world." The man looked at Sal like he had told him that the world was flat and hollow and filled with mole men. "But there is GPS tracker in the suit, and I sent a distress signal before it went offline. So, unless the GPS is broken..." He looked at Kennedy.

"It's intact," she said with a twist of her mouth.

"Dead, or assholes," Gregor said with an unhappy growl.

"Well, if that's true, then the best-case scenario is that they're dead and assholes," the specialist said with a grin.

The Russian chuckled and shook his head. "That is closer to my view of the world."

"I'll take that as a compliment," Sal said with a nod. With Madigan carrying the Russian's suit and the other man in his underpants, he was now the de facto gunner of their little group. As they moved to link with their squad, he also searched for the novelties that would pay for their trip there.

Even so, Kennedy wanted them to maintain a good pace. It was already past midday, and she didn't want to spend the night out there with only the three of them, especially with one almost defenseless man and her weighed down. That would only invite trouble, and Sal was sensible and experienced enough now to understand that it wasn't a commentary on his own skills as a gunner. There was only so much one man could do when the critters came at them in hordes.

Sal was sure that Kennedy would somehow make it about how she didn't trust him to keep her safe out there in the Zoo in front of the rest of the team. As he walked, he directed his excess mental energy into the amusing process of creating his comebacks for the inevitable war of words that would come once they reconnected with the others.

"We're coming up on the spot," Kennedy said and checked her map once again. "Unless the rest of the team ran into trouble, they should already be there."

"Keep up a steady ping for them once we get within range," Sal said. "Make sure that they know it's us. I've heard stories about folks getting trigger happy out here and shooting without looking."

She nodded. Of course, all the reports read KIA or MIA since nobody would own up to shooting their own man, but there was talk about it in the bar once the booze flowed and tongues grew looser. Nobody owned up to anything then either, but there had been too many hints dropped for it not to be at least a possibility.

It took them another half hour to climb through the underbrush that now became far thicker and a lot more aggressive. Sal could move through it without too much trouble, and Kennedy was able to simply push. Their new Russian friend, however, had considerable difficulty, which meant that Sal needed to drop back and open a path of sorts for him to walk through. It was slow going, and they estimated that the sun had begun to set by the time they received a response to their ping.

"I have your signal," they heard through the comms. "Is that you, Kennedy?"

She keyed her comm. "Roger that, Young. We are about one hundred meters from your location, and we have a guest."

"Oh...that fucking Russian was in need of some help, was he?" Young asked.

Kennedy glanced up to see Gregor's reaction and then remembered that he wasn't attached to his comm unit anymore. He looked at her, confused, and she turned and isolated the sound from her suit he wouldn't be able to hear it. Everyone else on comms remained connected.

"Yeah, he had some problems with his suit," she explained. "Since the purpose of our little excursion was to save his life, it seemed the obvious choice since the alternative was to send him into the Zoo half naked and with our best wishes."

"Half naked?" Young asked.

"Oh, yeah," Madigan growled, "there is that. The guy is boots, boxers, and shirt shy of being as naked as the day he was born."

"Roger...that," Young said, clearly confused. "Might I ask why the fuck the Russian has almost adopted a nudist camp's dress code?"

"Long story," she responded quickly before Sal could come in with an explanation. "We'll see you ladies in a bit."

"Roger that," Young replied.

"What was that about?" the specialist asked after he'd opened a private channel.

"I thought that it would be more amusing to let them try to come up with some sort of mental picture of you and me fighting over his clothes or something before we drop them back down to reality with the real story," Kennedy said with a grin, and he chuckled.

"What are you two talking about?" Gregor asked.

"Nothing," Sal said and quickly turned the isolation protocol in his suit off. "We're sharing some...proprietary information with the rest of our team."

"How long will you hold this proprietary thing over

me?" the Russian asked as Sal held a couple of bushes aside for him to walk through.

"About as long as you have Kennedy over there lugging your suit of armor around," Sal said. "Plus interest."

"You are paid to do that!" he protested.

"At slave wages," she retorted. "So get used to a little ribbing from us there, Greg."

"Is Gregor."

"Whatever you say, Greg," Sal chimed in. He tried and failed to suppress a broad grin.

# CHAPTER TWENTY

The rotors sprayed sand everywhere as a ruthless accompaniment to the helicopter's arrival. This was among the very long list of reasons why Anderson had no intention to ever spend more time than was absolutely necessary anywhere near a desert. The disparity of temperatures from day to night and the glaring brightness of the sun with no shade was bad enough without the unbearable amount of sand that went fucking everywhere.

No, he would not look back on this mission with any degree of fondness. And that was only partially because his meds made sure that his night's sleep had been light and full of dreams that were less than restful. He gritted his teeth and shook his head.

He'd ordered that the morning be used to debrief the rest of the squad on exactly what had happened the day before. The colonel didn't need to look at it or even be present for it as the team leaders had handled it. Instead, he used the time to write up his own report, and true to his word, he made sure to lay the full weight of the blame on himself and the suits that the men were equipped with. In addition, he'd firmly suggested that all future testing stages be run in controlled environments and stated in the strongest possible terms that field testing must not be held in locations with as many variables as the Zoo. Then again, there weren't many places on earth that had that many variables. Unless they'd made the mistake of unleashing alien goop anywhere else, this was the single worst place in the world to test suits of power armor.

Thankfully, he'd taken typing classes in high school and made sure to keep those skills honed. Over the course of the morning, he'd given the dumbasses in the Pentagon—and hopefully, Congress—thirty pages of scathing review that he would make sure they read. If he couldn't get them to come down there into the middle of fucking nowhere to do their own damned tests, he would make sure to take every inch of revenge he could, petty or not.

He owed it to Sergeant Michaels.

Anderson started to write up a few words to celebrate the man's many achievements when he heard the helicopter approach. It would be a few weeks until the ceremony in which they returned the man's dog tags to his family. They needed to play with the records first and provide both witnesses and paperwork that confirmed that Sgt. Michaels had never been within a thousand miles of the Zoo. Only then would they release the man's body for burial along with a horde of posthumous medals. He would make sure that they gave the family his full pension and the man full honors. It was the least he could do.

A few members of Blue team had already been lifted to the Staging Area for medical treatment, but the colonel was happy to see that at least one member had remained, a man by the name of Chief Petty Officer Vernon. He had broken a couple of ribs in the fighting, but he had refused to be shipped out earlier.

All remaining members of Red and Green teams assembled alongside the men who stepped out of the helicopter. The team members were all in uniform. They hadn't brought their ceremonial outfits, but out there in the middle of nowhere, it didn't really matter. They would have signed off on not being able to return and attend the dead man's funeral, so this was as close to honoring the dead as they would get.

The men from the helicopter didn't think that this sort of arrangement was strange. They wore combat fatigues as well and quickly moved past the assembled troops. A couple of men who had worked on the wall and even a few of the scientists were there too.

"Ten-hut!" Anderson shouted, and the assembled soldiers snapped quickly to attention and saluted as the officers returned with a coffin.

The colonel glanced around. He had spent most of his career in the Marines. There were a couple present, he saw by their uniforms. Navy SEALs, Green Berets, and even a couple of AFSOC men were present and held their salute stiffly as the coffin passed. In any other time or place, these men would crack jokes about how inferior the other men's branches of the military were. A handful would make themselves heard every time men from different branches gathered together. He was sure that the joshing would come later, but now was a time to respect the fallen.

The colonel's hand dropped to his side again as the

coffin was placed in the helicopter and the rotors spun once more. One by one, the team members peeled away and headed back to where they'd bunked. He knew these men and had hand-picked them for this. They wouldn't break under the pressure. Each one of them would stay until the mission was done.

They merely needed a couple of moments to process it all.

For Anderson's part, he wasn't even sure what the mission was now. The problems with the suit—especially the communications issues which were one of the major selling points from the parent company—put the whole operation dead in the water.

He was the last to walk away a few minutes after the helicopter took off. The other men had dispersed and left him to his thoughts for a long moment. Even out in the blistering sun, it felt like the place to do it.

"Colonel Anderson?" he heard someone say behind him.

His assistant stood there with a tablet in her hand.

"It's Carlson," she said softly. "He wants an update."

Anderson nodded. "I'll take it in my room."

He marched back to his temporary quarters, and his assistant followed him into the room to place the tablet on the desk before she left and closed the door quickly behind her.

The device came alive with the image of a blue horse with wings surrounded by a silver ring. **Pegasus** was emblazoned on the bottom. It vibrated gently as it asked if he was willing to accept a call from New York.

He tapped the accept button and sat as the screen came

alive with the image of a man with his white hair cut by the kind of person who charged three hundred dollars. The rest of his clothes were similarly expensive.

"Colonel Anderson, it's great to speak to you again," the man said with a broad and well-practiced smile—the kind perfected in front of a mirror for hours and which made shareholders believe he was a pleasant man. "How's the Sahara treating you?"

"A pleasure to see you again, Mr. Carlson," he said. Unlike his caller, he didn't have to smile. "The Sahara is hot and full of sand, as it's always been."

"Well, the same can be said about the beach." Carlson leaned back in his chair. "I was in Bali last week—got a fantastic tan, I have to tell you. My ex-wife is a dermatologist, and she always harped on at me about skin cancer and all that crap. Even after the damned divorce. Although I guess she wants to keep the alimony checks coming in and she can't cash them once I've died of skin cancer, am I right?"

Anderson had the distinct impression that this was the kind of man who liked the sound of his own voice—one who would invite a horde of people to his penthouse for cigars and brandy so that they could have what Carlson assumed was the pleasure to hear him go on about politics or sports. Yes, he definitely seemed like the guy who could go on a rant about how baseball was better than football, and it would come with graphs, quotes, and historical figures.

He looked at the screen and realized that Carlson still rambled on about his trip to Bali.

"I'm sorry, Mr. Carlson," he interjected. "I'm sure that

your encounter with the two young women while deep-sea diving was very memorable, but the internet connection around here is spotty. I think it would probably be best if we could get the business out of the way first. Just in case."

"Of course," the man said with a small smile. "I'm sure that you're a busy man too, Colonel, and I'd hate to keep you for too long. Yes, to business. How did the trial runs go?"

"There were a couple of problems," Anderson said. He tilted his head after a moment as he considered that response. People had died. It was time for politeness to go out the window. "Actually, there were many problems. I've sent you and the generals back at the Pentagon my full report on the matter."

"Of course, and I look forward to reading it," Carlson said with a nod. "However, I'd appreciate if you could give me the pointers. I have a meeting with the lead scientists in the project over dinner, and it would be best if I knew what kind of mess we'll walk into."

"All right," he said through clenched teeth. He didn't need to be polite, but it was probably in his best interests to at least be civil. "The first issues were found during the march to the first testing stage. Sand and grit entered the joints too easily and impaired movement which could, over long use, cause problems with the hardware of the armor as well as the electronics. There was also some problem with the movement lag of the power functions in the suits."

"We did talk to the scientists about that," Carlson interrupted. "The lag is caused by a few inhibitors kept in place for the earlier models. We'll refine the process and improve the training regimens for the people who will wear them from now on."

"Right," Anderson said. *Do not snap at the man for interrupting you. He's a billionaire company CEO, not a recruit in need of a few lessons in manners.* "Anyway, that was the first mission run. The second had a lot of other problems. First of all, there was a lot of interference with the comms while the team was in there. We lost the connection repeatedly, and there was stuttering and—well, all the details are in the reports from the engineers in charge of overseeing the tests. They'll have a much more informed report, so you should read that."

"Wait, but I heard that these radio problems were common in the Zoo," Carlson said, and Anderson could almost hear the cogs turning in his head. "Something to do with the radiation in…whatever it is that makes those trees and plants grow."

"I'm sure all that will be covered in the report," the colonel continued. "However, considering that the isolated comm frequencies included in the suits were one of the major selling points, this problem exposes some serious vulnerabilities that you may want to have your scientists look at and test for. The radio signals inside the Zoo are unique to this location, but only for now, after all."

The CEO nodded. "I was told that there were casualties during the second test."

Anderson closed his eyes and exhaled a long and eloquent sigh. "Sergeant Hugh Michaels. The men on his team managed to recover his body before retreating. Well…most of it."

"Most?" Carlson asked and raised an eyebrow.

"The animals that attacked them managed to tear a leg off," he explained, his tone curt. "Something else that you might want to bring up with your development team since we were told that the armor was impervious to most attacks, which we assumed included animal attacks."

"I'm not sure I appreciate your tone, Colonel Anderson," the caller said and leaned forward in his seat. "You need to appreciate that the amount of research we put into these suits is being funded for the betterment of the military."

"And you need to appreciate that one man died and three others were wounded in testing your company's suits, Mr. Carlson," he responded but managed to keep his tone even and make sure not to show any emotion on his face. "Men with families who will have to be told some lie about how their fathers, husbands, and sons were injured or killed in the line of duty. Don't you tell me to mind my tone."

Carlson leaned forward, raised a finger, and opened his mouth to retort. Anderson had the feeling that few people in his life ever talked back to him, and those who did were divorced rather quickly.

He brought himself under control, leaned back in his seat once again, and allowed the momentary tension to fade.

"I apologize," the CEO said in a more even tone. "I do realize that there are people dead and injured due to our lack of foresight."

Anderson said. "I'm sorry too. It's been a stressful day."

The man nodded. "I appreciate that. Now, with... Sergeant Michaels, you said that they recovered the body. I assume that excludes his leg and the armor in which it was encased?"

"You assume correctly," he replied.

"Not putting GPS locators in the limbs of the armor," Carlson said with a shake of his head. "Such an obvious issue in hindsight."

"We've considered sending a team in to recover the leg."

"Do you know where it is?"

"Well...no. Not a clue. The Zoo is a massive place in which to mount a search."

"Well, in that case, if you don't have an idea as to where it could be, I think it might be best if we leave it as is," Carlson said decisively. "There's no sense in risking any more of our men and resources on a search for something that the Zoo is probably consuming as we speak. No." He shook his head. "We'll have to outfit all our suits with locators on each of the limbs, but the risk to reward ratio of any attempt to recover a piece of broken hardware is too terrible."

*Risk to reward ratio*, Anderson thought. While he was happy with the decision not to go after the leg, he couldn't help but realize that it had actually been made by budgetary concerns. Still, looking a gift horse in the mouth and all that.

"Anyway, I'll put your thoughts to the team here in New York," Carlson continued. "For now, though, how long do you think it'll be before they get the tests back on the road, as it were?"

"That will take time," Anderson said. "The suits used by Blue team were heavily damaged. To repair them for the new team you send in and have all the other suits upgraded for use in the field—it'll be a week, at least, before we're ready for operations again."

"Look, every day that we run this operation inside the walls costs us a fortune," Carlson said with a shake of the head. "I can authorize a five-day delay, but that's it. Believe me, you could buy a house in the fucking Hamptons with the cost of two extra days, and I'll eat these extra costs myself."

"I understand," the colonel said. "I'll inform the team."

"Thank you for all your work, Colonel. We'll be in touch," the CEO said and signed off with a click.

Anderson remained seated for a moment and stared at the screen and the rotating Pegasus logo before he heard a knock on his door.

"Come in!" He pushed to his feet.

Dr. Bial pushed the door open and stepped inside, and the outside brightness seemed to follow him. "Colonel Anderson? Did you talk to Carlson?"

He nodded.

"Any word on new pilots for the suits?"

"They should arrive within the next couple of days," the colonel said. "They were pre-selected in case something like this happened, but they still need to go through the training course required to use them."

"All right, we can work with that." The scientist shut the door behind him. "What kind of time are we looking at to have the suits functional and fit them with the upgrades?"

"Carlson says five days before we need to work again," Anderson said. "Although you should probably tell your team that there's a four-day cutoff and act surprised but understanding when they need five instead."

"I'll keep that in mind," Bial said. "Did your drill sergeant teach you that?"

"No, I picked it up while helping my son with his homework," he replied with a smile. "Work will always expand to the allowed time."

"Huh," the man grunted. "I'll keep that in mind too."

# CHAPTER TWENTY-ONE

Sal peered into the jungle. Night had fallen, and the wary watchfulness that had become habit brought little comfort. He could see very little in the darkness and especially with the heating lamps activated. These provided a circle of light as well as a barrier from the icy night winds that seemed to cut through the trees as if they were still in the desert.

Even so, he had noticed while they set up camp and before the heat lamps went up that the glowing goop inside the trees was a lot more visible as darkness fell. It was an enchanting sight, and almost made up for the night sky that the tree cover hid from them. That brief glimpse was thrust aside when the lights came on, and now it was simply all dark with only a hint of something out there. It was also less enchanting and far more unsettling. The tiny pricks of light were barely visible and looked more like eyes that peered constantly at them, not clearly visible but always there. More than once, they caught his attention as he moved his head and each time he turned to look, he saw nothing there.

Oddly enough, even knowing what caused it, those glimmered reminders that the goop was always there made things worse.

"We can't break all the way to the northern wall construction to escort the Russian to his camp," Young growled. He and Kennedy had been at it ever since the rescue team returned.

"So what do you suggest?" she demanded and yanked her helmet off as she walked over to him. "That we simply leave him out here to die? Or force him to come back to the Staging Area with us—and lug his heavy-ass mother-fucking piece of useless junk suit all the while?"

"That suit has a lot of interesting mechanics," Young said with a shrug. "I'm sure that the people we work for might be willing to pay a hefty price for it since this is a research mission, after all. He can consider it payment for us saving his life out there, and maybe—just maybe—find a chopper to fly him back to his base when we're finished."

"That's not fair, and you know it." She shook her head. "And even if that seems like a smart thing to do now, you don't want the Russians to give our people the same kind of treatment. Would you like to be in the position where you have to violate contractual agreements to have your life saved?"

Young sighed and shook his head. She did have a point there. They would share this place with the Russians, and it was best to keep the relations as cordial as possible. He still didn't like it much, though.

"So, what do you suggest?" he asked finally as they

prepped the rations for their dinner. "Do you want us to put our mission on hold while we play babysitter and get him all the way back to his side of the Zoo?"

"We split the team up today, why couldn't we do it again?" Kennedy asked.

"Yes, that's a great idea," their leader retorted with blatant sarcasm. "We're heading deeper into a dangerous part of the world and the deeper in we go, the more dangerous it gets. Splitting our team up seems like a fantastic idea."

"I think everyone needs to calm down," Sal interjected and silenced the dispute, at least for the moment. While the two had talked, the other team members had looked on— or seemed to try not to while they went about their work. The most awkward one of all, of course, was Gregor himself. The Russian was incredibly uncomfortable about the fact that Young had insisted that they conduct this conversation like he wasn't even there. From the look on his face, it didn't look like he wanted to be there either.

Sal shared the feeling.

Both Young and Kennedy glared at him, almost annoyed by the interruption. She was the least peeved of the two, of course, but she still peered at him like she wondered what he tried to do. In all honesty, he had no agenda in mind for his interruption. He simply didn't want to have to listen to the two of them go back and forth in a heated conversation while they tried to eat and recover from a long day in the Zoo.

They had enough time for hostility and the like later. For now, they could enjoy the comparative peace and quiet. Of course, jungles were never quiet, and now that there were insect-arachnid hybrids out there, it was even less so. The song of what sounded like cicadas but of a different cadence eroded the near silence he'd grown accustomed to on his previous runs.

It wasn't unpleasant and was actually quite musical if he listened carefully, even if it remained constant with no sign that it might stop anytime soon. It would grate over time, Sal knew, but for now, it was less irritating than having to endure the awkwardness of being in the middle of an argument that they weren't a part of.

"We can figure all this shit out tomorrow," he said. To punctuate the statement, he opened his heated ration and drew a long breath of the steamed vegetables with spaghetti and carbonara sauce. "For now, let's eat and rest. Everyone's had a long day, okay?"

The adversaries both nodded. Sal had almost expected them to put up more of a fight at his attempt to take the reins, but he realized that they had to be hungry and tired too. He pulled out the recyclable fork that came with the meal and dug in. Ito heated up an extra meal and handed it to Gregor with an apologetic smile.

Courtney moved to sit beside Sal while they ate. He smiled at her as his mouth was too full for him to say anything. The red sauce on his lips made him wish that she had joined him later when he'd had the time to clean himself up. As delicious as he found pasta like this to be, it wasn't the most elegant meal, and he had long come to terms with the fact that the best spaghetti was usually also the messiest.

"How was your day?" she asked when she finished her diced chicken and rice.

He held a finger up as he slurped the last of the pasta and cleaned his mouth quickly before he answered.

"Well, we ran into a couple of new plants that look like they might have flowers similar to the pita plants, so I already made a point to take as many samples as I could. There's always a chance that it might prove to be something similar to the fluid sacs of the big critters," Sal said. He spoke quickly and paused only to take a quick sip of water from his canteen. "You know, an added revenue stream out here or something."

"Oh, I know," Courtney said and grimaced as she remembered that she'd very recently had to cut one of those sacs out of the massive creature.

"Aside from that and the rescue of our new unwilling team member—" Sal did what Kennedy and Young couldn't and kept his voice down when he mentioned Gregor. "It was fairly standard. No more animal attacks, although from what our Russian friend told us about how he got stranded, it seems like the combined hyena and panther attacks that we saw ourselves back there has become more and more prevalent."

"Did you—"

"Oh, I already noted it down as something of interest for further review," he said with a laugh. "If it's something that could help us and others survive trips into this place, do you think I won't at least put some thought into studying it?"

She chuckled softly. "I guess not."

"And how was your day?" He set his plate and utensils aside for recycling. "Did you find anything interesting?"

"Not really?" Courtney said, but she ended the

sentence like a question and her face scrunched into a frown. "I saw a couple of interesting things out there, don't get me wrong, but once the team knew where to find Pita bushes, they basically lost focus on everything else. There's no assurance of money from the research, and what they do get will be split with the rest of the teams. The bounty money isn't split—or it is, but between fewer people—so that was what they focused on all day."

"You guys cleaned the bushes out then?" Sal asked.

"It's actually a little scary how fast these guys can strip these plants down," she acknowledged with a small smile and a tilt of her head. "Well, impressive too, I guess."

He nodded with a chuckle. "Most of the folk are here to make money, so are you really surprised that they put that ahead of the research and the wonders of this place?"

"Not really," Courtney admitted. "It still annoys me, though. Don't they understand that what we research here could mean a lot more money in the long run?"

"I think they do," Sal said, "although they probably also know that they don't see a hot dime of that money themselves."

"Yeah, I guess," she agreed softly, and he smiled as he turned to look at the rest of the squad. Finished with their dinner, Kennedy and Young had resumed their argument over what they should do about the Russian, although they at least tried to keep their voices down this time. Kennedy glanced at him and gave Courtney an almost venomous look before she turned to Young once more. Sal frowned and wondered what that was about.

"How much did you guys collect?" he asked.

Monroe seemed distracted and dropped back into the conversation with a somewhat startled look. "Huh? What?"

"How many sets of the Pita flowers did you guys collect?" he asked again.

"Oh...twenty sets," she replied with a nod. "A pretty good haul by all estimations."

"Damn good haul," he said with a chuckle.

"You guys really need to tell me what you did to enable you to track these plants down," she said. "I mean, I understand that you want to keep it a secret from the people who run the Staging Area since this is something of a meal ticket, but since I'm part of Heavy Metal now, doesn't that mean that I get to know about it too?"

He nodded. "I'll fill you in on the details later when we get back to base. It was mostly luck anyway. I'm surprised that you guys didn't find out about it sooner."

"Well, we didn't, so I'll hold you to that promise to share with the rest of the class," she said, and he chuckled with real amusement as he leaned back. He could enter the conversation with Kennedy and perhaps apply his brains to find a solution to their Russian problem.

For the moment, though, he was done. He needed rest and time to think. It had been a long day, and he didn't want to watch Kennedy and Young go at it again with increasing intensity.

Sal pushed himself from his seat and moved to where Gregor had situated himself. Courtney's eyes followed him for a long moment before she turned away, shook her head, and moved to where she'd set up her space in the camp.

"Hey," Sal said. "How are you holding up?"

Gregor shrugged. "As well as can be expected. Your two commanders seem to be at odds about what to do about me."

"Well, can you blame them?" Sal asked and raised an eyebrow. "You're a bit of a wrench in this whole operation."

"Wrench?" he asked, his head tilted in frank confusion.

"Oh…we're out here to do some research, and there's only so much research we can do if we take you back home," he explained with a smile. "Not that we won't get you back to your base, of course, but it'll take a while to get past all the greed. These are good people, I promise."

The Russian nodded. "I take your word for it. And thank you again for saving my life."

"We can only hope that you would have done the same for us, Gregor," Sal said with a smile. He dragged a sleeping bag across the ground and handed it to the Russian. "For now, though, you might want to get some rest. It will be a long day for you tomorrow."

# CHAPTER TWENTY-TWO

"Okay people, listen up!" Young called.

Sal narrowed his eyes. Normally, he would make some sort of crack that the sun was too bright for him to be awake, but he hadn't slept well the night before. He had thought that his offer to turn his sleeping bag and tent over to Gregor had been a noble gesture. While it might have been that, there was also the small problem that it left him without anywhere to camp. He'd applied his impressive intellect to that for most of the night, but it had mostly ended with him snatching a couple of dozing naps which were quickly interrupted by someone's snores, eerie shrieks from inside the jungle, or merely the very real discomfort of sleeping in his armor.

It wasn't that uncomfortable under normal circumstances, but when he was stuck in it overnight, there was a lot to hate.

They all had breakfast, and Sal had raided the instant coffee stores after he'd found a reliable water source about fifteen paces from where they had set up camp. He felt vaguely human, although he couldn't promise that he'd be able to maintain the charade indefinitely.

"Since we're close enough to the Staging Area, we decided that it's pointless to hike all the way across the Zoo to get someone there on foot," Young said once everyone was armored and ready move. "We've come away with a fairly decent haul, so Kennedy suggested that we take what we have already and head back with Gregor. I'll accompany him and carry his suit for good measure."

Sal nodded. It was a step up from calling him the Russian, which was what Young had seemed to insist on doing every time he mentioned the man. Sal could see Gregor smirk, which told him that he appreciated the change in tone. The specialist knew that Kennedy had offered to let Young take their haul and split it between themselves.

"Nobody is told to do anything, though," Young continued. "This will be on a volunteer basis. I'll lead the team heading back to the Staging Area, and Kennedy will lead the team that stays out for the remainder of the five days. We'll still need a specialist on each team, and since I assume Jacobs will stay with Kennedy, that means that Dr. Monroe will come with me."

Sal saw Courtney grit her teeth and look away. There was something different about her. She acted strangely like she now looked more to him for direction than before. He wasn't sure that he disliked it, but it was certainly something he would have to get used to. Later.

Their haul from the single Pita plant had been enough to make up for anybody's cut in pay for the trip, so the split was fairly even. Ito and Carson chose to stay with Sal and Kennedy and try for another, similarly large haul while

Sousa agreed to head to the Staging Area with Gregor, Young, and Monroe.

"You'd think that this would be my dream," Courtney told Sal with a smile. "To head to the Staging Area early with a huge haul, but there were a lot of things out there that I wanted to study."

"Plants and animals too?" he asked with a small grin.

She blushed. "I didn't think I was that obvious. But yeah, you've helped me cope, and I'd like to find out how you do it so I don't constantly find myself in trouble."

Sal nodded. "I...don't actually know what to say to that," he said with a soft chuckle. "But take care of yourself, and take care of my pal Gregor." He raised his voice so the man would hear him. "I'll see you in four days. Or not, because we're in a dangerous place full of hostile plants and animals and we might all die before then."

"Don't even joke about it," Courtney growled and punched him softly in his power function arm. "I'll see you in four days."

Sal grinned. The team heading to the Staging Area was the first to leave, which meant that it was up to the rest of them to pack up. He realized that Madigan gave him the odd funny look too.

"What's up, Kennedy?" he asked with a quizzical expression as he lifted his share of the packs and attached them to his armor.

"Nothing much, Jacobs," she responded but averted her gaze quickly and busied herself with her own packs. "What's up with you?"

"Nothing," Sal retorted. "I'll simply look at you with an

accusatory and confused expression...oh, no, wait, that's you."

"You're talking crazy," she said dismissively and now avoided eye contact with him altogether.

"Sure," he said with a chuckle.

"If you two are done squabbling," Ito said and rested her rifle against her shoulder, "I think we have some ground to cover before you pull pigtails and yank shorts down."

"Come on, we're not in seventh grade anymore," Sal said with a chuckle.

"You did that shit in seventh grade?" Ito asked and raised an eyebrow.

"I skipped second, third, fourth and sixth grades, so yes, I was the only nine-year-old in my seventh-grade class," Sal said and tried not to make it sound like he was bragging. It wasn't like these people actually appreciated the work that it took for him to do that anyway. "Either way, I think she has some residual angry talk left over from her argument with Young. It's best that she gets it out her system now than have it stew in her brain all day until she explodes on one of us when we don't set the heating plates up right."

"That's very insightful, Jacobs," Kennedy snapped, her voice dripping with sarcasm. "But if you just go ahead and shut up and then fuck yourself, that'd be great."

"Do you think we have time?" Sal looked around. "I mean, I know we should probably move and explore, but I'll be quick. Help me get out of my armor and—" He stopped talking since he couldn't keep a straight face while she flipped him off. Even so, his words had the desired effect, and she had a hard time keeping a straight face as Carson and Ito laughed.

"I can help you get your armor off, but only if you give the whole team a show, Jacobs," Ito said with a chuckle.

"As quick as you are, Jacobs, I really don't think we have the time to watch you fumble with your armor like you've been dumped at the prom dance," Kennedy muttered as they pushed deeper into the jungle. Without having to adjust to someone out of armor, they were able to maintain a much better pace than they had the day before.

"I never actually got to go to my prom," Sal said and checked his weapon before he disengaged the rifle.

"Why, getting ready for a Mathletics competition?" Ito asked.

"Of course not," Sal snapped. "It was a chess tournament. Mathletics is for losers."

"Whereas we all know that chess captains are swimming in potang," Carson said with a grin.

"First of all, nobody says that anymore," Sal retorted. "Secondly, that's not what I mean. Theoretical stuff never appealed to me as much as something where I could get my hands dirty and actually be in the middle of the whole thing. It's why I picked biology as my major instead of theoretical physics. Those were the two most challenging fields I could think of that didn't involve me in a hospital wearing scrubs."

"So, if you had been more into not getting your hands dirty, you might be cooped up in some university-run lab watching reruns of Big Bang Theory?" Ito asked.

"The horrible knowledge that there's a version of me in an alternate universe doing precisely that keeps me awake some nights," he said with a nod. "Well, mornings, since that's when I'm actually asleep."

The conversation stopped abruptly when something hurtled out of the bushes and charged at them with a high-pitched hiss that made Sal's ears hurt. It wasn't particularly tall, but it was long and curled like a snake. The creature moved rapidly over the ground on dozens of small legs like a centipede. The head was definitely reptile-like, though, and as it attacked, the sides of its head flared, its jaw extended, and a foul-smelling liquid jetted out at Carson, who was the closest.

"Get down!" Sal yelled. He didn't recognize the creature, but he'd seen enough of the Zoo creatures to know that Carson would not want that liquid to touch any part of him or his armor.

The man did get down as Kennedy and Ito fired simultaneously, but a heavy glob of the acid still struck him in the chest.

"Fuck!" Sal scrambled forward quickly. He realized that there was a downside to the hybridity of his armor—restoring it to combat mode wasn't as instinctual as he had hoped. Either way, it didn't matter. Even though the pieces of the animal that had been severed still moved as if they worked independently without the need for a head, Kennedy and Ito could handle it.

The liquid that had come in contact with Carson's armor immediately smoked and released an acrid smell. Sal yanked his water canteen out—recently filled, thank goodness—and poured it over the armor. His plan was to wash the acid away quickly before it could reach the electronics and, more importantly, Carson himself.

He wondered if he was a bad person if his first thought was to save the armor instead of the man. The answer that came first was probably. He took an acid-resistant microfiber rag from his pouch and dabbed it over all the spots that still smoked, then continued until there were no more signs of the acid on the suit.

"What's the prognosis?" Carson asked. Despite the fact that he obviously tried to keep his voice as steady as possible, Sal was close enough to hear the slightest tremble. He didn't make any mention of it, though. Honestly, he couldn't think of a worse way to go than by acid that seeped through armor you couldn't get out of.

"It looks like the metal plate has warped a little," Sal said quickly as he continued to wipe the rag over the cracks in the armor. "How do you feel? Any itching or burning? Anywhere? And before you answer that, please keep all STD humor off the table until we're sure that you're all right."

Carson opened his mouth, probably with something along the lines of how it still burned when he peed on his mind since he shut it again quickly.

"No, no burn and no itch," he said finally. "Not of the acid variety, anyway."

"Kennedy, Ito, is that thing dead yet?" Sal asked as he examined the structure of the plate as rapidly as possible.

Kennedy dropped her boot down on the creature's severed head and ground her heel down into it. "It's a fucking pain to kill all the way, but I think the pieces that are left won't attack us anytime soon."

"Good," Sal said softly. "Because I'll need to pull the breastplate off to make sure that there isn't anything still in there. The last thing we want is for it to cause trouble when we are mobile again."

"Okay, what do I do?" Carson asked.

"Well, if you could run a quick diagnostic on your armor to make sure that there's nothing still in there," Sal said as he tugged and twisted at the levers that separated the chest plate from the rest of the suit.

"Already working," Carson replied and grunted as Sal yanked and pried until the piece came off.

"Ito and Kennedy, if you guys could keep watch so that nothing tries to eat us while Carson is in a particularly vulnerable situation," Sal said and didn't look up from his work.

"Will do, sir," Ito said. Sal didn't pay enough attention or even want to find out if she was joking or not. He used a couple of smaller tools to pull the pieces of the breastplate apart.

Kennedy joined him where he squatted and worked the pieces apart. He wasn't sure how he knew, but he was certain that she looked at him in that weird judge-y and yet unsure way as she had earlier. He didn't have time to look up and confirm it, though.

"At the risk of repeating myself," Sal said, his voice distracted, "what's up, Kennedy? And before you say nothing again, if you do, I will make you fix this piece of armor while I keep watch."

"Please don't say nothing again, Kennedy," Carson growled.

"Right," she replied. "It's just...I've noticed that you and Courtney have gotten closer than you were before."

"What's your point?" Sal asked. "She's a part of the team

—and, might I say, the only part of the team who I can bounce my ideas off without being insulted and called a geek and a nerd and…chess captain. Although I'm not sure how that last one can be anything but a compliment, the tone still hurts my feelings."

"Come on," she huffed. "I haven't called you any of those things in at least a month."

"No, but when I talked about the kind of tracheae through which the insect-arachnid hybrids breathe, I could hear your eyes glaze over from the other side of the camp," he replied. His voice retained the faraway quality that indicated that while his mouth talked, his mind was elsewhere.

"Sure," Kennedy admitted and nodded as she focused warily on the jungle with her weapon prepped in case any more of the creatures attacked. "But still, it seems like you two might be much closer than you were before."

"You mean besides the fact that she has recently been added to our company and this is the first time that I've been out in the field with another specialist for an extended period?" Sal asked.

"Ugh, fine," she muttered and shook her head. "I'll make a sweep of the area."

Sal nodded as she moved away, finished cleaning the breastplate, and connected it to Carson's suit.

"That was some fantastic deflecting you did back there," the man said with a grin.

"Thanks."

"So, what was all that stuff about, anyway?" he asked when Sal showed no inclination to continue the conversation. "Are you and Kennedy involved or something? You guys an item?"

The specialist didn't look up from his work. "Do you want me to deflect with you too? We don't know each other well enough for me to put some effort into not deflecting, you know."

"Oh," Carson said and nodded. "Ten-four, loud and clear."

"Excellent." Sal forced a grin as he looked up and patted the breastplate. "There should be some issues with the surface sensors there. It looks like they were caught by the acid before I could get to them. A simple repair job should fix that, though."

"Thanks, Jacobs." Carson stood again and ran a few mobility tests. "So you really won't tell me what's going on with you and Kennedy?"

"I have no idea what you're talking about," he said and forced a smile. "But I'll make sure to let her know about your interest."

"No...no, no, that won't be necessary," Carson said quickly.

"We'll see," Sal replied with a wink. "I think we're ready to move on again."

# CHAPTER TWENTY-THREE

She would never have believed that she would be less happy to get back to the Staging Area after a trip into the Zoo. It wasn't only that she didn't want to leave Sal and Madigan in there, but there were also a lot of things happening that she wanted to be on top of.

And she was actually quite happy that there was nobody around who could hear her thoughts right about now. She didn't want to think about how embarrassing this sort of thing would be if she had said something like that out loud. Normally, she would have assumed that crude jokes would be made at her expense, but all things considered…

It was annoying how much she cared about what other people thought of her these days. She had been such a strong, independent woman before, and because she got drunk and kind of raped one man, she suddenly became all needy and possessive?

She rubbed her temples gently as their JLTV pulled into the Staging Area. There had been very little actual resistance to their advance, and most animals moved quickly out of their way. That meant there was very little need for a specialist on their team.

Even so, she'd caught some pictures and taken a few samples. She might be off her game, but she wasn't the kind of person to let any personal shit interfere with her work. Usually, anyway. There were some truths about herself that she only now began to discover. Not all of them were good, but she was a scientist. Any learning experience was a worthwhile experience, in her book.

She merely hoped that these learning experiences didn't end with awkward conversations in the future.

The vehicle drew to a halt, and she jumped out of her seat. Back on the ground, she quickly completed the uplink between her suit and the SA's database and added all the information that they had gathered. It was automatic, but the connection logs gave her a decent view of what had been collected, and there wouldn't be a problem with them getting their cut for that. Although she reminded herself, it was probable that nothing would actually appear in her bank account from the sponsors until the other teams came in with what they had gathered.

"Okay, Gregor," Young said as he closed his comm. "I've relayed the mission statement to my superiors, and they'll relay that in turn to your bosses. We should hear from them any minute now, and they'll most likely send transport to pick you up. Soldier to soldier, it won't be first-class accommodations, but until then, they've set you up in the infirmary. I'll make sure to drop your suit off where your people can pick it up, and I promise that nobody will snoop into the mechanics of it."

"I appreciate that very much, Sergeant Young," the Russian said and offered his hand. "I will never forget that you and your team saved my life."

Young cracked a smile, probably the only one for the whole day. He took Gregor's hand and shook it firmly.

"I can only imagine that you'd do the same thing for any one of us out there," he said with a smile. "An ambulance will be here soon to take you to the hospital. In the meantime, I'll head to the commandant's office and see how much of a profit we'll actually make for this very short and yet very productive mission."

Courtney looked on as Young and Sousa headed off. It had been a long day, but mostly because nothing really interesting had happened to make it go by faster. She wasn't complaining, but at the same time, boring meant longer-lasting.

"If you could send my thanks back to Kennedy and Dr. Jacobs too, I'd really appreciate it," Gregor said to her.

"He's not...he isn't a doctor," Courtney said before she paused and smiled.

"But he's a specialist," the Russian said, clearly confused. "And one of the brighter ones too, especially for someone so young. Make no mistake, I think that you're quite intelligent too, but then you *are* a doctor."

"He's merely a very smart guy, is all," Courtney said. She needed a drink. No...no, maybe not. But she would like to have a hot shower and a real meal.

"I need to head out too, Gregor," she said with a chuckle when the ambulance rolled into view. "You take care of yourself, you hear?"

"I will do that, Dr. Monroe."

Kennedy still gave him the silent treatment, although he had caught her glaring at him when she thought he wasn't looking. Well, technically he hadn't, but his new suit had a very interesting set of cameras that could provide decent footage from the side and the back that filled him in on the details.

Why did she look at him like that? And why had she interrogated him about Courtney? Did she actually think that something had happened?

Well, something had, of course, but it had been while he was unconscious and one hundred percent not his fault or doing. What, did she want him to have put up more of a fight or something?

As the day wore on, he found her silence more boorish than usual. They were friends, despite everything, and he associated their trips together into the Zoo with the banter they always exchanged to pass the time. They did have a good rapport, both in and out of work, and all this silence made him miss the whole relationship more.

He broke away from his study of a new set of insects—ones that actually were insects. He even collected a few live samples and added them to his bag before he headed to where Kennedy kept watch.

"Are you finished with your samples, Jacobs?" she asked but didn't look at him.

"Oh, yeah, and we're ready to move once more," he said with a smile.

She merely nodded and keyed her mic to get the attention of Carson and Ito. "We're moving again. There's another Pita bush about five klicks away, and I want to get there before it gets dark. You all know the kind of pain that goes into collecting those fucking flowers after dark."

"I don't," Ito said and raised her hand.

"Well, I'm sure you're smart enough to infer how much of a pain it is," Kennedy responded shortly. "Let's keep it moving, people!"

She forged ahead, and Sal picked up his pace to catch up with her. With power function in his legs this time, it was actually easier than it had been before.

"Hey, Kennedy," he called.

"Anything I can help you with, Jacobs?" She focused her eyes resolutely ahead.

"Yeah, you could tell me what bug crawled up your ass," Sal snarked, his patience now worn thin. "Come on, you've been in a foul mood all day, and honestly, I'm sick of it. I don't see why I should put up with it. I'm the one who didn't get any sleep last night, so I'm the only one who's allowed to be in a bad mood, okay?"

She looked at him and narrowed her eyes. "Don't put up with it, then," she snapped and increased her pace.

"Except I have to, don't I?" he pointed out although he now had difficulty keeping up with her. "You're my partner in all this, Kennedy, and if something bothers you, the best way to get it fixed is to get it out in the open. So, tell me, or I'll continue to nag you. I don't want to do that because I don't like to run when I don't have to. Seriously, could you slow down?"

She finally slowed, took a deep breath, and met his gaze.

"It's nothing," she said finally.

"Yeah, because nothing says business as usual like cryptic interrogations and silent treatment," Sal retorted and rolled his eyes.

"By nothing, I mean it's something stupid," she said with a shake of her head. "Something that you shouldn't have to deal with. A personal problem, and something that I'll work through. And I don't need help."

"Wait," Sal said and raised a hand. "You asked me about Courtney. Do you have a problem with her? Did she say something about—" They immediately ended the conversation when the unmistakable sound of gunfire caught their attention.

"Did you guys hear that?" Sal asked. Ito and Carson both nodded, and the four of them prepped their suits and weapons for action.

"Where's it coming from?" the specialist asked.

"My sensors tell me that it's roughly in the same direction that we've moved in all day," Ito said. "Which means that they're probably between us and the Pita plants we've been headed toward."

"Fuck," Kennedy hissed. "Let's move. With our luck, it'll be the rest of Gregor's team still fighting for their lives like they were when they abandoned him to our tender care."

They hurried through the jungle with renewed purpose and rapidly closed the distance between them and the gunshots.

"You know, running toward gunshots and explosions isn't the best survival instinct," Sal said.

"It's the instinct we're taught," Ito growled. "It's not like we were born with the need to head toward the loud noises."

"So, Jacobs," Kennedy said, "you said something back there. You asked if my problem with Courtney was something specific, and honestly, it sounded like you had a particular something in mind."

"This is really not the time, Kennedy," Sal said. "Although it is good to know that you actually do have some sort of problem with Dr. Monroe. The first step to healing is admitting."

"Just…shut up," Kennedy snapped. "Fuck!"

Sal glanced at her quickly, alerted by the sharp edge to her tone. A scrape in the paint of her shoulder armor indicated that one of the bullets had struck her.

"If these motherfuckers aren't in trouble, I'll fucking kill them myself," she snarled. With that, she adjusted her grip on her weapon and headed in. The animal sounds of rage and pain told him that whoever these people were, they actually were in trouble. He couldn't tell if Kennedy was relieved or disappointed.

"Get ready for some action," she said and leveled her weapon.

# CHAPTER TWENTY-FOUR

Unlike the animals that had attacked them at first, these appeared to be mostly reptiles teamed up with the massive grasshoppers. There were a couple that weren't locusts, though, Sal realized. Not entirely, anyway. They had the same six legs and wings, but tails protruded from the back that made them look suspiciously like they might have merged with scorpions.

He shuddered because that was the last thing they wanted right now—the most numerous of aggressive creatures in the Zoo to suddenly grow pincers and poison-tipped stingers. Hell, knowing the kind of creativity with which these creatures were being created, maybe the pincers would contain poison too. Or they'd be tipped with acid, with their luck.

Sal held his weapon at the ready but made sure to record as much as he could of the tailed locust creatures before they were gunned down.

The animals seemed surprised with the sudden arrival of and attack by the four humans from behind, and after a brief battle, they backed away. Once the last scorpion-locust dropped, the remaining creatures quickly broke away and disappeared into the jungle again.

It wasn't always easy to ensure that both teams' lines of fire didn't place each other in jeopardy. At one point, he was worried that Kennedy might try to shoot them on purpose if another round impacted her armor. He knew that it had to hurt, but more importantly, Boulos would charge them through the nose to have the dents removed.

Sal looked around once the animals were all dead or had retreated. He could say with some degree of certainty that the party that they had saved were Russian, or at least equipped by them. He didn't give it too much thought, though, as he quickly applied his scalpel to collect the stingers of the new creatures as well as samples of the poison.

Kennedy moved in closer to the men. "Hey there. Correct me if I'm wrong, but are you guys from the Russian base?"

A couple of them responded in a different language that definitely wasn't Russian before one of them came forward.

"We are from the Russian base, yes," the man said, but his accent sounded South African. "We really appreciate that you lot stepped in and helped us out like that. We've run from what looks and feels like the same group of animals for days now. They've backed away and given us some breathing space, but they always come back harder than before. It felt like this time, they might have had us. We really appreciate the assist."

"Don't take this the wrong way," Sal said, "but Gregor

said that it was mostly hyenas and panthers that attacked you when he was separated from the group."

"Gregor is alive?" the man asked and looked shocked.

"I'd say alive and well, but he sustained some injuries and a destroyed suit that required us to evacuate him to the Staging Area," Sal said. "He thought that you were all either dead or merely assholes who left him behind."

"Well, that's some very serious language from him," the man said. "But we're glad to hear that he's alive. He ran our little team and kept a lot of us alive throughout the run."

"Well, I'm Sergeant Kennedy," she said and stepped into the conversation. "This is Corporal Ito and Corporal Carson. This is Salinger Jacobs, our specialist. Who are you guys?"

Sal studied the five men, including the one who had spoken to them. With the heavy helmets and armor, it was difficult to make out anything else about them, except that one had to be a medic since he knelt beside another. The patient lay on the ground with the left leg of the armor removed for treatment of what looked like a very serious wound.

"My name is Janko de Beer. These men are Kotze, Lutz, and Malan. The young man you see on the ground is Solaratov, the only other Russian assigned to our team," Janko said. One of the others whom he'd pointed out as Malan looked up from where he treated the Russian's leg.

"What happened to him?" Sal asked and moved closer.

"One of those new insects with the stingers managed to get some of the poison through a crack in his armor and under the skin," Janko said quickly. "Malan is our medic, but since there hadn't been any encounters involving venomous creatures, we didn't think to bring any anti-venom with us."

Sal moved to where Malan worked. "I don't have much experience," Sal said, "but if there's anything you might need from our medical pack, it's all yours."

Kennedy nodded. "I'd suggest that we move on before those animals attack again. I doubt that they're finished. If you follow us, we know somewhere with some open ground for us to set up decent defensive positions."

Janko nodded and barked orders to his men as Sal helped them to get Solaratov onto an improvised stretcher made from the tarp from their tents and the poles used to erect them.

Madigan had said that they were four or five klicks away from the Pita plants that they had headed to all day, and it took them almost an hour to cover that. By the time they finally set the stretcher down, the sun had already begun to set. Sal knew that because, unlike the last bushes they'd made camp next to, the trees seemed to avoid this group. It was larger than the last, although it had considerably fewer flowers. Or maybe the same number of flowers, but spread over more plant.

"There's a clear line of sight, so it should be easier to defend," Kennedy stated. "What's the situation with the wounded man?"

Sal looked up. The Russian had passed out during their walk, so he felt better about talking about him while he was present.

"It has reacted like some sort of hemotoxin, and I see a lot of neurotoxin activity too," he said and assisted Malan to settle the wounded man as comfortably as possible.

"So...it's a locust with a scorpion's tail that injects rattlesnake venom?" Kennedy asked and shook her head. "It would be shorter to list the kind of shit that the Zoo doesn't throw at us."

"Can you help him?" Janko asked. He looked genuinely concerned.

Sal opened his mouth to respond, but the medic, Malan, answered before he could. His accent was harder to make out, though, like he'd learned English as a third or fourth language.

"The venom is too deep in his system now," Malan rasped. "It's already started to degrade the muscle tissue in his foreleg and thigh. Even if we had some anti-venom for this particular sting, he might still lose the leg, if not his life."

Kennedy looked pointedly at Sal and gestured with her head for him to follow her a short distance away so that they could talk in private.

"Why don't you do that thing with the Pita flowers that healed my leg all the way back when?" she asked. "I mean, I realize that there's no certainty that it'll work when it comes to this new kind of fun and adventure, but there can't be any harm in trying, right?"

Sal shook his head. "It could take me hours to distill enough to heal that much damage. And by that time, it won't matter anyway. I...I do have something that might help, though."

She narrowed her eyes. "Really? What?"

"Well...it's a company secret," Sal said and scrunched his face. "Something that I've sat on for a while that we might be able to sell for a good price. I'd normally simply do it, but since we're partners in this, I thought I should run it by you first."

"If it'll save this guy's life, I say go for it," Kennedy growled. "But try to make sure that they make some sort of verbal agreement about how we can sue if they try to steal it or something."

"I'll take care of it," he said and moved quickly to where he'd left his pack beside the stretcher. He rummaged through the bag for a few moments in irritation. Of course, the damn thing would have to be all the way at the bottom for the very obvious reason that it would be difficult to find. That caution had backfired a little right now, he realized, but still.

Kennedy narrowed her eyes when he returned with a syringe with 'Madie' written on the side, but he put that aside for the moment.

"Look, we have something that might help," he said to the rest of the men. "But since we're freelancers, it's a trademarked formula. We'll need a verbal agreement from you that you won't try to replicate it if it works."

"What if it doesn't work?" Malan asked.

"Well, I doubt you'll want to replicate it then anyway," Sal said. "I know it might not be published in any peer-reviewed journals, but I've tested it before on the sergeant, and it works to help repair damaged tissue."

"It's not like we have a lot of options out here," Janko said. "If it helps, we will make sure not to cause any problems for your freelancing team."

Sal noted that the man made no such promises if it didn't work, which was a source of concern when it came from an almost two-meter tall Adonis, but he couldn't worry about that at the moment. He had a life to try to save.

The syringe contained what he planned to take himself over the duration of the trip, but with a life in the balance, it seemed like a fair enough trade.

He shook his head and turned his attention to the man's leg. The skin was mostly gone, or if it was still there, it had been blackened beyond recognition by the venom. He continued to search and finally managed to find the spot where the venom had been injected. Carefully, he slipped the needle into the same place and pressed the plunger. It had taken almost a full week to carefully extract the stuff milliliters at a time to get as much as he had in the syringe, and it disappeared depressingly quickly. He couldn't see any immediate reaction, but the goop was in there. He watched the wound attentively for a few seconds and the goop didn't come out again, so at least the body hadn't rejected it.

"Is something supposed to happen?" Janko asked and peered over Sal's shoulder.

"It takes medicine a while to work," Malan said. "Have some patience, and we will check on his status later." He looked at Sal to confirm that this was indeed the case.

"I do remember that it started slowly," Sal replied with a nod. "Give it a few hours."

"In the meantime, let's set up some defenses," Kennedy suggested in a voice that was more a command. She checked her weapon and looked around. "I'm uneasy about how long it's taken these creatures to go on the offensive again. When they wait this long, it usually means that they're getting ready for a knockout punch."

The other men nodded, which indicated that they had at least some knowledge of English. Or maybe the concept of 'get ready, we'll be fighting soon' transcended the language barriers. Sal stood from where he knelt beside the litter, but she waved him off.

"It's best if you keep an eye on how our Russian friend is doing since you're the closest thing we have to an expert in all this goop...stuff."

It seemed like they were back to the silent treatment after that. He wasn't sure what it was that he'd done this time, but he was sure that it was better to talk about this when they weren't surrounded by foreign mercs and animals that wanted to get intimate with the taste of their collective bone marrow.

Sal nodded and dropped to his haunches. He watched as they set up some motion sensors at the perimeter. Cover didn't matter unless they had to deal with something that could shoot projectiles, and it was better to keep a clear line of sight on all sides to make sure that they didn't get caught unawares.

As the sun finally set in full, they all wisely decided to keep the heating lamps in their packs. Virtually everyone would keep their suits on, and after some discussion with the men equipped with Russian gear, it was clear that everyone had something to protect them from the elements. Besides, they didn't want anything to interfere with their night vision when they expected a fight.

"So...why did these creatures attack you anyway?" Sal asked. "They aren't usually this determined to kill people unless you do something to piss them off—like try to pull one of the Pita plants or kill one of the big creatures."

"You mean one of those big dinosaur monsters?" Malan asked and looked up.

"I see you've been introduced," Sal said with a small, apologetic smile. "Yes, yes, I do mean the big dinosaurs."

"One of them attacked us," Janko growled. "When we killed it and tried to move on, the creatures swarmed us."

"Well, if you get the chance, you might want to keep a mental note of where you killed it," Sal said. "You can find some sacs right near the medulla that go for a hefty price on whatever market that you guys run on."

"It's mostly the Russian government," Janko said with a grim smile. "They don't really trust the corporations to get their hands into the dirty business."

"Yeah, because the Russian government is the paragon against corruption," Malan added with a smirk.

"If you guys are done being political, some of the motion sensors have gone off," Kennedy warned and raised her weapon to aim toward the jungle. A few seconds later, they could hear the tell-tale chittering of the locusts. As his night vision-motion sensor vision kicked in, he could see that they were surrounded by a veritable horde of them, with more than a few scorpion tails in evidence.

"I don't suppose you have more of that blue stuff on you, do you, Jacobs?" Kennedy asked.

"Nope."

"Well, I suggest that everybody avoids those damn scorpion stings."

"I'd say that's probably a good call." He retrieved his weapon and stood over Solaratov while the rest of the squad, including Ito and Carson, formed a staggered circle around them. They were all dressed in the same kind of armor, so aside from Malan, who was the medic, Sal couldn't tell if any of the Russian team were specialists.

It didn't matter now anyway.

It took the locusts a few minutes to gather what Sal assumed was the courage to charge at the group, but the night filled rapidly with the sound of gunfire. Even in the dark, he could tell who was shooting by the different sounds of the rifles. The Russian rifles had a loud clatter. He didn't know enough about weapons to have any real opinion, and he was sure that weapons weren't usually purchased by how pleasant they sounded. It wasn't like the eardrum-shattering noise would ever be a priority.

Sal heard the now familiar growl of one of the panthers a few seconds before it broke through the line of fire. It seemed that it either didn't want to get tangled with the locusts on the ground or was maybe smart enough to use them as meat shields. Exoskeleton shields?

*Not the time, Sal, not the time.*

He raised his weapon and realized that the rest of the team had their hands full with the horde that surrounded them and were unable to deal with the one that got through. Sal fired a couple of shots into the creature and scored a round to the shoulder and another to the neck. It emitted a gurgled roar before it dropped to the ground and its blood soaked into the dirt.

Malan spun and looked for whatever it was that Sal had shot at. As he did, the locusts surged and three of them powered past him, knocked the medic to the ground, and tried to attack the team from behind. Sal kept his weapon leveled and opened fire. The massive gun kicked into his powered shoulder. Six shots blasted through the creatures and opened massive, smoking holes in their bodies as the other man quickly regained his feet.

A pinged thumbs-up appeared in his HUD. Malan nodded as he moved into his position in the line. It didn't matter, though, since for the moment it seemed like the locusts had decided to retreat. They backed away quickly, and their mandibles chattered incessantly almost like they were talking.

"Well," Sal said softly, "it looks like they're done for the night."

"Agreed." Kennedy paused to glance at each member of the group. "Do you guys think we should set up camp for the night, or should we get moving again?"

"Neither," Janko responded immediately. "From this location, we can send a signal to the base to send a pick-up team."

"Really?" she asked. "Do you guys get radio signals around here?"

"Not exactly," he said with a small smile and drew a flare gun from his pouch.

"Low tech," Sal said, impressed. "Respect." He stopped when she looked at him with a small smile on her face. "I can't pull that off, can I?"

"Not even remotely, sorry," she replied, her smile now apologetic. She focused on a quick weapon check and refilled the mag. "So, how do we call in a pick-up team?"

"Like so." Janko raised the flare gun and fired. For a split second, Sal was almost blinded by the brightness of the flare. It reached its peak after a couple of hundred meters of flight, erupted into an even brighter explosion, and sailed slowly down to the ground.

"So...you simply hope that someone will look at the sky at the right moment?" Sal asked, a little confused by the logic of it.

"Firing this flare activates a GPS beacon that leads them to our location," the man explained with real amusement at the scientist's astonishment. "Given where we are, it might take them a couple of hours to get out here. Until then, we wait and maintain the defense. On the other hand, how is Solaratov?"

Malan moved to where the Russian still lay on the stretcher. "It looks like his fever broke. And the discoloration from the hemotoxin seems to have receded as well. It's too early to tell if he'll make a full recovery, but the signs are good."

Janko grinned. "Well...that's some impressive shit, Jacobs."

"Thanks," he responded with a smirk.

# CHAPTER TWENTY-FIVE

A real meal, a hot bath, and a decent night's sleep worked wonders, and Courtney felt the change in her body after she dragged herself out of bed. It was late—half past ten in the morning—but she decided that she deserved the rest, all things considered.

She groaned and shuffled to the kitchen, where she put the coffee on. Her body reacted and seemed to insist that she go back to bed and maybe spend the entire day immersed in the base's limited collection of films and series on the public server. Or she could read a journal. There were a couple of very interesting studies on macrobiology that she really wanted to dig her teeth into when she had the time.

For some reason, though, she had no impetus to do anything at the moment. She was plagued by thoughts about how she was nice, safe, and warm in her own cozy apartment while the other members of her team—since that was what they were now—were still out there. They risked their lives and made advances in her field of study, and she sat at home and waited. It simply didn't seem right.

She sipped her coffee and made a face as she added milk and sugar. There were many things that she wouldn't miss about being stuck out there, and one of them was fucking coffee. No matter how fresh it was, it always tasted stale, which meant that she needed to add milk—since cream wasn't even a remote possibility—and sugar to make it even marginally palatable.

After a few minutes of the sweet, tasteless coffee, she finally made the decision to go to the hospital. Gregor would still be there, she reasoned. He had his fair share of injuries, among which were a couple of broken ribs, so they would probably keep him there for most of the day for observation, right?

She decided not to wait around in case he was transferred to his own base.

Courtney threw some clothes on and made sure that they were comfortable since she didn't know how long she would be gone. With the team still out in the Zoo, she had a considerable amount of time to kill between now and when they got back. She could use it to make sure that all the information gathered over the two days that she'd spent in there was correct and maybe do some editing and proofreading before it was submitted for approval to their sponsors. But that was shit that she could do tomorrow.

She walked to the hospital. It was only five blocks away, and even though the sun was already blisteringly hot, a cool wind blew in from the south with a surprisingly small amount of sand.

Despite everything, she actually enjoyed the short stroll.

She'd grown up around hospitals. Her mother was a nurse, and Courtney had been a very inquisitive child with a fair amount of willpower when it came to obeying—or not obeying, in this case—orders of the "sit right there" variety.

She talked to a nurse who directed her to where they had placed the only Russian on the base under observation. It took only a couple of attempts to get through the "only close friends and relatives" bureaucracy.

"Dr. Monroe!" Gregor called from his bed. "How nice of you to visit. Missing me already? My charm is known to do this among women."

"I'm sure," she responded with a laugh. "And, well, I didn't exactly have real plans, considering that I was supposed to be in the Zoo with animals trying to eat me for the next few days. I thought I might come and see how you were doing. How…are you holding up, then?"

"Bed is comfortable, slept like baby," Gregor said with a nod and scratched at the dark stubble that shadowed his chin. "After I spent most of a day in a ditch and thinking that there won't be a chance for me to ever see outside of Zoo again, even a hospital bed seems close enough to heaven for comfort."

Courtney smiled and sat on one of the chairs placed beside the hospital bed.

"I'm really happy that you're doing better, Gregor," she said. "What did the doctors say about your condition? Will you head home soon?"

"Over a couple of bruises and a broken rib or two?" he

asked and shook his head. "All this is only thanks to some problems with the suit, and they want to make sure that I'm all right. I only need a few weeks in recovery for ribs, and I will be ready for action again."

She didn't think that she would be that cavalier about her own life, but that was why she was a specialist and not a gunner. Before she could say anything in response, though, a man entered the room. He wore a deep green uniform, one that was clearly not American or even one that she recognized. The Cyrillic lettering on the literal blanket of medals that covered his chest told her that he had to be Russian.

Gregor stiffened visibly and spouted a couple of quick words in Russian. The newcomer smiled, shook his head, and snapped a sharp salute before he turned to Courtney and offered his hand.

"My name is Brigadier General Sebastian Petrov," he said in very concise English when she took his hand.

"Dr. Courtney Monroe. Nice to meet you." She withdrew her hand and rubbed it surreptitiously to restore the feeling he'd all but crushed out of it.

"Are you treating the sergeant?" Petrov asked.

"Oh...oh, no," she said quickly. "I'm not that kind of doctor. I have a Ph.D. in biology. I was part of the team that helped to recover Sergeant Popov from the Zoo."

"Ah, you have my thanks then, doctor," the general said with a smile. "I've just spoken to your commandant about a reward to those responsible for rescuing our men from some very trying circumstances in that jungle."

"Oh," Courtney said with a smile. "That's very generous of you. Although, if you put money in for me, I'd suggest putting it into the account of Heavy Metal…Incorporated? I think?"

"You work for a freelance company then?" Petrov asked and seemed surprised. "Of course, we can wire the payment to whichever account you prefer, but are you sure you want it run through corporate? This is a private reward, after all, for private actions."

"Well, all the members of my team were involved in the rescue of your man here," she explained with a smile. "Actually, a lot more than I was if the truth be told. It doesn't seem fair that I get paid and they don't."

"Well, if you mean your compatriots Sergeant Madigan Kennedy and Dr. Salinger Jacobs—"

"He is not doctor," Gregor said with a grin.

"Well, Mr. Salinger Jacobs then," Petrov said and looked mildly confused. "They have already contacted the Russian base this morning. Well, last night, but we didn't know it was them until this morning. They helped to rescue the rest of Sergeant Popov's squad and brought them back to the base, so they will be adequately recompensed for their actions." He added a few details of the Russian team's experience for the patient's benefit.

It had only been twenty-four hours, but she was relieved to know that Madigan and Sal were both still alive and well.

"Either way, I'd still like my payment to go through their corporate account first," Courtney said.

"As you wish, Dr. Monroe." Petrov nodded and studied her with new interest. "I have to say, you are one of the most trusting people I have met out here. It is quite… refreshing."

"Well, I trust Kennedy and Jacobs," Courtney said. "And I know that my trust will be rewarded."

"As you say." The general nodded before he turned back to Gregor. "The...medical doctors have told me that you will be released from their care in the afternoon. I will give you a ride back to the base in my helicopter once you are cleared for travel."

"Thank you, General," the patient said. The man saluted again, spun on his heel, and left the room.

"You guys spoke English for my benefit, didn't you?" Courtney asked.

"Probably," Gregor said with a nod.

"So, helicopter ride back to base, huh?" Courtney said with a smile. "That's impressive."

"Well, it pays to be good friends with the commandant's son." The Russian grinned with real humor. "Although I really hope that he is still alive. From the sound of things, it seems like Kennedy and Jacobs pulled them out of what you Americans call some...hot water?"

"So, if the son isn't alive, could you head back to a court-martial or something?"

"That is a stereotype I do not appreciate. Even if it is true," he responded with a chuckle. "But I am not worried. If there's anyone to blame, it will be the damned mercs who left me there. Although I do understand why they wanted to leave since it seems that they needed to stay on the move due to the animal attacks, I suppose."

Courtney smiled. "Well, I'll leave you to your rest here. I need to go and get some food from the mess hall."

"Do not miss me too much when I leave, Dr. Monroe," Gregor said with a grin. "I know the look of desire in your eyes, but it would never work between us. I am happily married and could never be with another woman."

"It's tempting," Courtney said with a laugh. "I'll be a mess, but I think I'll be able to move on one day. Feel better, Greg."

"Is Gregor!" he called after her as she closed the door behind her.

# CHAPTER TWENTY-SIX

E ven after a trip of a few hours, Sal still wasn't sure how they managed to get vehicles this deep into the Zoo. They didn't appear to have anything special or which could indicate an advantage in the jungle conditions. The ride itself was bumpier than he was used to and he attributed it to the fact that the vehicles had been fitted with special tracks.

Even so, they'd arrived in the dark, and it was still difficult to tell if there was anything different about these beasts. Maybe, like with the flare, the Russians simply relied on low-tech solutions to the problems. He'd heard the story that had been passed around social media about how the US government had put millions of dollars into research so that they could have a specialized pen that worked in zero gravity for their astronauts during the cold war. The Russians, on the other hand, decided to solve the problem by giving their cosmonauts pencils.

It was complete bullshit, of course, the kind of thing that appealed to mass humor. He wasn't sure if the

Russians had actually done that, but the practical problem with taking pencils into space was that lead and wood shavings would get into their air filters and burn the shuttles into an early retirement.

While he had to concede he'd been too busy to properly research it and so had no reason to really believe it, there did seem to be a general trend when it came to the Russian military that gave the rumor some weight. He still didn't entirely believe it, since they didn't exactly have cosmonauts to spare back then, but they did seem to enjoy the low-tech, low-cost solutions to problems that his own people dropped millions into various attempts to solve.

It had taken most of the night for the vehicles to reach them in the Zoo. They had sensibly decided to remain in the location the flare had provided in its GPS signal. After a few more uncomfortable hours in the ponderous vehicles, they were finally out in the clear again.

It should have been difficult for him to actually sleep, but considering that he'd had less than eight hours of sleep over the past forty-eight, he nodded off despite the rough ride that they had to endure. When Kennedy punched him in his non-powered shoulder to wake him, sunlight streamed through the thick, round windows. Unimpeded light, he realized, with the kind of brightness that clearly indicated that it wasn't filtered through layers and layers of foliage.

"We're here," she informed him and made sure that he was awake before she heaved herself out of the vehicle, which Sal realized was now empty except for him.

He stepped out as paramedics lifted Solaratov clear. He was still in the litter and seemed to be unconscious, but his color had definitely improved from the deathly pale face that Sal had seen last. The leg was bandaged by professionals this time, but it looked considerably less swollen than it had before.

"He's doing much better," Janko said as he stepped from behind Sal. "Whatever you did to him, Jacobs, it seems to have at least helped to keep him alive until we could get him back here. I have to tell you, saving him saved all our asses."

He turned to the man questioningly. "How do you mean?"

"Well, Corporal Ivan Solaratov is the son of Commandant Ryen Solaratov, the man who hired us. He is not the most forgiving to men who get his children killed."

"Does that sort of thing happen a lot around here?" he asked. "Commandants' sons getting killed?"

"Well, no," the man replied with a smirk. "But people court-martialed for pissing the commandant off happens frequently. I likely would have gotten a couple of weeks in the brig until my contract here is up, and it would not be renewed, which would leave me to find work out here in the middle of butt-fucking nowhere. But there's always a chance that something worse happens, I suppose."

"Right," Sal said. *Way to live up to your stereotypes, Russia.*

"Anyway, if you'll follow me, I'll help you and Kennedy to the mess hall where you guys can get some food if you're nice to the guy who runs the place. Your other two team members have chosen to join a convoy that will leave shortly—unless you want to join them?"

When both Sal and Madigan shook their heads, he led them briskly to an area where they could strip out of their armor first. Sal was very thankful that he, unlike Gregor, was fully dressed when he emerged from his suit. For some reason, he was even happier that Kennedy was similarly dressed.

The mess hall was different in a lot of ways from the mess at the Staging Area. Not in bad ways, necessarily, merely different. It was very clear that two very different cultures were involved in the building of the two separate sites.

Either way, they were both military installations established to feed their personnel, which meant that the functions were essentially instinctive. Sal and Kennedy quickly filled up on beef stroganoff with beets, cabbage, and potatoes on the side, as well as small sips of the vodka that the man in charge of serving the food assured them was made not too far from where they currently stood.

The specialist didn't know enough about the vodka distillation process to know if this was a good or bad thing, but he definitely intended to look into it. He wasn't sure if the vodka was any good either, considering that he hadn't been legally allowed to drink for that long and hadn't experimented much, but Kennedy told him that it was very tasty and spouted words like smooth and lush and clear, which he took as a good sign. It could have been wood alcohol for all he knew—or even cared right then.

And dammit, it burned like wood alcohol all the way down to his stomach. He assumed that had been the case, though, as he didn't actually taste the stuff beyond the burn.

They finished and sat and talked with some of the other men and women in the room who had heard about what they'd been through before a couple of men in uniform entered. They looked around, homed in on Kennedy, Sal, and Janko almost immediately, and weaved between the tables toward them.

"Oh, shit," the South African said.

"Good morning." The officer kept his tone and face pleasant. "Commandant Solaratov would like to speak to you."

The three of them stood, but the man waved Janko off quickly. "Not you. Only the two newcomers."

"Oh, right." The man sat and looked distinctly relieved. "Good luck, you two."

"Thanks." Sal grinned and did his best to look unperturbed.

They exited the mess hall and approached a military vehicle that waited for them outside. Sal still didn't feel like he'd had sufficient sleep to have a conversation with a very powerful man about how his son might die of snake venom from a giant locust with a scorpion's tail.

No, he would never adjust to that startling image. Somehow, the new creature they'd encountered had his brain in a knot—he honestly didn't want to hear or think about it, or even imagine it, for that matter.

They drove up to one of the largest buildings in the area and the officer led them inside. There was something different about the building, even though it followed the same basic structure as all the others, but for the life of him, Sal wasn't sure what it was. It wasn't the color or even the room placement. Merely...something that prickled at his consciousness.

They were directed into an office with a window that

looked out into the Zoo, where a hefty, corpulent man sat behind a desk and watched a video on a social media feed.

"You actually have an internet connection here," Sal said as he complied with a gesture that they should sit. "I can't believe I'd actually say this, but I'm really very jealous about it."

"I'll take that as a compliment, Dr. Jacobs," the man said with a grin.

"Not a doctor," Sal and Kennedy said in unison.

"I—what?" he asked as the officer who had led them in backed out again quickly.

"It's a long story," Sal said, "but I'm actually a doctoral candidate, not an actual doctor."

"Oh...well, then, Mr. Jacobs, and Sergeant Kennedy. I must thank you for taking the time to join me," the man said with a pleasant smile as he turned the screen of his computer off.

"You're very welcome...Commandant Solaratov, I presume?" Sal asked. "Did we have a choice?"

"Of course you did. There is no trouble," the man said hastily with a smile. "Would you like something to drink?" He didn't wait for them to answer but filled a trio of crystal glasses with a clear liquid from a matching decanter. Sal didn't think that his guess that the liquid was vodka could be questioned. Their new Russian friends seemed determined to live up to the stereotypes.

Kennedy took her glass without any encouragement, and the commandant took his as well. Sal, who didn't want to drink too much while he was there, was the last to raise the small glass.

"*Za Zdarovje*," Solaratov Senior said with a grin before

he downed the contents of the glass. Kennedy followed suit and Sal, again, was last. He winced as the stuff burned all the way down to his stomach. This time, he felt every inch of its journey. He gasped and his eyes bulged, and the man on the other side of the desk laughed with unbridled amusement.

"You are not a habitual drinker then, Mr. Jacobs?" Solaratov asked with a grin.

"True words," he responded, his voice unusually hoarse.

"Now, with politeness out of the way, we move to business." He opened a couple of paper files on his desk with a brisk movement. "Reports tell me that you first helped one of our officers, Sergeant Gregor Popov, as his suit was damaged and the man himself in need of medical assistance. Then you helped the rest of his team when they were attacked by the monsters inside the fucking jungle."

"How do you already know about Gregor?" Sal asked.

"Well, we received a message from your Staging Area base about one of our soldiers who was recovered," Solaratov said with a smile. "Part of your team abandoned your mission to help him return to civilization for medical treatment. We are deep in your debt, and we will be sure to compensate you all for the money that you might have made from your mission if you had not helped."

"Well, we want to ensure that the relations between our two bases remain as cordial as possible," Sal said smoothly. "If only because we'd like to think that if your people were faced with a similar situation, they would do the same."

"Absolutely," the commandant assured him. "Your gesture of good faith will not be forgotten, my friend. And now, we move on to you saving my son's life. I know, as member of the military, I am not to show favorable treatment. But since I am personally grateful for your actions, I will reward your team most generously from my own private funds."

Sal raised an eyebrow. "That's...very magnanimous of you, Commandant."

"You saved my son's life," Solaratov said, and his tone became grave. "The doctors tell me that he has improved so much that they may not even need to remove the leg. His foot might also be saved as well. I don't know how you did it, and the men who saw what you did refuse to tell me how it happened—"

"It's a proprietary recipe," Sal interjected and smiled to take any possible slight out of the words. "We're actually independent contractors and work from a very small startup, so our profit margins depend on things that we've developed personally during our time here."

"I can respect this." He nodded. "Either way, it will take a few hours for me to be able to withdraw my funds all the way out here, so I invite the two of you to spend some time with us. Living arrangements are being prepared, and you can spend the night. Your payment will be wired in the morning, and once that is in order, we will find way to escort you safely back to your base—or anywhere you want to go."

"That's...incredibly generous of you, Commandant," Sal said again and stood as the man pushed himself slowly from his office chair, which squeaked under the weight.

"Please," he said and offered his hand for Sal and Kennedy to shake. "It is the least I can do. Now, get some rest. You will find your accommodations completely furnished and well suited for a short stay."

"Thank you, Commandant," Kennedy said and grinned as she rubbed her hand. "If it's not too much to ask, could you perhaps assist us to have our armor cleaned and repaired? The suits got a little banged up while we were out there."

"Of course. We will have it handled immediately."

The officer who had led them there waited outside the door when they exited. It seemed that he already knew where they were going and he simply directed them back to the vehicle. They complied and took a short drive to what Sal was surprised to see were a couple of small apartment buildings.

Actual buildings. With multiple stories and various apartments, not tiny little houses.

Although, once they had been taken to the second floor and the accommodation that had been provided for them, he realized it was extremely small. Even smaller than his place, as a matter of fact, but he was sure that wouldn't be a problem. It wasn't like they would stay there long.

"Dibs on the shower," Kennedy said once the door closed behind them. Sal chuckled but allowed her to go first. He knew from experience that she still lived the life of a military woman in that she went the "navy shower" route that only lasted about five minutes. The whole building was plumbed to an ancient boiler system for hot water, so he could stand to be sweaty and sticky for five minutes more if it meant he would step into a piping-hot shower. He needed the kind that made you feel like all your troubles were burned away in righteous flame—or, in this case, scalding liquid.

While he waited, he set his pack down in the small living room-kitchen and used the time to inspect the food they had been supplied with. It wasn't much and mostly the typical ration-type packages that would be found in any military installation. Everything had, of course, been dehydrated and efficiently packed.

He'd lived through worse, he recalled. There was a time when popcorn and ramen noodles had been his food of necessity rather than choice. It felt like a lifetime ago, even though it was less than six months.

He wondered who would recognize him back home after only half a year. He caught a glimpse of himself in the bedroom mirror. He had put on weight during the months there, but it was almost entirely muscle mass. If the truth be told, he had been rather scrawny when he first arrived. Kennedy had to have been insanely drunk to even consider getting into bed with him.

Literally and metaphorically, Sal thought with a smile.

They'd given them an apartment with two bedrooms, both with queen-sized beds which took up virtually all the space. They looked comfortable, even though the place had a motel vibe which extended to the generic art that hung from the walls.

He would never have thought that Russians would even put art, generic or not, on the walls of their accommodation. It was like they actually expected people to live here.

Ten minutes later, the lock turned on the bathroom door and Madigan stepped out of a very steamy bathroom wrapped in a clean white towel.

"Ten minutes?" Sal asked, with a small smile on his lips. "Your control is slipping, Kennedy."

She smirked, clearly in a better mood than before. "Get in there, Sal. The water's nice and hot for you. Oh, and there's an extra towel hanging in there."

"Thanks." He closed the door but didn't bother to lock it as he stripped down, placed his clothes on the lowered toilet seat, and stepped into the small shower stall. The water was scalding, exactly the way he liked it. He let it wash over him for a full ten minutes before he actually scrubbed himself.

The steam was almost impenetrable by the time he stepped out to shave and brush his teeth.

"Thirty minutes," Madigan said with a grin. "And you have the gall to criticize my time? For shame."

"Hey," Sal said and secured the towel that wrapped his midsection as he joined her on the living room couch. "You're the military woman here. You're a sergeant. I'm not even a doctor. You need to be held to higher standards than I am. It's the way of the world."

Madigan grinned. "Former sergeant, remember? I turned my papers in when I decided to sign on with your sorry ass."

"You didn't think my ass was sorry that long ago," Sal said. "Or is that why you insist on grabbing it so much while we have sex?"

She smiled and tilted her head as she looked at him with an odd expression. It was similar to what he'd seen when she had stared at him before.

"You're wondering if Courtney and I slept together, aren't you?" Sal asked. It was a blunt way of going about it, but if she wouldn't do it herself, damned if he would beat around the bush with her.

"Well…yeah." Madigan looked confused for a second but quickly came to terms with the fact that they were having this conversation. "I mean, I don't judge you for it. Believe me, I know that the fact that we live out here and risk our lives almost every day makes all the societal rules that would usually surround us a little warped. But I'd have appreciated it if—if you did have sex with her at all, of course—you had simply come out and told me about it."

He nodded and chewed lightly at the inside of his mouth. To be honest, he had expected her to be a lot less understanding. Her candor caught him off-guard for a second, but he regained his composure quickly.

"I'm not the best when I have to express myself," he said and created a metaphorical net for him to drop into if needed. "I think I'm even worse at it when it comes to all this…" He wasn't sure what "this" was supposed to be, so he merely made a hand gesture and was relieved when Madigan nodded. "I'm not any kind of player. Honestly, I didn't have much of a sex life before I got here, so when it comes to knowing the rules and stuff…well, I don't."

"Get to the point," Madigan said with a laugh.

"Right, sorry," he said quickly. "The point is that while it's more complicated than that, the short of it is that…well, yes, Courtney and I did sleep together. Well, we had sex. Not much sleep."

She nodded, and an odd smile touched her face. "Well, thanks for being honest with me, Sal, I really appreciate it. I don't suppose I can persuade you to share what about the whole situation makes it more complicated than simply two people who have a lot in common having sex? I mean, she told me that she had something of a crush on you, so it's not really a surprise that you'd have one on her too."

Sal shook his head. "I'm sorry. Again, all the unspoken rules aren't that clear to me, but I feel like whatever needs to be said about the situation shouldn't be said by me. She should probably tell you about that."

Kennedy leaned back in her seat and shoved a strand of wet hair out of her face. "Okay, but if you think that the fact that I have to wait until we see Courtney again means I won't dig into this stuff, you'd better have another think coming, and fast."

"Why are you talking like you're in a standoff in a Western movie?" he asked.

"Shut up," she retorted with a grin and pushed to her feet. "I need to get some sleep. The bouncy ride in that vehicle last night did me no favors, I'll tell you."

"Hey, Madigan." Sal stood and caught her attention before she disappeared into the bedroom on the right side. "Are we okay? Did this talk help?"

"Yeah, we're good, Sal," she said, and her smile was genuine. "I merely need a second to collect my thoughts is all. Thanks for being honest with me. You know, eventually."

He grinned as she vanished behind the closed door. For a moment, he wondered if he should go in after her, but the moment passed, and he slipped into the left bedroom instead. He needed a nice long nap too.

# CHAPTER TWENTY-SEVEN

S al muttered unintelligible curses and yanked the soft, thin pillow over his head in the hope that the knocking would go away. It was too soon. He needed his sleep. Honestly, it didn't even need to be beauty sleep. Ugly sleep would work as long as it was uninterrupted.

He finally popped his right eye open when the knocking resumed for the third time. He would have thought that people would take the hint by now, but apparently not.

"Fucking hell," he grumbled under his breath. The pounding on the door sounded like drums—those in the deep that he used to have nightmares about. Unfortunately, there was no way to wake from this nightmare. He would have to get up and answer the door if he wanted to silence the noise.

There was the random and somewhat confused consideration about whether he would prefer to face a room full of goblins and a cave troll instead of getting out of bed. It was quickly settled when he slipped out from under the covers in only a pair of boxers and stumbled around the tiny room to the door. He stifled a massive yawn with his hand. The knocking resumed, more insistently now.

"God damn it. I'm coming, I'm coming." He yanked the door open and immediately regretted his choice of words when he saw Madigan waiting on the other side. A grin spread across her face as she stepped into his room without waiting for an invitation.

"I hope you're ready to go again soon, Sal," she said with a teasing grin and brushed her fingers across his lean stomach as she passed him. "Although this has to be some kind of record. It's the first time I've ever gotten a guy to come before he even saw me."

"Ha ha." Sal laughed sarcastically. "Very funny. There was a time when people would have simply said 'phrasing' and moved right on."

"Was this time recent, by any chance?" she asked. He realized that she still wore the towel that he'd seen her in last and nothing else. When she sat, it rode up higher on her lean legs.

"Not particularly," he replied, effectively distracted at the suddenly very disturbing woman on his bed. Madigan noticed his stare and smiled as she crossed her legs coyly to push the towel up further. "You know me, though. An absolute sucker for the classics."

"I do know you," she said and smiled even wider at his dumbfounded look. She liked that she still had this effect on him, despite all the time they had spent together. "Although, knowing you, I would have expected you to be down and out right now."

"Is that why you tried to break my door down?" Sal asked, sidetracked once again when she leaned back on the bed. Invitations for him to join her on his bed didn't come much clearer than this.

"A girl has needs," Madigan responded, and her full lips pouted. "Do you think you can recuperate?"

"As you like to point out, I'm still young." Sal moved in closer so that he now stood over her. "My recuperative powers are impressive."

"Oh?" she asked and raised her right eyebrow. "How impressive?"

"Not to be competitive, but much better than yours," he said with a smirk.

Madigan chuckled and pushed herself to a sitting position once again. Sal could tell that she wanted to stand and stare him down, but he was too close for her to do so. She elected to remain on the bed and looked up at him while she bit her bottom lip.

"If you're trying not to be competitive, you've failed pretty miserably," she said finally, and her eyes drifted to where there was little left to the imagination by the boxers he wore.

"It's a good thing I didn't try to not be competitive, then."

"Just to be sure that we're both on the same page..." She moved closer to where Sal grew rapidly larger and let her towel fall open. "You're saying that you can outfuck me here, right?"

Sal tilted his head and pretended to take a moment to think. "I'm saying that I can outlast you and keep going until you beg me to stop—and until you can't take it anymore."

Madigan smirked and ran her fingers over Sal's growing cock through his boxers. "Nobody, and I mean nobody, has ever been able to outlast me when it comes to fighting, drinking, or fucking. I'm not bragging, by the way, but I think you ought to know what you're claiming here."

"I'd never think that I could outdrink you," he said honestly. "And I'll wait for a while before I think I can outfight you. But I do think that I can leave you walking bowlegged like a cowgirl after a long ride. A very long ride."

Sal wasn't sure why he'd become this cocky. He figured that if he had to brag, he might as well go hard—pun intended—or go home. He simply wasn't sure that he could live up to his claims. And if he didn't, she would never let him live it down.

Unless he actually managed to fuck her to sleep. It was the best way to prove her wrong, he supposed, although he somehow had difficulty focusing on the thought.

"Do you want to make this interesting?" Madigan asked and yanked his boxers down to lean in to press her lips to the heavy head directly at eye-level.

He needed a moment before he answered and his eyes fluttered shut as she teased him. Driven by pure instinct, he ran his fingers through her hair.

"Bragging rights are in there," she said and held her mouth close enough that he could feel her hot breath on him. "Let's say that if you fall asleep or take ten minutes or more to get going again, you forfeit."

"Well, that's hardly fair," he growled.

"It is a game rigged in my favor," Madigan admitted with a teasing smile. "But it'll make it so much sweeter if you win."

"When I win," Sal growled in response. He placed his hands on her shoulders and pushed her roughly onto her back. She squealed with delight. "And you never said that I can't rig the odds in my favor either."

He tugged her towel free and left her completely naked on his bed as he dropped to his knees between her spread thighs and leaned in hungrily to kiss at her lower lips. While he had a certain confidence in his stamina, that didn't mean that he would simply go for it without tipping the scales in his favor.

---

"Oh…fuck!" Sal gasped and ran his hands over her back as his hips bucked against her again and again. He'd left a couple of handprints on her ass and they were still red, so he might as well give her a rest there. A light sheen of sweat coated his skin, which was a sight better than the sweat that dripped from Madigan.

She was thoroughly drenched, he thought, and pulled out of her. She dropped to the bed, and her thighs shuddered as she rolled onto her back.

"Five," she declared and looked at him with a determined expression on her face. "Is that…" Her voice trailed off as an aftershock from her last orgasm rippled through her body. "Is that all you got, Jacobs?"

Sal grinned. She looked like she was a bare step-and-a-half from done, but then again, he was the one who did most of the work, at least after her second orgasm. After she'd coated his cock with her cum, she had been more than willing to let him take the reins in their time together.

"Where have you hidden all that?" she asked when she saw he was still hard and even now, simply watched while he waited for her to recover instead of the other way around.

"I'm a geek, remember?" he said with a grin, only slightly out of breath. "All I think about is sex and science, and not necessarily in that order. Ready to go again?"

She grinned and gritted her teeth as he took hold of her ankles, dragged her back toward him, and spread her thighs for his hips.

---

"I haven't conceded yet," Madigan panted, and her eyes closed momentarily with a sweet feeling of relief. She looked at Sal, who had withdrawn after he rode her from behind in her prone position on the bed. It was obvious that she had long since given up on her ability to take any kind of control for now. Sal had felt her go limp a few times, but she simply insisted that she'd needed a moment to recover.

"Well, we are in double digits now." He grinned. A healthy burn started in his muscles, and he'd lost count of how many times she had climaxed as he'd had a hard time staying focused himself. "Nobody would blame you if you called it."

"Nope," she retorted and pushed away from the bed. "I only need a quick...break."

"The ten-minute rule applies to you too," Sal said. "Remember that."

He allowed himself the pleasure of watching her leave. She had a fantastic ass, toned and muscular and yet with a delicious amount of give that he'd tested more than a few times tonight. Even so, his eyes were drawn to the way she walked for the first few steps—like she ached between her thighs. She paused and realized that he was watching, straightened, and now walked normally though significantly slower.

It was tonight by now, he realized. The shades were drawn on the windows, but no light penetrated anymore. He'd left his watch and anything else that might tell the time on the other side of the room, and right now, he needed to conserve his strength.

"I just might have this," Sal said aloud and smirked as he tucked his hands under his head.

---

"It's...not...normal," Madigan gasped, her words broken with each thrust as Sal pushed himself inside her. He had begun to flag, he knew. There were other matters to consider aside from his sexual stamina, among which—and probably more importantly—was his physical stamina. He was still rock hard, he realized, even after going two more times, but there was a price to pay for fucking for... however many hours that they'd been at this. He still wasn't sure. It could be hours from sunset or minutes. All he knew for sure was that the sun had been shining when they'd started.

"I can keep going for hours," he said and decided he would no longer give her the usual pause between orgasms. He would keep going until she gave up or he dropped. In all honesty, he thought he had at least one more round in him, but *she* didn't.

Finally, she patted the bed and then his arm, which he had pressed into the sheets beside her shoulder. "I'm tapping out, Sal."

"Say what?" He kept going.

"Please…just…enough…" Her eyes closed and her hand fell back on the sheet as he slowed gently to a halt.

Sal grinned and leaned forward to place a light kiss on her lips. "I won't stop until you say it."

Madigan shoved her hands between them to push against his hips in an effort to prevent him from thrusting inside her again. "Please…no. You win, you win. I…can't. Fuck…"

She called it, he thought as he pulled himself from her drenched pussy and brushed her clit gently with his thumb. Her thighs closed instinctively and a shudder ran through her body.

"Holy fuck," she gasped, her eyes wide as he moved across and dropped onto the bed beside her. She lay there for a few moments and stared at the ceiling, her arms stretched above her head and thighs as he'd left them like she didn't have the strength to do anything for the moment.

"I'll take that as a compliment," he said.

She glanced at him with something between amazement and annoyance in her eyes before she groaned and turned on her side to face him.

"What the actual fuck?" she protested, her voice rough. "What did you eat for breakfast today? Viagra-frosted cornflakes?"

Sal smirked. He'd actually never even seen one of those pop-culture famous blue pills, and considering that they'd both eaten the same breakfast in the Russians' mess hall that morning, it was a moot point, but still. His scientific mind told him that it wasn't even a possibility—unless the Russians sprinkled it into everything they served—but he did suspect that another blue substance was to blame.

"If you think I'll give you the satisfaction of walking out of here bow-legged, you have another think coming," she added and leaned in to kiss him gently on the lips. "I'm spending the rest of the night here, Super Sex Man, and if you'd rather not sleep with me, you can go ahead and use my room. The sheets are probably less...messy there anyway."

"I'm fine here," he said with a smile, but she didn't wait for an answer. She merely rolled over and pulled the covers from the floor where they'd been pushed off the bed in their throes of passion. After a second, she shared them with him.

Sal smiled. She fell asleep quickly, but since she usually wasn't the type to cuddle after sex, he decided not to spoon for the moment. Instead, he pulled himself up and dragged his pack out from under the bed. He retrieved his tablet after a fair amount of rummaging. A couple of very secure encryptions kept it safe from intruders. He dealt with those in short order and opened a file labeled Madie.

"Impressive sexual stamina, possible side-effect of the goop," he tapped quickly into the digital keyboard and tagged it with a reminder for him to come back to it later once he'd had more time to research. He stowed the tablet and pushed his pack under the bed before he shuffled down into his place beside Madigan.

Damn it, he'd forgotten to check the time.

# CHAPTER TWENTY-EIGHT

"Talk to me here, Dr. Bial," Anderson demanded as the technicians and engineers worked single-mindedly on the suit upgrades. With the amount of work imported from Pegasus, he wondered if it wouldn't actually be cheaper to simply take everything away and start from scratch with whatever these new upgrades were. They had to be tied to the feedback that the scientists had sent back.

He assumed so, anyway. They had sent him the specs of the improvements, but it provided innumerable details that were supposed to be in English but didn't seem to be in any kind of English he could understand. The colonel had minored in computer sciences back in college, so he got the gist of what they talked about when it came to the software upgrades. But even then, it was leagues and leagues ahead of any of the coding he'd studied, which explained why he was out there to oversee this rather than comfortably seated in New York where he'd be paid six figures to develop this crap.

His real trouble, as if he didn't have enough others, was when it came down to the specs of the hardware upgrades. He liked to think that a college degree enabled him to get a good grip on the coding. But no amount of dozing off in elective classes for extra credit would get him anywhere when it came to the electrical and developmental engineering that went into a multi-million-dollar project like this.

It took aliens to beat aliens, he thought with a small smirk.

"How can I help you, Colonel?" Bial asked and glanced up from his own copy of the specs.

"I may have failed high school chemistry," Anderson said and pushed from his chair in the operation center to walk to where the researcher stood. "Well, not so much failed as forgot to take, but I've seen the periodic table of elements, and I don't ever remember seeing something called..." Anderson took a moment to check the name again. "Eurtonium?"

Bial nodded. "I was curious about that too. It turns out that it's a proprietary element created and trademarked by Pegasus. These days, the trademark laws allow them to withhold the precise details about the creation and even the atomic density of their elements for up to twenty years. That includes anything from scientific journals to high school chemistry textbooks."

The colonel nodded. "Well, hot damn. I wondered what I could do with the elements I discovered and couldn't make any money from."

The scientist smirked. "Yeah, well, they made me sign about fifty non-disclosure agreements before we started on this fucking project, which means that their proprietary designs are legally safe."

"They made me sign the same NDAs," Anderson confirmed and folded his arms as he watched the engineers who worked on the suits. They'd been flown in almost minutes after the reports had been sent out, and word was that the new pilots they would bring in wouldn't even be military. At least, not any branch that he was aware of.

Because that wasn't fucking shady at all, he thought snidely.

"From the look of it, I'd say it's a mineral used when they make the metal that they put into the armor," Bial said. "It makes the metal less dense but with a firmer molecular grip. It has a low melting temperature, so it's easily malleable, but once it cools, it will maintain its integrity under even the worst pressure."

Anderson rolled his eyes, and his companion laughed. "That means that it's light and easy to work with, and at the same time, is capable of absorbing gunfire and other kinds of impact without breaking—and even absorbing kinetic energy, it appears."

"So...along the lines of Kevlar made into a steel plate?" he asked.

"It's obviously more complicated than that, and I assume it cost millions to develop, but yeah, that's it in a nutshell," Bial confirmed.

A little intrigued despite his frustration with the entire project, the colonel watched as the engineers drilled into the plates with what looked like diamond-bit drills. He assumed that was what it took to penetrate them. He'd heard of armor-piercing rounds with diamond bits built in, but with the amount of difficulty that the man had to make even a tiny hole in the piece he drilled into, Anderson suspected that even diamond-strengthened slugs would have trouble making any real impact.

"What are they doing?" Anderson asked.

"The first order of business was to fit all the individual pieces with tracking markers," the scientist answered. "My guess is that they don't want any more legs to go missing with chunks of trademarked metal in them."

"That's the first order of business? We have only four days in which to prepare everything for the next trial run or this whole operation is dead in the water."

"That's their call, not ours," Bial replied and tapped lightly on the clipboard he held. "Our people are relegated almost entirely to support roles right now, while the people that they brought in do all the work. It seems they want to pass the blame for the mishaps onto us rather than their own development teams."

"You'll still get paid for all this though, right?"

"Oh, yeah." The man chuckled dryly. "Still, I didn't come out here for the money."

"I wish I had come out here for the money," the colonel muttered. He wouldn't even have the satisfaction of a pay bump from this entire fiasco.

He looked out the window and studied the changed environment. A few years ago, this had been the second largest desert in the world. Now, it was dangerous for a whole myriad of other reasons. Heavy machine guns still covered the angles of the Zoo and men alternated on a twenty-four-hour schedule to maintain the couple of kilometers that were still free of the trees between the construction site and the Zoo. Satellite images revealed that the Zoo was already within spitting distance of other sections of the wall that were already completed.

Beyond the limit of his vision and shrouded by the rampant growth, something moved in the underbrush of the Zoo. The creature stood almost at the edge of the tree line. Four eyes were spread over an elongated skull. They all moved independently from each other like a chameleon's, but at that moment, all were focused on the encampment across the open space. Very little could be seen of the animal, even by anything or anyone closer to where it stood. The eyes blinked one at a time before the beast growled, a low, deep rumble easily lost in the noise of the jungle before it withdrew slowly between the trees.

# CHAPTER TWENTY-NINE

Madigan shook her head and opened her eyes when the glare of the sun bothered her. She peered at the window, annoyed to find that the shades were pulled but that the sun shone through them easily. Just like the Russians to go cheap on the shades, she thought and muttered her irritation.

It took her a few seconds longer than she would have liked to realize that something else had woken her. The sun had been the catalyst, of course, but something else had penetrated beyond that to draw her out of her instinctive grumbled protest about not being able to sleep. She scowled and focused on the strange surroundings to identify the something that dragged her into full wakefulness. Someone whistled on key but off rhythm enough to scratch at her internal senses.

She growled incoherently as she pushed her legs off the bed and winced when she realized how sore she was. At that moment, she had approved of how roughly Sal had man-handled her, but in retrospect, she probably could have done with a bit less macho through the marathon. Her tits and ass were red and tender, along with her aching pussy. All three would probably remind her for a couple of days of the experience. Although, she mused, there was something hot about being marked by Sal. She wasn't sure what that was about. It was like he'd established his dominance last night and made sure she wouldn't forget it anytime soon.

Kennedy pushed past the memories and stood carefully. She swayed a little as she tried to keep her balance while resisting the urge to spread her sore thighs too much. Her gaze paused at the clothes from her pack that were now hung over the back of the chair in the room, and she narrowed her eyes. She hadn't brought them there. No, she had come with only a towel on since the idea had been seduction.

The towel was gone too, she realized.

Before any thought of dressing, she needed to take a shower. She smelled of sweat, sex, and cum, both hers and his, and while it had been hot in the moment, it was now much less so. She snatched her clothes, shrugged, and simply walked out of the room.

The whistling came from Sal who worked happily in front of the stove. She could smell breakfast food, and while her mouth watered, she forced herself to head to the bathroom first.

"Morning," he said with a smile when he heard the door open.

"Morning," Madigan responded and turned. He watched her with an amused grin and she realized too late

that it was because she still walked bow-legged. "Oh...
bite me."

He pointed at her shoulder where, sure enough, there
were a couple of bite marks. "Already done. I'm efficient
like that."

She chose to say nothing in response and simply flipped
him off.

"We can do that next time if you feel up to it," he said with
a grin. She shook her head but felt a tremor between her
thighs at the thought. Quickly, she pushed the sensation
aside. She was in no shape for a repeat and probably wouldn't
be for a while, although she knew that she would knock on
his door for the next round before too long. She would,
however, refrain from making any bets against him this time.

"There are some pain meds in the mirror cabinet," Sal
called before she closed the door. She peeked out at him,
suspicious about how he knew that already—and how he
knew that she would need them.

He shrugged at her unasked question. "I might be Super
Sex Man, but I'm not Man of Steel yet. I'm still not at a
hundred percent after last night either."

She smiled and looked away. "Thanks."

"No problem." He turned back to his cooking. "Think of
me while you shower, okay?"

She blushed and flipped him off again, unconcerned
that he couldn't see it before she shut the door behind her.
Even so, she couldn't help but think about him in there,
especially while she washed where he'd thrust into for
most of the night. The exercise stirred conflicting feelings
and sensations, and she was tempted to explore these

further. Common sense prevailed. She knew that if she fell, she might need to call Sal to help her up.

There was no way she would ever live that shit down.

It still meant that she had been left with an ache of need and more than a little wetness to disguise when she pulled her clothes on. She shook her head and gave up her attempt to come to terms with all this before she took Sal's advice, stole a pill from the cabinet, and swallowed it smoothly. It would take a few minutes to kick in, so she was unfortunately damned to make another walk of shame from the bathroom to the kitchen.

At least he didn't tease her about it this time.

She sat at the table and watched Sal work at the stove. A couple of minutes passed before he turned to put a plate with a couple of bacon strips and a stack of pancakes in front of her.

"I...didn't know that you could cook," Madigan said, impressed, as he put some butter and jam beside the cup of hot coffee that he'd prepared as well.

"Well, I could make a couple of cracks about how much there is about me that you don't know," he said, "but there were a lot of occasions to learn how to make some good breakfast food when I was a teenager. Breakfast is the only thing I really know how to make. When we get back, I'll make you some killer eggs Benedict. They only had dehydrated eggs here, so...yeah."

"So you can't cook a decent steak, but you can make eggs Benedict?" she asked, her mouth half full of pancake that she'd smeared with butter and raspberry jam.

"I can make a decent steak," Sal said and sat across the table from her. He dug enthusiastically into his own pile of pancakes. "Decent baked potatoes. Pretty much anything that doesn't require days of work, which means...yeah, breakfast foods and snacks."

"Since when is steak a breakfast food?" Madigan asked. She sipped her coffee and winced.

"I know," he agreed. "Russians make up for their good vodka with terrible coffee. Anyway, where I come from, steak and eggs are the go-to breakfast. And bacon was in everything, so it mixed into breakfast too."

"Yeah, in a diner," she sniped.

He didn't actually have anything to say to that. In all honesty, he liked diner food, especially when it included fries, steak, and no judgment for someone who had lived on coffee and popcorn for the past week or so.

"How do you feel?" he asked after she demolished her first stack and he served her a second.

"Don't even ask," she protested. "I'm not even sure how you managed that, but you did. I might be ruined for life."

"You might want to see a doctor about that," Sal said and looked genuinely concerned.

"Not physically, dumbass." Madigan laughed. "Well, maybe a little bit, although it's nothing that shouldn't be rectified in a couple of days. Hopefully. I will see a doctor if it doesn't."

"How do you mean, then?" he asked and his face twisted with disgust when he sipped his coffee.

She smirked. "Well, unless guys who can marathon like that have been in hiding all my life, I don't think I'll find any other guy who can do it like you can. The guys I've been with before couldn't, and that includes you. Not that our sex before wasn't fun and enjoyable, but never…that fun and enjoyable."

He smiled and nodded. "Well, I guess I'll take that as a compliment and look to improving my performance for next time. That's…assuming that there'll be a next time?"

"Provided that the both of us haven't died before then, you can bet your nail-marked ass there'll be a next time," Madigan said and grinned.

He smirked. "Well, I am happy to hear that. Although I need time for recovery, and I'm sure you do too."

"Hey, my recuperation skills might not be as impressive as yours, but I don't think it'll be too long before your bones get jumped once more," she said and winked.

Sal looked like he might actually be blushing when he looked down. If she were that kind of woman, he was the kind of guy she could have eating out of her hand. He was still young, energetic, and passionate about things. She wasn't like that, though. Even though he'd probably ruined her for other guys, she didn't want to be the kind of woman who ruined other women for him.

She took another sip of the coffee and coughed. "Fuck, is there any cream around here? This stuff is atrocious."

"There's some milk in the fridge." Sal pointed at the mini refrigerator behind him. She nodded in thanks and poured a hefty amount into her mug.

"They've transferred the money that the commandant promised us into the company account," he said once the pancakes were gone. "Even the stuff that they said was for Courtney. I already pushed that into her personal account. I know I should have checked with my partner first. I'm sorry about that. It only occurred to me after the transfer was made."

"So long as you don't touch the money I help make without my consent, it's all good," Madigan responded with a smile. Even with milk, the coffee tasted like it had been harvested a decade before. "You're the senior partner, so I trust you to do the right thing. For now, anyway."

Sal nodded. "Thanks, I appreciate that."

She finally put the mug of coffee down with a snort of disgust. "I swear to God, I need to make this stuff Irish or something."

"I don't think that the whiskey will be any good around here," he said. "Do you call it Russian coffee if you mix it with vodka?"

"Isn't that a black Russian?" Madigan asked.

"Nah, that's with Kahlua, I think." He'd had some group projects with students who worked part-time as bartenders. Of course, he had only been a teenager at the time, so he had to go on what he'd heard them discuss. It really wasn't that much to work with, but still, when you had a bear trap for a brain, things stuck around.

Madigan didn't seem to know any better, though, and she merely shrugged and scowled sourly at her coffee mug. "The vodka here is pretty good, though."

He nodded, still prepared to take her word on that. "You know, if it's good and cheap, we might be able to get some money on the side if we used what we got here to buy a couple of crates of it and flipped it to the bar."

"That way, we might even get to drink some of it too." She paused when she noticed that Sal looked at her with narrowed eyes. "What?"

"Nothing," he said and looked away quickly. "I thought you would think that it was a stupid idea."

"I know how much money there is in alcohol here," she said with a chuckle. "Believe me. I'd say that I know better than most."

"Considering that you constitute about half the money that goes into the bar, I most definitely believe you," Sal said with a grin which persisted even through the venomous glare that she threw his way.

"Well, with breakfast out of the way, why don't we go ahead and do it now?" Madigan asked.

"What time is it?"

Madigan checked her watch. "Half past ten."

"The commandant communicated that the convoy to the Staging Area that we'll hitch a ride with will leave at sixteen hundred, so we have some time to kill," he said with a nod. "Let me get the dishes and we'll go."

"Why bother?" she asked and pushed out of her seat. She still had trouble keeping her balance. "It's not like we'll make any more food here anyway."

"Because it's the nice thing to do," he said, and his jaw jutted stubbornly.

She rolled her eyes.

---

"What do you think?"

Sal winced as he tasted the vodka. It was strong, that much was obvious. He could feel the vapor burn his nostrils as he swallowed, and the sensation continued all the way down his esophagus.

The man who made the sale tilted his head at his reaction. He quickly shook his head.

"I'm not that used to vodka," Sal explained as he still tried to process the burn in his mouth and throat. He coughed gently. "I don't actually drink that much. If you want a professional opinion, ask her."

The liquor rep, a pot-bellied man with a look that suggested he'd been in the military some decades before, looked at Kennedy. She regarded the glass with an impressed look on her face.

"This is some good shit, Vlad," she said with a chuckle. "Nice and smooth. How much of it do you have?"

"We are still small operation," he said with a thick accent. "We are all former soldiers and mostly sell to former soldiers, so while our product is good, it is still made in the small scale."

"How much do you have to sell in bulk to us now?" Sal asked.

"Twenty crates." He grinned. "Twenty bottles each."

"How much for each crate?" Kennedy asked.

"I sell bottles at fifty dollars each," the man said. "If you buy crates, the price is reduced to thirty dollars each bottle."

"How much is that?" Kennedy asked.

"Six hundred bucks a crate," Sal interjected before the Russian could say anything. "Twelve grand for all twenty."

"That's not even that hard," Kennedy snarked at his math skills and rolled her eyes before she shifted her focus to Vlad. "That's a really reasonable price. What's up with that?"

"Production costs are lower," he said with a shrug.

"Besides, it's not a big brand, so we have to keep prices low for sales."

Sal nodded. "Fair enough."

"Although," Kennedy cut in, "there will be problems if we find out that you filled half the bottles with wood alcohol of the break-your-bones variety."

Vlad started to chuckle but cut it off quickly when she gave him an icy look.

"It's fair," he said quickly. "We are here on legal contract, so any complaints from customers, especially from outside of Russian compound, is huge problem and it compromises our sales."

She nodded. "That's a good point. Besides, if this stuff sells well, we'll probably come back for a return visit. You can't ever have…too much pocket change."

"We can't take it out of the company funds, though," Sal said. "We'll have to buy it with our own personal accounts."

Kennedy nodded. "So we split the costs of…shall we say, ten cases?"

Sal nodded.

"Excellent!" Vlad said with a big grin.

"What are the transportation costs?" Sal asked quickly.

"What are you talking about?" Kennedy asked.

"Small operations like this always charge transport costs," Sal said and looked at Vlad. "Look, we leave at sixteen hundred hours, so how much will it be to have the cases dropped off at the convoy?"

"Shall we say fifty dollars?" Vlad asked.

"Sounds good," Sal replied. "We will need an invoice, of course."

"Of course, I print up right now. Drink to seal deal?"

"Better than any handshake," Kennedy said as the Russian grinned and poured another three shot glasses full.

"Cheers!" she lifted her glass, and they all clinked and swallowed the contents quickly. She glanced at Sal as he set his glass down. Normally, after two shots in such short succession, he would have been flushed and grinning like an idiot, but there was no sign of drunkenness now. Interesting, she thought and tilted her head to regard him curiously.

"What?" he asked.

"Nothing." She shook her head as Vlad headed back into his office to print their invoice.

"How much do you think we can flip these cases for in the Staging Area?" Sal asked.

Kennedy shrugged. "I have no idea. If anything, I'll pay you for some of them and use them to drown my sorrows."

He nodded. Usually, he would have cracked something funny about what kind of sorrows she might have after last night, but he stopped himself. He still needed to maintain some level of professionalism when they weren't in private.

She smiled and winked at him, having apparently come to the same conclusion.

# CHAPTER THIRTY

Sal and Kennedy were among the first to arrive at the area where the convoy prepared to leave. He wasn't sure why the Russian base would send a convoy to the Staging Area since they had only recently set up, but it was rather fortuitous timing.

"I heard that they offered helicopter rides for people yesterday," Kennedy informed him. "One of the officers headed to the Staging Area to check up on our friend Gregor and apparently, they try to save as much money as possible with these things so when someone goes, it's a tentatively open invitation to virtually anyone who needs to get over there. However, since there weren't that many people who had business on the other side of the Zoo, the chopper was almost empty."

"Well, we'll have to settle for ground-based travel with the rest of the non-VIPs," he quipped with a small grin. Since the convoy wouldn't actually pass through the Zoo and the vehicles themselves were all equipped with armor and weapons, they hadn't needed to suit up. That was a relief since Sal wanted to have the suits inspected before they went back into the jungle with them. With an efficiency that surprised him a little although he wasn't sure why, the suits were already delivered and placed beside the crates of vodka when they arrived fifteen minutes before the convoy was due to start out.

So, barring a bounty hunter raiding party or—and Sal really hoped that this wouldn't become a thing—the animals came out of the Zoo and attacked the roads, they would be relatively safe. Even so, he opened the crate that he'd packed his suit into, pulled out the sidearm that had come with it, and tucked it into the belt of his pants. Kennedy did the same.

"Can't be too careful, right?" he said when a couple of the crew members sent them questioning looks. The men chuckled and spouted a couple of words in Russian that Sal hadn't heard before. Considering his time spent on international multiplayer forums, he had picked up little more than a smattering of the language.

"They think that we're being smart," Sal said when Kennedy looked confused. "Or something."

"Oh, well, color me reassured," she retorted and made sure the weapon tucked into the back of her pants was covered by her shirt.

It was thirty minutes past four before the teams that were supposed to head out trickled in, and an hour after that before everyone was finally ready to go.

"It looks like these guys are worse at punctuality than we are," Kennedy commented as they settled in.

Sal nodded. "Do you regret where you put your gun?"

Kennedy nodded. "Oh yeah."

He grinned as they got underway. It was a good thing that she wasn't bothered about what they'd done the night before. While he did like teasing her about it, there was also a need to be professional, and that would be difficult when all it took to get his mind in the gutter was to see how she walked. He was usually so good about stuff like that.

His scientific mind reminded him that his "usually" had slipped considerably and protested the reality that he'd been impractical and had not run more tests. He reassured himself that he would have plenty of time for that later if all went well and neither of them died. Now was not the time to draw conclusions about what he was or wasn't good at.

It wasn't that long a drive. The Zoo took considerably longer to cross because it was difficult to get vehicles through—and actually impossible in the roughest terrain—and moving on foot was even slower. Sal still wasn't sure how the Russians had managed to get their vehicles in and out so quickly to evacuate him, his team, and the Russian-merc squad, but he would definitely look into it. From what he'd heard, all their own attempts had ended when the Hammerheads broke down and more had to be sent in to get them all out again.

As things stood, the drive around the Zoo took them the rest of the day, all night, and halfway into the morning of the next day before he caught sight of the expansive complex that comprised the Staging Area. With the jungle spreading as quickly as it was, they had begun to put up walls and defensive perimeters around the complex. These emulated the concept of the walls that they tried to build around the Zoo itself but in reverse.

A few hours later, the vehicle with their belongings finally managed to pull up at Kennedy's apartment.

"I can store the booze at my place and we can look for a buyer together," she said with a grin that almost dared Sal to make a joke about it.

He liked to think that he was unpredictable and decided to prove it by ignoring the opportunity. Her quick look of surprise was satisfying. "I'll get the suits to Boulos and have him do what's needed. We should be able to move back into the Zoo by tomorrow if he doesn't try to pull anything."

Madigan still looked mildly disappointed but nodded. He grinned because he so easily read her mind, but he gripped her by the shoulder before she turned to unload the crates. "Stop by my place later. I have something I want to show you."

She tilted her head in sudden interest. "Well, I think I can make it over later today if that works for you."

"That works. I'll see you then."

---

He didn't have the rapport with Boulos that Kennedy did, and he certainly lacked the kind of intimidating look that normally kept the armorer in line. Even so, the man seemed to associate Sal with Kennedy and so gave him less trouble over the pricing for the repairs than usual. It was a relief. He had been cramped in a tight, bumpy vehicle for hours on end and the entire trip hadn't been conducive to real rest or sleep. Added to the strenuous activity of the night before that, he was exhausted, even though it was barely an hour after noon by the time he actually returned his place after picking the key card up at the commandant's office.

Surprisingly, Kennedy stood outside, waiting for him.

"What…what are you doing here?" Sal asked.

"You said you wanted to talk to me about something," she replied with an easy grin. "You almost never want to talk to me about something that's not important."

"Well, yes, it is," he admitted as he opened the front door to his little apartment. "But I didn't think you would take it seriously, especially since there are two hundred bottles of supposedly prime vodka stacked in your house."

"Please," Kennedy snorted as he took her hand and dragged her inside. "I have some self-control. I also have functioning muscles capable of carrying my sexy ass all the way over here, so I don't think I need you to hold my hand, Sal."

He smirked and released it. "Sorry. I'm just excited."

"Look, I can give you a blowjob, but I think that's it for me now," she said pointedly as they moved into his bedroom. "I still need a couple of days for recovery."

"What?" he asked and moved past the bed toward the closet where his safe was. "No, that's not what I was talking about. I need to show you something."

He gestured for her to sit on the bed as he tapped his long, complicated passcode sequence into the safe's keypad. They waited in silence for the couple of seconds for it to unlock before he retrieved a cubic container. It was slightly rectangular and tall, but it wasn't heavy. Sal put it down on the bedside table for Kennedy to see. He removed the film that was supposed to keep the contents of the glass container hidden.

"Holy shit," she murmured as she leaned in closer and narrowed her eyes. "Is that what I think it is?"

"Well, if what you think it is happens to be a fully formed and blossoming Pita plant..." Sal paused for dramatic effect but couldn't restrain his grin. "Then yes, that's exactly what it is."

"Fuck." She stared at it in obvious disbelief. It still wasn't fully grown. Most of the plants were bush-sized, at least a meter tall, and spread evenly and thickly over the ground. It seemed that the lack of natural light—the down-side of keeping it in a safe—had affected the growth pattern.

"Do you know what the standing price for one of these is?" she asked when she managed to drag her gaze from it and the four blooming flowers. "There are a couple of companies that offer upwards of seven million, and there's talk of ten."

"Well, yeah, I do know," Sal said with a small smile. "I call her Madie."

"How do you know that it's a girl?" Kennedy asked, and then her eyes widened. "Oh, 'Madie!' That explains so much."

"Okay?" Sal said and narrowed his eyes. He decided it was safer to ignore all that might imply. "Moving right past what her name explains, the flowers of the Pita plants have both stamens and carpels, which means that, like most flowering plants, it's hermaphroditic. That's not...not really important, but yes, she's a she, and she's called Madie. Named after you."

Kennedy smirked. "I think I'm flattered. Anyway, when did you get 'Madie' out? I don't remember us surviving the kind of shitstorm that comes with plucking these babies."

"Sure you do," Sal said. "It was on our first trip in. It hadn't blossomed yet, so I took the chance that we wouldn't call down all the kinds of hell that comes with pulling a plant out. I was...half right. They were still pissed, but not as much. And only the ones that were around. Remember? You got shot in the leg by those bounty hunters?"

"Oh, yeah," Kennedy said with a smirk. "Fun times."

"Fun times?"

"Yeah. But that's not the point right now. I mean, you weren't even close to a Ph.D. then, and you managed to pull something that not even the best, brightest or most funded—not necessarily in that order—were able to do."

"I'm still not a Ph.D.," Sal said with a grimace. He would have to finish his dissertation sometime. Eventually. One of these days.

"You should have told me," Kennedy said. "We're partners in this, and I have to be able to trust you to tell me the truth about things."

Sal nodded. "I know, and I'm sorry. I honestly didn't trust anyone when I got her, and while I've run tests, I wasn't sure if I could tell anyone about her. It seemed easier to keep you out of the loop, and I made up all kinds of excuses, like giving you plausible deniability—" He paused when she snorted derivatively. "Yeah, I know, bull-shit, but still. That's why I'm filling you in on it now."

Madigan nodded. She supposed that he could have kept it a secret indefinitely, and the fact that he had opened up to her about something that had happened before they were partners was a sign of trust.

She sighed and shook her head. "Why haven't you sold it yet?"

Sal shrugged. "I'm not really sure. It's not that I don't want the money. I could probably push the price up to at least twice what they're offering once I give them the results of the tests that I've run. But I'm not sure that I'm ready to trust anyone or any corporation willing to drop that much money on this."

Kennedy narrowed her eyes and paused to think about what he'd said. When she finally arrived at her conclusion, she looked at him in surprise. "What? You've tested this stuff on yourself—is that what you're telling me? Is that why you can fuck for that long?"

He backed away instinctively as her voice rose. "I've taken small doses of the unfiltered stuff from the flower. There is a correlation to my dosing myself with the blue stuff and my newly acquired…ahem, prowess, but considering that my sex life wasn't even that active before any of this, I'm not sure if it's actually a direct result of that, or maybe the fact that I'm young, and you have the ability to get a boner out of— Nope, nope, I will not make that joke."

She grinned. "Thanks for that. And thanks for the compliment, no matter how badly you worded it."

Sal chuckled. "Well, yeah. I kind of had a crush on you ever since our first trip. I'm not really sure that I would have believed that you ever came here that first night if you hadn't left your panties with your initials on them. Well, the panties were the giveaway, the initials more…pointed the finger, I guess."

She pushed from the bed and approached him with a small smile on her lips. "So…a crush, huh?"

Distracted, he lowered his eyes to trail his gaze over her form. "Well…yeah."

"You named your plant after your crush?" Kennedy asked with a smile and leaned up to kiss his lips softly.

"I did name my ten-million-dollar-plus plant for my crush, yes," he said with a small smile. "Do you want to fuck?"

"Unless you give me a dose of that blue stuff from Madie, I don't think I'll be able to," she said regretfully and kissed his chin.

"Well, you did say a blowjob was on the table," Sal said with a sly smirk. "But if you like, I can give you something for the pain."

"Well, I guess we could start off with a blowjob anyway," she murmured and leaned closer. "I seem to recall that you liked that. But I'll want a rematch for the sex Olympics in a week or two."

"Well, give me a moment and I'll be right with you." He kissed her gently.

# CHAPTER THIRTY-ONE

Courtney looked up from her empty breakfast plate when there was a knock on the door. Supplies arrived every week, but she'd had enough of the dehydrated stuff and the repetitive food that they served at the mess hall, so she'd put some work into stocking up on fresh food. It wasn't the best. Getting groceries out into the desert was always troublesome, but occasionally, the variety and freshness made it worth the effort.

She washed her hands quickly, went to the door, and opened it. Sal stood outside.

"Well, good morning, boss," she said with a soft, almost awkward chuckle.

He grinned in response as she gestured for him to come inside. "Well, I'm not technically your boss, but I appreciate the deference."

Monroe chuckled softly. "Well, considering that there's only one doctorate in this room, I guess I should call you 'partner,' then."

"Junior partner," Sal retorted and narrowed his eyes.

"Let's not get carried away. Heavy Metal is my baby, and you're crazy if you think that I'll let her go without a fight."

"The company's a woman now, is she?" Courtney asked.

"Well, yeah, since there are more women than men staffing it," Sal said smoothly like he'd expected her to say that.

"Can I get you some coffee?" she asked.

"Please. You wouldn't believe how bad the coffee is on the Russian side. Seriously, we could make a fortune simply by smuggling this stuff over to those poor, poor comrades."

She laughed. "Well, we can look into expanding our business into smuggling coffee later, I think."

"We've already expanded it into buying vodka from them," Sal said. "I guess we forgot to tell you, but they sold the stuff for bananas, so we brought some crates back with us to sell to the bar here. We thought we'd be able to make some money on the side with that."

Courtney nodded and set a mug of hot coffee on the kitchen counter where Sal had taken a seat.

"I got your message," she said after he'd taken a couple of sips. "I really appreciate you giving me the full bonus."

"You did the work, you get the money," he said with a shrug. "And I looked into the tax laws around here, and I can actually get some tax breaks if I pass the money on to you, so...thank you, actually."

Monroe laughed. "The breaks aren't that substantial. Anyway, I appreciate it. I'm glad that I'm finally in business with someone whom I can trust. Someone who's got my back, as it were."

Sal smiled. "We're partners in this. If we stab each other in the back, we'll all end up dead."

"That's not how the guys who wrote my paychecks before saw things," she reminded him and raised her mug to toast silently with him. "Any word on the actual pay from our little trip into the Zoo?"

"Well, it was cut short, so it'll be a couple of days before we send out invoices," he said. "But we did manage to bring in a substantial amount of data, so that, plus the salaries owed us, even if they're half-rate, should net us some good income. Oh, Young sent me a message with what we're owed for the sets of Pita flowers that we turned in, but those will also only be deposited once the rest of the teams come back in and all the money is paid out."

Courtney nodded. One of the downsides of actually paying attention to how her money was handled was that she wasn't great at keeping track of things. Maybe she should take notes or something.

"Can I ask you something?" Sal asked.

"Of course," she replied and snapped out of her train of thought. "What's on your mind?"

"Well, you've probably already made something of a name for yourself as the specialist who's gone out into the Zoo the longest," he said. "You could probably get tenure in a university or a seven- or eight-figure salary in one of the corporations that are interested in this place. Why are you still here? I mean, sure, it's fun, but don't you ever feel tempted to go back to civilization?"

She settled her gaze on the mug of coffee cradled in her hands. "There's always the temptation to head back, I guess, and I've actually talked with a couple of corporate headhunters about cushy job back home, but…it's complicated."

Sal seemed content to simply sit and wait for her to explain. He even leaned forward, and the gesture prompted her to continue.

"Well, you should probably know that my dad is Dr. Hartley Monroe," she said. "You know, the—"

"Yeah." he nodded. "The whole thing with the monkeys in Los Angeles. I remember."

"Right. Anyway, he's the one who got me this job with the goop before it became all Zoo-ified. So yeah, I've put out some peer-reviewed stuff that's been well received in our circles, but I've looked for something…spectacular. Something that would put me on the map and kind of… well, show that I earned my place out here and I'm not merely riding on the wave of my father's success, you know? Plus, I want to one-up him a little. So yeah, I stick it out in the most dangerous place in the world, fighting for my life, to make myself *the* Dr. Monroe, not Dr. Monroe's daughter."

"I get that."

"Overbearing parents on your side too?" Courtney asked.

"No, not really," Sal replied. "They were always the kind of people where a job was something that they did in order to live and never let their jobs be their lives. Which is a good thing, I guess, but I was born different. They knew that, and they loved me in spite of my brains. To them, I was simply one of their kids. It's vanity, I know, but I've always wanted to be more than that to them."

She laughed. "Yep, I get that you were one of those kids. You're special, and you want everyone to know about it."

He opened his mouth, but shut it again and shrugged. "That's actually pretty darn accurate, but I do want you to stop describing me...forever, so let's change the subject, shall we?"

"Sounds like a plan. What did you have in mind?"

"Well, I was over at the armory yesterday, and I talked to Boulos about upgrading your suit to something new and snappy. I thought that you might want to get something more dedicated to a specialist's duties and not a hybrid like mine is."

"That sounds about right," she said with a nod.

"Anyway," Sal continued, "I need to charge it to the company's account, and for that, I'll actually need to finish your working contract. Boulos will send me a list of the specialist suits that they have available for us, so if you could get all your contracts sorted out for me today?"

"I need to pick up my residual checks from the other guys this morning, and they'll sign off on my severance this afternoon," she said. "I'll have them all to you by then."

"That would be great." He finished his coffee and stood. "I'll give Kennedy the specs on what to look for in the suits regarding budget and you can tell her what you're looking for with function. Based on that, we can find something that works for you. We can meet up for dinner at the bar and exchange all the info if that's okay."

"Sounds good to me."

"Awesome," he said with a wink. "I'll see you then."

Courtney escorted him to the door and shut it behind him with a soft sigh. It wasn't like her to pine after a guy or wonder what he meant by every tiny little detail. It did make her wonder why he jumped so quickly to all business when they had a real, earnest discussion.

"You're overthinking this," she scolded herself. She needed to finalize the contract issues, so she put the dishes in the sink to be taken care of later and grabbed her bag and keys.

She didn't like that he had apparently friend-zoned her now that they worked together, but considering everything that had happened, she wasn't too surprised about it. If he wanted her to stick around because he liked her brains, she could live with that. It would take some getting used to was all.

Monroe nodded, steeled herself, and put all those thoughts aside for later—maybe never—as she exited her apartment.

# CHAPTER THIRTY-TWO

Courtney stepped into the bar. The sun had already set which meant that this would be the peak hours at the place. Most of the tables were already full, as were most of the bar stools. She did feel the need to have a drink, if only to help calm herself. It hadn't been too stressful a day, and it was always nice for the ego when the people whom she worked for in the past asked her to come back. It also showed that they didn't realize how shitty they had treated her, which was depressing too.

She looked around once more, reluctant to have to stand until one of the loud teams left a table, and finally saw Madigan in the corner near the kitchen, waving her over. A wave of relief washed over her as she joined her. It was a table for two, but three chairs were spaced around it. Considering the sour looks that Kennedy received from the people who stood at the larger tables around them, Courtney wondered if she hadn't wrestled the extra chair away from them.

Monroe really wished that she had that sort of gall. Her

companion simply sat there, sipped her drink, and didn't give a single fuck about the people around her. She obviously also knew that nobody would try to take the chair back because she would happily fight them for it.

Of course, she would be kicked out for the night, but then again, so would the others. Nobody wanted to risk getting cut off for the night over a stupid chair.

Madigan knew that which was why she sat there in such peace despite the noise around them.

"Hey," Courtney said with a smile. "Thanks for saving me a seat."

"No problem." She nodded in greeting. "You going to drink anything? I have a tab open."

Of course, she did. "I'll have a diet Coke. I'm still traumatized by the last time you and I drank together."

The other woman smirked, headed to the bar, and returned with a soda in hand. "Sal is finishing off a whitepaper that he has pending. It's a way for him to bring some money into Heavy Metal while we're not in the Zoo. There are some testing contracts that we've worked on too. You're welcome to join in on those, by the way."

"Thanks," Courtney said with a smile and sipped her drink. "How long do you think he'll be? Sal, I mean."

"Oh, that depends." Madigan drank from her own pint of dark, frothy beer. "He could be bored and have it finished in fifteen minutes, or he could be interested and do it all night."

"Which do you think is most likely?"

"With Salinger Jacobs?" She raised an eyebrow. "I honestly couldn't say."

"He mentioned something about a new suit for me to

work in," Courtney said. "Something about passing the budget-restricted list of suits to you for me to pick out."

"Oh, yeah." Kennedy tapped at her thigh to indicate her phone. "But that can wait, I think. We're having dinner, and I'm starving. It's always best to avoid shopping when you're hungry."

"That's a myth, isn't it?" Courtney asked.

"Not for me. I've kept myself under control with that in mind for a long time now."

She grinned. "Well, I can give it a try, I suppose. Sorry if I'm overeager, but I'm happy to finally work with people whom I trust to watch my back, you know?"

Madigan nodded. "I feel the same way."

"And I like the work," she continued. "I'd be happy to take everything that he can put in me."

"Phrasing," her companion grumbled.

"What was that?" Monroe asked.

"Nothing. I just approve of your choice of words."

"Oh…" Courtney blushed. "Sorry, I didn't mean it that way."

"Sure," Madigan said with a grin to tease the woman across from her. "So, Sal told me what happened between the two of you while we were over in the Russian Base."

She caught her breath and tilted her head, and panic careened in her stomach. "Oh…really? What did he say?"

"He didn't give me any specifics," Kennedy said with a shrug. "Only that the two of you slept together and that if I wanted to hear the dirty details, I'd have to ask you about it. That's not to say that I want to hear the details."

"Well—" Courtney said and stalled for time as she tried to get a read on what the other woman thought. She had raised the conversation, after all. In this lighting, it was impossible to tell. That smirk could be malicious or teasing. She had no idea. "I...how do you feel about it?"

Madigan shrugged. "I think that we're in a very dangerous business, and life is way too short to have to bother with the drama and complications that come with relationships that regular society approves of. When you can get your ass killed the next time you walk into the Zoo, all those rules and regulations don't really have relevance."

"Huh." She had no idea where to go with that.

"What I mean is..." Madigan started and paused to collect her thoughts and word this right. "What I mean is that I'm not some catty bitch who will start a fight where no fight exists, you know?"

Courtney nodded. "I appreciate that. I mean, I really like working with you, and I wouldn't want some drunken mistake to get in the way of our working relationship—and hopefully, a friendship."

"I feel the same way. Although you'll have to tell me how it was that you managed to get Sal drunk during the day. I can barely get him to drink at night."

So he really hadn't told her any of the details, Courtney thought. Well, if he hadn't wanted to tell Madigan about it, she didn't intend to pop that bubble. She really did respect the woman, and she had the feeling that if she told her about how she had sex with her man while he was asleep, she would take that seriously. It was way better to avoid the possibility of a fight with her—catfight or otherwise.

"Look, if you want to get into bed with Sal, I have no problem with that," Kennedy said. "Although you should probably challenge him to something of a fuck-off first. I can tell you something, there aren't many people out there who can handle him. If you can't, maybe he's too much man for you."

Monroe narrowed her eyes. "Come on, guys can't outlast women, that's a scientific fact. Except maybe Arnold in his youth." She pronounced the former body builder's name in his native Austrian accent.

"Scientific fact, eh?" Her companion leaned forward with a smirk. "How many times have you had the chance to put that fact to the test?"

"Oh..." Courtney hedged as she hadn't expected that question. Madigan had been candid with her, though, and she didn't want to take that away from her. "Well, no specifics, but it's been more than one and less than twenty."

She felt her stomach drop when Kennedy leaned back again and looked skeptical.

"Well, if it's a fuck-off," she said to move the conversation forward quickly, "forewarned is forearmed, so thanks for that. I have a couple of tricks up my sleeve that'll guarantee me the victory."

Madigan opened her mouth to reply but shut it quickly when Sal arrived and moved toward their table. Even in the dim lights of the bar, they could see that his eyes were bleary and he looked tired, which meant that he hadn't felt at all inspired by what he'd worked on. Which explained why he was there so early as opposed to not at all.

"How was the whitepaper?" she asked.

"Well, it was an incomplete that they wanted me to finish," Sal said. "So of course, I had to edit the whole damn thing, and of course, it was riddled with errors. After all that edit work, I didn't feel like putting too much effort into it. I finished it off without any flourishes and came here. Fuck, I need a drink."

Madigan waved her hand to the bartender, who nodded, filled up a pint of lager, and handed it to one of the waitresses to carry to the table. Madigan winked at Courtney as she took the glass and handed it to Sal.

He drank quickly, and even Madigan raised her eyebrows as she called for another. Sal attacked that one as well, then accepted the third with a little more civility.

"That bad, huh?" Madigan asked.

"Oh yeah," he replied. "I mean, I know that the Zoo has defied all logic and even laws of physics, but I'll believe that there's a fucking T-Rex when I fucking see one."

"But there are legitimate dinosaurs walking around out there," Courtney said.

"Like I said, laws of physics out the window," Sal said and raised his hands. "But the big critters that we ran into are not DNA replicas of the fossils that we've encountered before, and I doubt that the goop has watched Jurassic Park to replicate it."

Madigan raised her eyebrows when she saw that he had already finished his third beer. It wasn't like him to drink and certainly not this much, and like before, it didn't seem that what he'd consumed had even mildly affected him. She didn't doubt that it would but pounding that much alcohol usually ended up with a man on his face to sleep it off prematurely.

"I think you need something stronger," she said, waved the waitress over, and ordered a boilermaker.

Sal nodded his approval of the choice, which made Madigan even more suspicious.

"Yeah, I have to agree," Courtney said after a sip of her diet Coke. "I mean, the big guys are definitely large reptiles, which makes them dinosaurs, but at the same time, they don't follow any kind of genetic code that we know of. We do know that the goop is able to take away from and mix and match the DNA of different animals. Whether the dino stuff merely makes the reptiles that the goop has been exposed to bigger, or if maybe there were a couple of fossils that it could draw from, or if the DNA is actually from wherever the goop came from... Well, we can't be sure."

"Well, all this geek talk is my invitation to exit," Kennedy said with a laugh. "We can do all the suit business tomorrow once you've got this out of your systems." She gesticulated to the two of them. "Sergeant Kennedy out." She headed toward the bar to pay her part of the tab but paused when Sal was distracted by the waitress who arrived with his drink.

"Have at him, tiger," she whispered, leaned toward Courtney, and patted her on the shoulder.

Monroe looked almost shocked for a moment before she realized what Madigan meant and felt something cold and full of anticipation stir in the pit of her stomach as she turned to him. He had already poured the shot of whiskey into the pint glass.

"Are you sure that you should drink that much?" she asked, suddenly not sure how to even begin to seduce the man of her dreams.

Sal looked up and smiled. "Believe me when I say that I've earned it. The T-Rex was one of the more believable items of the whitepaper they sent me. I swear, the guy in charge of writing this shit up must have been fired from the job."

She smirked. "I think we've all been there. Those people who want fame more than recognition will jump at anything to get their names on some big headlines and hope for a movie or book deal to come along because of it."

He nodded and took a long sip from the pint glass. After a few seconds, he straightened and shook his head with a laugh. "Come to think of it, maybe you're right. I might be going at this a bit too quickly."

"Hey, if you need to unwind, you need to unwind." She chuckled. "Although, if you're in the mood to unwind in ways that don't kill your brain cells and attack your liver, I think I might have a couple ideas."

Sal leaned forward curiously. "Oh? What did you have in mind?"

"Well, I've been told that you like stamina-testing sex marathons," she said. "A fuck-off," she added quickly when his eyes widened.

He wasn't sure how to respond to that and immediately wondered where she'd gotten the idea from. He turned quickly as Madigan slipped out the door without looking back. She couldn't have...

Then again, putting Courtney up to something like this did seem like the kind of thing that she was capable of, now that he thought about it. It wasn't something that she would become known for, but it was the kind of stunt she would pull to keep him on his toes with her. Now, he simply had to figure out whether she wanted him to decline the offer or not.

Maybe it was the alcohol, but he wasn't in any mood to

play games. If she wanted him to be monogamous, she would have told him. That was the kind of woman she was.

He turned to Monroe, and a smile teased his lips before he took another long sip from his drink. "Let me finish this and we can get started on our stamina-testing sex marathon."

She blushed furiously and looked around to make sure nobody had heard him say that. Thankfully, enough people were drunkenly loud to mask what he'd said from anyone even close by.

It didn't take him long to finish the drink, and they paid their bill before they stepped outside.

"Your place or mine?" Sal asked without even the slightest hint of a slur.

Courtney thought about it for a moment. She wasn't that prolific, but she knew enough to make an informed decision.

"My place," she said. "Definitely mine."

---

She gasped for breath and could half believe that her eyes actually bulged out of her face as she dropped back down to the bed.

*Breathe. Just keep breathing.* That was the key.

"Are you ready to give up?" Sal asked as he tilted his head in a challenge and grinned. He was sweating, but he still looked like he could go for a while yet.

She shook her head in answer to his question, not ready to talk yet. To distract him, she grabbed his wrists and pushed his hands against her breasts. He kneaded them gently. The sensation as his rough, callused palms rubbed against her nipples didn't help with the low, needy ache from where she could still feel him filling her.

"It's not possible," Courtney finally managed to gasp. "I'm a scientist, and I say that nine times is not scientifically possible."

"Well, you know that the Zoo has all kinds of ways to flip off the laws of science," Sal retorted with a grin. He leaned forward to press a kiss to her lips. "Besides, my current record is twelve times, and I still think that I could have gone for a few more."

She gaped at him, but her competitive streak flared. Twelve times? It had to have been with Madigan, she realized. She had been the one to set this up.

"That bitch," she breathed.

"What?" Sal asked. He gripped her nipples between his fore and middle fingers and tugged them gently in a way that made the wet ache in her pussy harder to resist.

"Nothing," she growled. "Fuck it, I don't think I have it in me to go to twelve, but I think I can make double digits at least."

"Your call," he said with a grin and kissed her neck as his hips pumped in and out of her again.

"Fuck, yes..." she whispered, her teeth gritted as she held him close to her.

# CHAPTER THIRTY-THREE

Morning had arrived, and she wasn't insanely hungover and in need of coffee-based medication to keep her from murdering anyone who so much as looked at her wrong.

She was getting old, Madigan realized.

At least she made up for it by being at the bar for breakfast and sipped some coffee infused with Irish whiskey. The coffee there was better than anywhere else in the Staging Area, but that didn't mean that she couldn't make it interesting. She smirked, took a sip, and picked at the grilled cheese she'd asked them to make for her breakfast. The drinks were great. The food was greasy and strictly comfort-based. It was good for when her head pounded, and she needed something to take the edge off of that and an upset stomach. Right now, though, it wasn't that appealing.

What did appeal, she decided, was who had strolled in through the door. There were customers there even in the morning, so that wasn't a surprise. People kept all kinds of hours around there, but right now, this was their slow time.

Which meant that when Courtney stepped into the bar, she easily became the focus of Madigan's attention. The way that she alternated between a stagger and a shuffle revealed all too clearly that she had gotten lucky the night before—although luck was subjective in this case. She'd obviously taken Madigan's advice, but challenging Sal to a fuck-off did have its consequences.

Monroe sat across from Madigan and glared at her. She opened her mouth to speak but stopped as a tired-looking waitress came over to their table.

"What can I get ya, honey?" the woman asked in a practiced tone.

Madigan answered for her. "We'll need coffee. Lots of it. Just…bring a pot and a mug. Plus, as much protein as you can get on a plate for her."

The waitress nodded, apparently unfazed by what had to be a common order around there, and headed back toward the kitchen.

"You…bitch," Courtney accused as soon as the waitress was out of earshot.

Kennedy chuckled softly. "I don't exaggerate, Courtney. Best you get used to that. Now that we have him, how do we make sure other women don't? I mean, it seems like you took the workout pretty well, so I see that I made a good choice."

"Are you kidding me?" her companion asked. "He's a fucking machine." Madigan smirked at the pun. "I'll be sore for a week, and that is even though I had to alternate between my mouth and my pussy after round five."

A pause ensued as the waitress returned with a pot of coffee, a mug, and a plate full of bacon and eggs heaped on a thick steak. It looked greasy and delicious, and Monroe immediately attacked a piece of bacon.

"And twelve times?" she asked, speaking with her mouth half full of bacon. "What do you have, titanium labia?"

Madigan laughed. "Honestly, I was ready to throw the towel in at nine, but he had this cocky smile that I wanted to fuck right off his face. I didn't succeed, but it was an honest attempt. How many times did you go?"

"Ten," Courtney admitted. "But that's only because he said that he'd gone twelve times with you recently, so I had to get it up to double digits at least."

"Alternating though?" Kennedy stole a strip of bacon from Courtney's plate. "That's cheating."

"Believe me, it was necessary," the specialist growled. "My jaw still hurts a little too. I mean, I've only ever been with two guys before, so my experience is thin, but there's something that tells me that there's nothing natural about it. He has to be unique in the fuck-me-blind ability."

Madigan nodded and sipped her coffee thoughtfully before she responded. "I've been around enough to have had a decent control group. Even Arnold couldn't compete."

---

Sal stepped out of the shower. There wasn't an extra towel for him to use, and he didn't want to try out the razor that he'd found in the stall. He would need to head home to complete his morning ritual.

For now, though, he took advantage of the still slightly damp towel that Courtney had left behind to dry himself before he stepped out. He had made sure that he was alone in the apartment before he took a shower. Well, it wasn't like he had anything to hide from anyone who might arrive. He'd simply assumed that Courtney didn't expect any visitors.

He kept her towel wrapped around his waist to be safe as he returned to her bedroom where his clothes had been discarded the night before. He'd taken them off fairly early in the evening. Well, Courtney had, anyway, but the point remained. They were still clean enough to wear, at least to get back home.

There was, however, a matter he needed to consider. He was now in a physical relationship with the other two founding members of Heavy Metal. That wasn't a simple situation. He wasn't great with women. Hell, he hadn't even been in a physical relationship with anyone but himself before he was shipped out there, so he knew less about it than most.

"I'm so fucked," Sal growled, shaking his head. "Then again, they have been fairly intense relationships, so if I go out with a shot in the back in the Zoo, it'll be with a smile on my face."

That was assuming he would have a face left, of course.

He fucking talked to himself again, he thought with a shake of the head. Maybe this was another sign of taking that goop in raw—going crazy. That he'd hooked up with two different women, both of whom had ready access to guns, was another sign that he was borderline fucking nuts.

It had been worth it, though. He grinned and nodded before he pulled his shirt on over his head. Still, his bravado about how Madigan would feel about him with Courtney had faded along with the alcohol. He didn't look forward to talking to her about it.

He looked down as he pulled his pants on.

"You had better be happy with those two and not get me in trouble with a third, or the next time we go out into that fucking jungle, we may not make it back out," he growled as he buttoned himself up.

And he had talked to his dick now, huh? Insanity definitely loomed.

---

Anderson dragged himself out of bed and rubbed at his eyes as he looked out the window. What kind of work base didn't have a steady supply of coffee, anyway?

Well, they did have a steady supply. The people who worked on the wall there were required to be functional and sharp enough to handle heavy equipment at all hours of the day or night, so that wasn't the problem.

The problem was that the supplies were all shipped in from that cesspool of capitalism that was the Staging Area every week. Since the whole operation was required to be one hundred percent under wraps, the supplies had to match the number of people who were supposed to work there, which excluded the black-ops team that tested new combat armor suits. Add that to the extra personnel who were brought in, and supplies were running out, fast.

And since scientists and engineers needed obscene amounts of coffee to maintain their work habits, it was no surprise that coffee was the first thing to run out.

Thankfully, the sun now rose on day five of this debacle, and that was the last one that they were paid for. If the suits weren't ready by now, the plug would be pulled, and hopefully, someone else would be called in to handle round two of testing these pieces of high-tech crap.

As he stepped out of the little hut that he'd called home over the past week or so, he saw that the open ground in the construction site had been put to good use.

Finally.

The new pilots weren't of the same cut as the special forces that Anderson had worked with. They were harder and tougher—hard-core black-ops operatives. They might have had the likes of SAS, French Foreign Legion, SEAL, and Green Beret attached to their credentials, but they had been out of it for almost a decade. Since then, they'd worked with security companies and ran the operations that even the US black-ops teams were afraid to implement.

The message was clear. After the previous bungle, Pegasus didn't want anyone associated with the military involved in what they did there.

The suits looked bulkier than before, and yet Anderson could see that the movements were smoother and easier and lacked the lag that he'd noted in the previous test runs. The weapons were new too, and not the bottom-of-the-basement stuff that the military liked to use. It was all new, high-tech, and top-of-the-line stuff.

It was a pity that it took the death of a good man to introduce all these improvements.

One of the team—the one out of the suit who oversaw the dry runs—turned when he noticed that Anderson watched their training.

"Colonel." His profile had called him Iver Corran, former SAS and one of the more highly recommended operatives among the new arrivals. "The engineers finished their work last night, so we've taken the opportunity to bring the new and improved suits out for a little fresh air."

"Corran, right?" he said. "I hope it's not too big a change from the overthrow of democratically elected governments to work on testing suits of armor."

"This is our overtime," the man responded with a smirk. "We keep the coups and political assassinations for the weekdays." He gave the officer a quick once-over and paused when his gaze reached the burn scars. "What are you, army?"

"Marine Corp, actually."

"Fantastic." He chuckled. "Even more sanctimonious."

Anderson nodded. If the truth be told, he wasn't that sanctimonious, but people like these guys were the lowest of the low. They were men of skill and talent who elected to do terrible things because it meant they received an unhealthy number of zeros in their bank accounts, all paid for by the Pentagon's defense contracts.

"Do you think you'll be ready to move soon?" Anderson asked to change the subject.

"Absolutely," Corran growled.

"At what time?"

He shrugged. "I can have them suit up properly right now if ya want. We might need time to make sure the supplies are ready. Let's say maybe an hour?"

Anderson nodded.

"Anxious to get out of here, are ya?" he asked with another smirk.

"I've been in this hellhole for a week now," Anderson rasped. "You cunts get this shit done today, and I can go home." He wasn't sure why, but he didn't want to talk about his family with a bunch of high-paid mercenaries.

"That sounds like a plan." Corran turned away with a shrug. "I'll let ya know when the time comes."

The colonel nodded and headed back to his little hut.

# CHAPTER THIRTY-FOUR

"This is Overwatch." Anderson spoke into his mic as he lowered himself into his seat in the operations center. "Are you ready, Falcon Team?"

"Fucking hell," one of the men cursed over the comms. "Do we really have to use these ridiculous call signs?"

He rubbed his temples. All work and no coffee made him a very dull boy, apparently.

"This is an official operation," he retorted and hated that he had to explain this to the men like they were toddlers. "Names and nicknames will be kept off comms at all times. Use your assigned call signs when you attempt to communicate and keep comms as clean as possible as much as possible. Is that understood?"

Silence was the only response from the other side. He knew that was an attempt to goad him, and it wouldn't work. He'd been in this game far too long to be outplayed by a bunch of mercenaries with over-inflated egos. Anderson shook his head and leaned back in his seat. Let them pretend to be high schoolers. He didn't give a damn.

"Overwatch asked you maggots a question, Falcon Team," Anderson heard Corran prod in a rough tone. He sounded like he felt similar irritation at their antics.

"Understood," came a series of three voices in quick succession. It annoyed him that they respected Corran more than they did him, but not too much. These guys were assholes, and their opinions mattered very little in the bigger scheme of things.

"Now, if you keep a southwestern heading, you'll encounter a mass of heat that we've picked up on the satellite feeds," Anderson informed them. "Keep your senses alert, though. There are many creatures in that mess of a jungle that don't show up on heat sensors. In fact, I'd go so far as to say that the most dangerous ones are those that don't show up."

"What was all that about keeping the comms clear of unnecessary chatter?" one of the voices asked with a laugh.

"Shut it, Patterson!" Corran snapped.

The colonel rubbed his temples. "That's Falcon Four to you, Falcon Leader."

"Oh...roger that, Overwatch," the man said and had the grace to sound chagrined.

Anderson shook his head. It really wasn't his problem if these dumbasses caught themselves in an international scandal while they ran an unsanctioned operation on foreign soil. They would simply be relocated and made to sit in some office in San Francisco until the heat cooled and they could operate out of the country again. It wasn't any trouble for him, so why did he stress so badly and insist that this mission went right and by the book?

Well, it was in his bones, he had to admit that. Any

mission that he was involved in had to go well, or it would be a lesson for him to obsess over and learn from for the next one. He might not have a next one after this debacle, but again, that wasn't his problem. If they found some cushy desk job for him too, he would be more than happy with that. It would mean he wouldn't have to travel all over the world and it meant he'd be home at a reasonable hour and attend soccer practices and piano recitals. Date night with the wife. No watching good men get killed over the profit margins of a company that had more lobbyists in Washington than there were politicians.

He also wanted this mission to go right because the last one had gone so poorly, he realized as he remembered the teams that had been sent home and those men who would be delayed since they couldn't be moved from where they were currently treated. And the one who wouldn't go home at all.

Why did that man have to die?

Anderson shook his head and closed his eyes. Let these guys have their fun. At least they weren't used to make sure the CIA had enough black-ops money to hide from the rest of the budget committees. Better that they were there, clearing out some of the bugs, lizards, and other awful creatures for the boys and girls in the Staging Area.

"We're making our approach now, Overwatch," Corran stated over the comms.

He checked the screen again. They had made decent time. Falcon team wasn't supposed to approach the spot indicated by satellite imaging as a large group of the Zoo creatures.

"Overwatch, my sensors pick up some automatic gunfire a short distance away," one of the men said softly.

"Roger that, Falcon Three. We pick that up on our end too," Anderson responded. It was difficult to determine the make and model of the gun used, but the clatter indicated that it had to be a power suit mounted model.

"Do we have any orders on how to proceed?" Falcon Two asked.

"They're probably only bounty hunters," Corran said but sounded distracted. "They have an open engagement protocol in effect on non-authorized personnel, right?"

"That's a positive, Falcon Leader," the colonel affirmed. "Although it would probably be best to keep the human casualties to a minimum. And make sure to identify whether they are hostiles or friendlies. We do have people from the Staging Area who run patrols in that area."

"Fine, spoilsport," one of the men growled.

"Shut it," Corran snapped. "Keep your sensors tuned and make sure that your Friend or Foe ID scanners are on at all times, understood?"

"Roger that."

Anderson could see from the HUD-mounted cameras that they all had their weapons out, and the FOF scanners were already engaged. It was a new system, one that worked off the ID chips that most of the military issued suits already contained. It would help to keep an eye out for civilians and the like in real application of the suits in war zones.

He wondered if these men had been selected to try these suits out because they were the ones who would use them out in the field. It made sense. The security companies that they worked for could always send the bill for the suits to the government and have the costs deducted from their taxes. It was such a common practice these days that Anderson wasn't even annoyed by the blatant corruption anymore.

Well, he was still annoyed. It had merely ceased to surprise him a long time ago.

"Weapons live, we have hostiles," Corran warned as a pair of the massive panthers hurtled from between the trees and attacked the five men in armor. The animals went down quickly, unsurprisingly, and the team leader motioned rapidly for them to proceed. Even though the state-of-the-art suits had voice isolation tech that would allow the men to talk without concern that hostiles would hear their voices, the hand motions were engrained in every inch of their DNA. They would probably continue to do it if they used nothing but these suits until the day they died.

Anderson knew that it wasn't good form to wish death on people who were supposed to be in his operation, but he really couldn't help himself. These guys were class-A assholes.

"I have a malfunction on my FOF ID scanner," one of the men reported.

"Roger that, same here," another said and tapped lightly on his helmet.

"It looks like the geeks back in the home office still have some bugs to iron out," Corran said with a touch of levity in his voice. "Disable the software and let's keep moving."

The colonel shook his head as he watched the FOF signals on the screens disappear one by one. The firing drew closer, and the men prepped their weapons for combat once more. The darkness of the jungle made it difficult to make anything out particularly clearly now.

"We have monsters," Falcon Two shouted. "Three o'clock."

Two of the team members shifted and opened fire on a group of massive locusts with stinger-pointed tails that charged forward.

At that moment, there seemed to be a convergence of the creatures. Orders were shouted, but gunfire and the monsters' roars from every angle quickly overpowered every other sound around them.

Anderson hated these bastards, but he had to admit that they were some of the best that he'd ever seen in the field. They didn't waste shots, downed one creature quickly before they targeted the next, and never focused on one hostile for more time than was necessary.

"We have humans, six o'clock," Falcon Three advised.

"They're shooting at us. Take them down," Corran bellowed.

"Belay that order—" Anderson shouted over the comms, but whether the sound was lost in the attack or if they simply ignored him became irrelevant. His order wasn't heard, and the group of five men in power armor suits were quickly shot down by the superior firepower of Falcon Team.

"Shit," the colonel cursed, but before he could reprimand Corran for acting without orders, one of the screens went dead. Screams echoed over the comms for a few moments before they faded into what might have been a whimper. The other screens pivoted to see what had happened while the remaining creatures seemed to beat a hasty retreat.

It was difficult to discern anything in the dark conditions. Four eyes were easy to see, though, as they reflected what little light that there was. The beast was long with a serpentine tail, but six legs protruded from what looked like a very mammalian body.

"What the fuck is that?" Falcon Three asked as the creature dug its talons easily into the new and improved armor. A massive jaw lowered quickly to crunch through Falcon Four's helmet. One last scream was heard before the man's body went limp.

Falcon Three shouted what sounded like a Samoan war cry and opened fire on the beast. It roared in response and the seven-meter-long tail whiplashed to crash into him. It tore easily into his armor around his neck. With a quick twist, it jerked the man's head off before he even had a chance to react.

"Open fire!" Corran screamed, and the two remaining members of Falcon Team emptied their clips at the creature. The bullets had an effect, but nothing significant until they finally shot into the long head. The creature opened its massive jaws to roar at them, and the soft tissue inside its mouth was immediately shredded by their fire. It screeched in pain, dropped back a few steps, and hit the ground with a heavy thud.

The two men worked quickly to reload their weapons, but before they could, another of the creatures, even larger than the first, swung silently from the trees above them. It landed without making a sound.

Unlike the dead one, though, this monster didn't seem

interested in them. Instead, it picked up the body of its kin and, before the men could reload, disappeared smoothly back into the jungle.

"What...the fuck was that?" Corran asked.

"Unknown," Bial said, his first communication since they'd started the mission. "There's no match for something like that in our databases."

"Your databases are fucking shit!" the team leader retorted belligerently." Get them updated ASAP."

"We can't," the scientist said. "This is an off-the-books operation. Any evidence has to be vetted by Pegasus before it can be released to the public."

"Whatever," the man snapped. "Diaz, let's get what we came here for and get the fuck out."

Anderson didn't have even the energy to tell them not to use their names on comms. It wasn't like anyone was listening. At least the engineers had fixed the problems of comms from inside the Zoo. There was little to no interference on their end right now.

He followed Corran's HUD camera as the man moved to the bodies of his men. He placed a beacon on them.

"You're not recovering them yourself?" Anderson asked.

"That's a negative, Overwatch," he replied coolly. "Our job is to collect the merchandise and get out. Recovering bodies is secondary, if that."

"What merchandise?" Anderson asked.

"That is on a need-to-know basis, Overwatch," Corran replied. He kept his tone even and clipped and looked to see what Falcon Two was doing.

Anderson switched to the man's footage to see that he had pushed the bodies of the men that they'd killed aside.

He held a digging implement in his hand and quickly ripped dirt and roots from the ground before he retrieved heavy chunks of metal and tossed them to Corran, who bagged them.

The colonel leaned in closer and narrowing his eyes. With the cameras reduced to night vision and motion sensors, it was difficult to tell the make and the model of the suits. They were all the same make, though. All uniform.

They were all military issue, he realized.

---

"You son of a bitch!" Anderson snarled.

Corran looked up from taking his helmet off in time for Anderson's fist to collide with his face. The suit of armor added an easy ton to the man's weight, and even without it, he wasn't small. Despite that, the rage that powered him produced an impact that knocked the operative back a few steps. He would have been on the ground if it weren't for the stabilizer units in the suit.

The result was that the team leader's head hung back for a few seconds as Falcon Two, the man who had been referred to as Diaz, quickly grabbed his gun and aimed it at Anderson.

"Come on then, asshole!" the colonel challenged and walked forward. The suits really were impressive, and it took all his willpower to not back away as the massive assault rifle was leveled against his head.

He was pissed enough that he didn't really care about that, not on a conscious level.

"Shoot me!" Anderson snapped and opened his arms as if to invite the shot. "It's not like you cunts care who the fuck you shoot at. Friend or foe, just gun him down!"

"Our FOF systems were down," Corran said, now recovered from Anderson's punch. "We couldn't tell who the guys were while we were in the middle of a firefight. It's unfortunate, but there wasn't anything we could do."

"Bullshit!" he roared, and his anger rippled through every inch of his six-foot-three frame. "The engineers ran a diagnostic on your suits once you came back into range. There was no malfunction. You fucking turned the systems off."

The man opened his mouth to say something but shut it again and shook his head before he waved at Diaz to lower his weapon. The man growled a protest, clearly unwilling to let the punch pass without some payback, but he followed the order.

"We were protecting proprietary Pegasus property," Corran said, his voice soft and even as he began to remove the rest of his armor. "We were authorized by the US government to do so regardless of who intruded on the acquisition and covert nature of our operation. No exceptions."

"What the fuck are you talking about?" Anderson said.

"It's in the updated contracts," the team leader explained as he pulled his breastplate off. "Fine print. You should read it. Either way, your hurt feelings do you credit, Colonel, but unfortunately, I don't have the time to deal with them. We've already been called back, and another operation will be mounted to recover the men and the armor we left behind. We got what we came here for, and that's what matters."

"Matters to who?" Anderson asked, his voice cold.

"To me, for one," Corran said with a nod. "To Pegasus, for two. And that's really all you need to know. Write up a report about what happened, and it will immediately be classified and redacted. Do what you want. I really don't give a shit." The man looked at some of the engineers who had come out to see the confrontation. "Don't fucking stand there, folks. Come on and help me out with this armor."

The colonel turned away, disgust roiling in the pit of his stomach. He knew how this would go. He needed to submit a report about what happened, but Corran was right. Any results and witness statements from this operation would be vetted by Pegasus before they were released to the Pentagon, which meant that nothing would change. The suits would be sold for the use of men like Corran, and Anderson would return to his office to file the paperwork.

"Fucking bullshit!" he roared once he was inside his room. He snatched up the mug that he'd left on his bedside table and threw it across the room. The ceramic shattered against the prefab surface, but there had been no coffee in it, so it merely dropped to the ground in dry, unsatisfying fragments.

# CHAPTER THIRTY-FIVE

They were headed back into the Zoo. While it was perhaps too soon, it really wasn't that difficult a decision to make. Teams had to go in to support the people still in there collecting data, so it was only natural that those folks who had to return early were given another chance.

In the meantime, of course, they still had a shit ton of booze that they needed to get off their hands, so Sal called Kennedy to hire a vehicle to carry their product and take it to the bar and arranged to meet her there.

She'd told him that she would arrive at fifteen hundred. It was fifteen minutes past, and Sal checked his watch a little impatiently. He supposed that he should be used to her showing up fashionably late to anything that didn't involve a trip back into the Zoo, but it still irked him for some reason. No matter what his own personal habits, his parents had made sure that he knew that being on time was something that wasn't up for discussion. Being late was money that you wasted without getting anything back, was what his mother always told him.

Needless to say, Sal had been late all the time as a kid and even deep into his teens before he got the picture. Now, he was angry at others for making the same mistake that he had.

A bit hypocritical? Sure. Would he stop doing it? No.

The sound of a vehicle caught his attention and announced Kennedy's arrival a few minutes before she rounded the corner. She drove slower than she usually did and steered the vehicle carefully within the lines. Sal didn't have to guess at the reason for the extraordinary care. There was six thousand dollars' worth of booze in the back.

He smirked as she pulled in close and put the vehicle in park before she dragged at the emergency brake.

"What?" she asked and scrambled out.

"I should have known that the only way to get you to drive carefully was to put some booze in the back," he said with a laugh.

"Not just booze," Kennedy said. "It's an investment. I drown in alcohol, but I'm careful with stuff that makes me money."

Sal stopped laughing and nodded. "That's a good point, I'll admit."

She regarded him with narrowed eyes. "Okay. Well, where's our buyer? Wasn't he supposed to be on time?"

"What's that, kettle?" he asked and leaned forward. "Calling the pot black, now, are we?"

"What the hell are you talking about?"

He shrugged. "Nothing. But he's the one doing us a

favor here, so he's allowed to be fashionably late—especially since he has a business to run."

Madigan rolled her eyes but immediately adjusted her behavior when their client stepped out from the back door of the bar. He was an older man, at least by Sal's standards, and his full, thick beard sported as much gray as brown. That, combined with the sharp army haircut and the powerful build, told of his time with the military.

Some might call it the perfect salt-and-pepper look, and it was supposedly very sexy. Sal could personally take it or leave it, and there wasn't much that he could say about it. Him acting jealous would be insanely hypocritical on his part right now.

Even so, he couldn't resist the tiniest twinge when the man gripped Kennedy's outstretched hand firmly. He wondered if there were classes one could take for hand-shaking. If there were, they were probably in the same building where they taught guys how to grow their beards and trim their hair like that.

"Sergeant Kennedy," the man said in a deep, sensual voice. "It's odd to see you out here without my having to send you away myself."

"Yeah, laugh it up, Spencer," she said with a chuckle. "I seem to recall you being as drunk as me when you try to throw me out."

Sal waited for the banter to stop before the man turned and offered his hand. "It's Dr. Jacobs, right? I see you in here all the time with the sergeant."

"It's not 'doctor,'" he said with a smile. After a few seconds, Sal retrieved his hand with a dull ache in the bones.

"Well, I've heard folks talk about you two working together, and they seem okay with calling you 'doctor.'"

"That's nice of you to say."

Spencer smiled and nodded. "Well, you folks called this meeting. How can I help you?"

"We were recently over at the Russian base for operations," Sal said, "and it turns out that they have a small business that offers decent Russian-grown vodka that they're selling cheaply."

"Is that so? Do you mind if I make the judgment for myself?"

Kennedy pulled a bottle from one of the crates. Impressively, it still sported the seal. She handed it to him.

"So...are you giving bottles away, or what?" Spencer asked and looked at the two of them.

"Let's say that if you like the taste, you can buy it along with however many crates you want," Sal said. "If you're not interested, you can keep that bottle by way of an apology for us wasting your time."

"That's might reasonable of you." The man smiled, ripped the seal off, and popped the cap before he took a firm swig straight from the bottle. Sal raised his eyebrows, but Kennedy didn't look at all shocked at his actions.

"Oh, wow," Spencer growled and took another look at the glass bottle. "That's some good shit right there."

"That's what I've heard," Sal said with a smile.

"How much of this do you have to sell?" he asked.

"We've got...ten?" Sal confirmed with Kennedy—and to be sure that she hadn't taken any personal tastes of the product herself—before he turned to the bar owner. "Ten cases of twenty bottles each."

"Really?" Spencer asked.

"Yeah, they were cheaper if bought in bulk," he said quickly.

"Oh...well, that makes sense," Spencer said. "How much are you selling them for?"

"We thought somewhere along the lines of forty bucks a bottle," Kennedy said before Sal could.

"The stuff is good," he hedged, "but since it's not a known brand, I don't know that I'll be able to sell it."

"We all know that's bullshit, Spence." Kennedy folded her arms.

"Right, but it still won't be as popular as the established brands," he protested.

"What kind of price can you give us?" Sal asked.

"Well, considering that the two of you are my best customers, and if you promise to ask for a shot of this stuff each time you come in..." Spencer tilted his head and made some mental calculations. "I can take all ten cases off your hands for...let's say thirty-five bucks a bottle?"

Sal glanced at his partner. They would net a little under a thousand bucks in profit, but since they were together in this, he would need her to sign off on it too. She shrugged and nodded.

"That sounds like a plan," Sal said. "Do you want an invoice?"

"Not really," Spencer said. "I think I have seven grand in the safe inside. Cash isn't a problem for you guys, right?"

"I...don't think so." Kennedy shrugged and glanced at Sal, who shook his head.

"Does that mean no, no cash, or no, cash isn't a problem?"

"Cash isn't a problem," Sal explained.

"Excellent." The man smiled broadly. "I'll go inside to get the cash and some guys to help carry this stuff in."

About a half hour later, Sal and Kennedy drove away with a small pouch containing a stack of dollar bills.

"I guess we're good at this whole booze-selling business," she said with a grin.

He nodded. "I mean, we could probably work with a more established line of supply. Maybe undercut all of Spencer's other vodka suppliers and—"

"We're getting ahead of ourselves." She laughed. "This was a quick way to make some pocket money which turned out…really literally."

Sal nodded. "Well…congrats on your first pocket money sale. And not drinking any of the vodka while it was at your place."

"Again, it was an investment," Kennedy retorted. "I don't drink money, Sal, that's not good business. Now, let's get some sleep. We have to leave early tomorrow."

# CHAPTER THIRTY-SIX

S ome might call him crazy. Others might use the word wuss or coward, but he still didn't like to head out into the jungle with only the two specialists. They could handle themselves, and with Kennedy to cover their backs, they were more likely to survive than most, but it was still a risk. This was a jungle full of plants and animals that wanted them as dead as possible and came up with new and inventive ways of making that happen all the time.

But company matters required that they run alone a couple of times. They'd hitched a ride with one of the teams that headed in to support the people on the research operation. There had been news that an entire squad had gone missing, so numbers needed to be bolstered with anyone they could get their hands on. Sal, Courtney, and Kennedy made the cut, and so they were out there again in less than two days after they'd returned from the last trip.

The squad they went in with didn't much care that they broke away inside the Zoo once Sal pointed them in the direction of the largest Pita concentration in the quadrant. There was the usual warning that if they weren't back in time, they would be left behind to walk all the way back to the Staging Area through the desert.

Kennedy didn't like walking. Sal knew all her complaints by heart and was tired of hearing them, so he would make sure that their little expedition didn't take too long. They were still on the payroll of the sponsors, so anything that they came across would only add to what others had already found. He maintained a wary watchfulness and kept his weapon primed. They hadn't run into any trouble five hours in, and that made him decidedly nervous. He didn't like trouble, but when it took a long time to arrive, it usually meant that what was coming was bad.

"Is it just me," Courtney asked as she took bark samples from a new kind of tree, "or is this place getting creepier?"

"Define creepier," Kennedy replied and held her weapon at the ready. All her motion sensors were set to the highest level.

"I don't know how to say it, precisely," Monroe continued as she bagged her samples. "It's like the faster the Zoo expands, the less earthly it is. Like whatever makes it grow this fast also makes it more and more alien. With each transformation, it seems to become more industrious and determined to break down the DNA and recreate it into newer and more horrifying monsters."

"It's not only about monsters, you know," Sal said. "There've been studies that show that the greenhouse gasses have taken a significant downturn across the globe, and the radiation levels in locations like Chernobyl and even in Japan are starting to drop to unprecedented levels."

"Do you really think that this is causing that?" She packed up the samples that she had collected and turned to rejoin them.

"There's nothing certain about it yet," he said. "But the drops seem to correlate with the times of the sudden growth spurts in the Zoo. There is implied causation in that kind of correlation."

"So what?" Kennedy asked as they set off once more. "Are you telling me that this goop is the answer to problems like global warming and radiation disasters or something? And the only price to pay is that this same goop still seems intent on killing all of us in the process?"

"It's more complicated than that," Sal explained. "And we'd need access to the records of what they studied about the goop before it became the Zoo to arrive at any definitive theories."

Courtney nodded. "They isolated all the different research projects, and once they were cut off, everything was heavily classified. It was bullshit, but I guess I wouldn't want something like this to hit the open market just yet either."

"Yeah, that might have been a good call," Kennedy said and aimed her weapon at the admittedly creepy jungle all around them.

She realized that Sal had come to a stop, his weapon leveled at a shady spot among the trees. The three of them looked in that direction, and after a moment, they saw that the shadow moved. The black fur was barely visible in the tiny beams of light that filtered down from the leaf cover.

A few seconds later, the massive panther saw the three humans. The four stared at each other in a deer-in-head-lights moment. Something long was clenched in the creature's jaws. It resembled a chunk of an animal that it had possibly hunted.

The panther lowered its head and put its food down before it turned to face the three humans and moved forward slowly to study them intently. After a few steps, it crouched as if it was about to pounce. Its lips lifted to reveal the long fangs that dripped with venom.

The jaws snapped open. A powerful roar echoed through the jungle around them, but was suddenly cut off by the sound of a single gunshot. The round went through the creature's open mouth and out the back of the skull. It dropped to the ground without a whimper.

Sal turned instinctively. A light trail of smoke drifted from the barrel of Kennedy's gun.

"What was that?" he asked.

"Sorry." She shook her head. "Pure instinct. I saw those big poison fangs and pulled the trigger."

He wanted to berate her for killing an animal that hadn't attacked them, but he couldn't honestly say that he wouldn't have done the same. He remembered that his first kill in the Zoo had been one of those panthers. He'd saved Lynch's life using a scalpel that had been in his pack. Instincts remained. He didn't want to have to face one of those bastards one on one like that again.

"Do you want to go investigate?" Kennedy asked.

Sal shrugged. "Sure, why not?"

They moved to where the massive panther sprawled on

the ground. She crouched beside the corpse and patted the fur gently.

"Sorry, big guy," she said softly. Sal and Courtney both heard her, but neither wanted to give her any grief for showing a soft side.

Monroe moved to what the panther had dropped before it turned to face them. She had thought that it was the remnant of a meal that it was saving for later. Leopards and panthers were known to hide their food up in the trees so that they could return to it.

As she came closer, though, she realized that the chunk had a metallic sheen, and of all the animals that they'd run into, none had metal for armor. Some had exoskeletons, even when they weren't even based on insects or arachnids, but never metallic.

This wasn't a Zoo animal, she realized. It was a leg. A human leg still encased in armor.

"Holy shit," she breathed and dropped to her knees. Sal, who had taken a defensive position while both his partners were engaged in investigation, hurried forward.

"Is that a leg?" he asked, his eyes narrowed.

"It is," Courtney confirmed and pushed the leg in his direction. "The armor isn't standard military, though."

"It's not Russian either," Kennedy observed. "They don't make them that sleek."

"It looks light," Sal added. "That should weigh a ton, but you pushed it easily."

Courtney nodded, annoyed that she hadn't noticed that herself. "I've looked at armor suits over the past couple of days, and I haven't seen any of them designed like this."

"A prototype, maybe?" he asked. "We weren't informed about any field testing in this area."

"It's a leg," Kennedy said and shook her head. "Whoever it belonged to could have been killed anytime, anywhere."

"We'll have to pull it out, won't we?" Monroe asked in a disgusted tone. "Thank God that this new suit is fitted with air filters, otherwise I'd be gagging right now."

Sal smirked, and Madigan scowled at him. He didn't see her but thankfully refrained from any jokes for the moment, even without her warning.

Courtney retrieved a couple of tools from her pack and as she moved around the leg to try and tug the leg out, she suddenly saw something move and jumped out of the way.

"Oh, fuck!" she gasped as Sal and Kennedy both aimed their weapons at a patch of black that moved through the bushes. They relaxed marginally when something small and fuzzy with black fur leapt from the undergrowth and bared unformed fangs at the three of them.

"What…the fuck is that?" Kennedy asked. She held her weapon raised but removed her finger from the trigger.

"That…looks like a venomous panther cub," Sal said. "I didn't know they had cubs. We haven't encountered any young creatures around here before, right?"

"There aren't any on record," Courtney said and shook her head in disbelief.

The tiny panther, which was the size of a beagle, circled the three of them and found the corpse. The little one nudged it, meowing pitifully.

"Well, crap," Kennedy muttered. "Like I don't feel shitty enough."

Sal patted her gently on her armored shoulder.

Monroe, in the meantime, went back to work on the leg and tugged gently at the limb that was still stuck inside. She made a disgusted noise when what came out didn't look much like a leg anymore. The basic skeletal structure remained, of course, but the meat had already begun to peel from the bones and disgusting red goo seeped from the flesh.

"There are signs of tearing," Courtney said softly. "It looks like this limb was ripped off. I can't really tell if it was pre or...post mortem. Guys?"

Kennedy had dropped down next to the cub and ran her armored hands gently across its neck. It snarled at her and turned to bite. The weak fangs sank into her armor but didn't get very far, and there was no sign of the milky venom.

"I'm sorry, little buddy," she said and raised her arm, but the cub already had vice-like jaws and lifted with her arm.

"That's fucking adorable," Sal said, unable to resist a broad grin.

"We have to take him back, right?" Kennedy asked. "Oh...her back, rather."

"Why?" Courtney asked as she still tugged chunks of leg from inside the armor.

"Well, we killed the mother," Madigan said in a tone that implied that she thought the question was beyond stupid. "She would die if we left her out here on her own. Besides, we haven't seen any sign of young or reproduction. If we took her back, she would be the first live animal we were able to bring back from the Zoo."

Sal nodded. "It sounds like a good call to me. As long as you feed, water, and potty train her—"

"Shut up, Jacobs," Kennedy growled. She drew the small creature against her chest and rubbed her gently behind the ears. "I'll call her Shuri."

"Shuri?" Courtney asked.

Sal faked a tear on his helmet. "I'm so proud. You do listen."

"I do not," Madigan snarled. "Everyone and their mothers have seen those movies."

He shrugged and turned back to Courtney. "What have you found out about that leg?"

She shook her head. "This metal isn't like anything I've seen before. It's light, it's hard, and I haven't been able to remove any of the plates."

"Can't we simply take the leg?" Kennedy asked.

"It's light, but not that light—still in the two-hundred-kilogram region, so unless you want to lug it around and explain it to the guys at the Staging Area when we get back—"

"Just take a sample and tag it with a GPS marker," Sal said impatiently. "We'll see if we can't come back and pick it up on a later run or send someone to do that for us."

Courtney nodded. There were a couple of chunks that had been torn off by whatever it was that had severed the leg. It still took some work to free the pieces, but she bagged them and sealed them in her pack.

"Okay, let's head back," Sal said. "I'm sure that they'll understand if we get back early again and if not...well, we'll bring the first live specimen back from the Zoo."

"The first?" Kennedy asked. "Really?"

"Yes, the first," Sal said firmly, and she nodded quickly in understanding.

"Let's get on out of here," he announced. "You keep an eye on the tiny thing. She's your responsibility."

"Yes, boss." Kennedy snapped a quick salute. "And her name is Shuri."

"Whatever," he said and shook his head.

# CHAPTER THIRTY-SEVEN

It took most of the day to reach the JLTVs, and after a quick discussion, Kennedy said that they had enough space in one vehicle to carry the rest of their squad out, so Sal signed off to take the extra one to transport them back to the Staging Area. They had little resistance since they carried some very valuable cargo.

Sal had to listen during the whole ride back to what Kennedy thought of him for calling Shuri cargo.

When they arrived and had to declare what they had found, Shuri was the talk of the commandant's office. A location to keep live animals had been set up when the Staging Area had first been built, but the problem with actually acquiring live animals had left the place to fall into disrepair over the year and a half since then. It took considerable time for them to register her since the company officials tried to make the argument that since Shuri had been recovered on their company's time, she should belong to them.

Sal responded by advising them that Heavy Metal now

waived the financial compensation for all teams sent in on the fact-recovering mission.

The lawyer left in a huff when he realized that he'd been out-lawyered by a twenty-two-year-old doctoral candidate.

In the meantime, they were told that it would take a few hours before the holding locations could be prepared to host any live animals, and Sal asked if he could break away early. They didn't need three people to keep an eye on Shuri, who had been given a bottle of warm milk and a small cage to rest in. The furball had obviously had a long day and was fast asleep in fifteen minutes.

Kennedy agreed, and Sal headed on home. He'd told her that he would work on whitepapers, but the fact that he picked up the shards that Courtney had collected from the leg armor revealed that he had lied.

Neither Courtney nor Kennedy complained, though, as they sat in silence and waited for someone to come to tell them where they could take Shuri to spend the night.

"You know," Monroe said softly, "Shuri doesn't need two people to stick around with her either."

Madigan looked up from where she performed some repairs of her own on a piece of her armor.

"What are you talking about?" she asked and set both the piece and her tools down.

"Well, I wanted to head over to talk to Sal about the piece of armor we recovered," Courtney said. "Plus some... other things."

Kennedy immediately grinned. "Hey now, I want to talk to him about Shuri...and other stuff too."

"But you brought Shuri back," Courtney argued. "She's

bonded to you and—yeah, I know, that's bullshit. I couldn't even finish that sentence."

Kennedy grinned. "So how do we decide this? Rock, paper, scissors?"

Monroe thought about it for a few seconds and finally nodded. "Sure. Best two out of three?"

Madigan nodded, and they raised their hands. Courtney won the first one with paper beats rock, but the other woman quickly took the next two with a rock and scissors win in succession.

"Fuck," the loser muttered.

"You have a tell," Kennedy said with a smirk and pushed from her seat.

"A tell? In rock, paper, scissors?" Courtney asked skeptically.

"Absolutely." She headed toward the door.

"Hey, Madigan," Courtney called, "would you mind if I showed up after Shuri is tucked in for the night?"

Kennedy glanced at her for a second and shook her head. "Sorry, I don't think I'm there yet."

She nodded and looked away when the panther cub woke with their talking and now stared at her with huge, black eyes.

"No, it's not that," she said like she could read the tiny cub's mind. "Of course we want to hang out with you. It's just...we'd like to hang out with Sal, too."

Shuri tilted her head and meowed softly before she rested it between her paws once more.

Sal opened the door, surprised to see Madigan there and changed into her civilian clothes.

"Hey," he grunted as she pushed into the house without waiting for an invitation. "What are you doing here? Is everything okay with Shuri?"

"Huh?" She looked blankly at him. "Oh, yeah. Courtney's looking after her. We thought it might be a while, and we didn't need two people watching her, so she let me go."

"That was...nice of her?" he said. It was interesting to sleep with two women. Both knew that he was sleeping with the other, and both seemed to be on talking terms with it. He was in uncharted territory, though, and he wasn't sure what to make of it.

"What are you up to?" Madigan asked and fixed him with an enquiring look as he shut the door again.

"Oh, apparently, Shuri's arrival has made some waves, even at this hour," Sal said and moved back into his room. She noted that he'd set up what looked like an intensely improvised lab around the chunks of metal pried from the leg of armor.

"What kind of waves?" she asked and sat on the bed while he resumed his place in his "lab.?

"The...money spending kind, actually," he replied with a chuckle. "It's been...what, three hours since we announced her arrival, and I've received fifteen messages from companies who want a crack at studying the first animal to be brought in from the Zoo." Madigan opened her mouth and Sal waved her off. "No, don't worry, I made sure to let them know that a shitload of contracts against animal cruelty would have to be signed before any kind of deal could be struck. It turned out that I had so many offers for exclusivity, I put it up for auction."

Sal pulled his phone from his pocket and unlocked it before he tossed it to her.

"Holy shit," Madigan said with a laugh. "The bid is at three million and still climbing."

"Yeah," he said. "You know, I've been thinking while I worked that we might need some new digs. A real lab and an actual, proper base of operations of our own. If these guys are serious about paying that much for Shuri, I think that's what we should invest in."

Kennedy nodded. "It would be nice not to have to store our equipment in our homes."

He nodded. "Right? I mean, I know Heavy Metal is mostly about us working without government interference all up in our asses, but...I don't know, I've had some thoughts that maybe we should make it something bigger, something more than only about money, you know?"

Madigan nodded and lay on the bed. She had arrived with the intention to get him naked and on top of her, but with him this excited, she assumed that he wouldn't notice if she stripped down and gave him a lap dance.

A part of her resented the reality that her plans would have to be shelved, but this was a part of him that she actually liked. He was passionate about these things, and while right now, it meant that she would probably not move him from that chair, it wasn't something that she would ever want him to change about himself.

Sal seemed oblivious to her thoughts as she suspected he might be.

"While I wait for the money guys to top themselves

out," Sal said, "I've looked at these pieces of metal that Courtney recovered. The mineral composition seems to have had some work, but once I've isolated the different minerals involved, it's…well, impossible."

He looked at her and Madigan nodded. She did that sometimes—simply tuned out all the science talk but didn't want it to seem like she was ignoring him, so she nodded when he expected an answer from her. He knew that she wasn't that interested in what he had to say, and he appreciated that she let him talk.

And he really wanted to talk about this.

"There are some hints of silicon and steel in there, but there's nothing that can bond iron to silicon among the known elements. But here it is. The molecules are bonded by something that allows the steel to retain structural integrity while it allows the silicon to fill in the gaps. That makes it less dense and…well, stronger. It's hard to say how it's possible, but the evidence is right here."

Sal didn't wait for her to respond this time. "I'm trying to study the bonding mineral, but in my defense, all I really have to use is the microscope function in my helmet's HUD, so there's not much that I can do. Either way, it looks crystalline and is obviously a bonding agent, which you would think is impossible since the two are usually mutually exclusive in nature. I'd like some closer looks at this and maybe to find someone more qualified, like a metallurgist. Still, even a better, good-quality microscope would probably be…best…"

His voice trailed off as he turned and saw that Madigan lay on his bed. She'd brought her knees up near her chest, and her eyes were shut. Well, he supposed that he should be used to putting women to sleep these days.

Sleep. That was probably a good idea right now anyway. The people running their auction wouldn't be finished any time soon, and there really wasn't much that he could realistically do with the pieces of armor at this point.

Sal pulled his shirt off and turned out the light, careful to climb into bed without waking Madigan. He draped his blanket over her shoulder and curled up himself. It had been a long day. A good day, but definitely tiring. It wasn't long before his eyes shut as well, and he was fast asleep.

---

Sal groaned. Something tugged and jerked at him. He rumbled a protest. He didn't want to wake up. Let him sleep. He could look at stuff later. Whitepapers could wait, dammit!

Finally, he realized that he wasn't asleep and wasn't likely to be so again unless he addressed whatever it was that had woken him up.

His eyes snapped open, and he pushed himself up to lean on his elbows to see what was happening. The first thing he noticed was that he must have had some of the best kind of dreams since he was rock hard and tented the shorts that he'd fallen asleep in.

The second thing he noticed was that Madigan had moved from his side and now laid between his thighs. She nuzzled her nose and lips gently against his cock through the fabric as her hands worked desperately to get the shorts down.

"Madie?" he asked tentatively.

"Yeah?" She lifted her head, which marked the first time that she'd ever responded to the shortened version of her first name.

"What are you doing?"

She shrugged and continued to tug at his shorts. "I noticed that you were rocking some morning wood and I suddenly wanted you in my mouth. Do you think you can help me?"

Sal pushed himself up higher. "Are you naked?"

She shook her head.

"Get naked."

Madigan huffed with frustration. she rolled off the bed, yanked her shirt and pants off, then her panties, which she tossed at him. In the meantime, he had pulled his shorts down and kicked them the rest of the way off. She settled back onto the bed with a hungry smile as she leaned in and wrapped her lips around his head.

"Fuck," he gasped, and his head dropped back. At least he wasn't asleep for this one.

# EPILOGUE

Five point two million dollars.

Sal had never thought to see that much money in his whole life, much less a single payout.

Now that they had successfully cut the government out of their business, not much of it vanished into government coffers. Of course, there had been some provisos and conditions, one of which Kennedy had absolutely demanded. It was that they be allowed to see and visit Shuri while she remained in the Staging Area. Considering that she was a Zoo creature whose venomous fangs were already in place and developing venom, she wasn't likely to be moved anytime soon.

Sure, the condition had knocked three hundred thousand from the price, but Pegasus hadn't been too difficult. That was the company that had paid out the massive amount to have the first shot at running tests—all animal-friendly, they were assured—and made things incredibly interesting for Heavy Metal.

Upgrades for the suits came first, of course.

After a few days of scouting, Sal had found a location that would work for them to set up shop in. It had been built by another similar startup that had also come into a lot of money. They had unfortunately lost a couple of their money makers to the Zoo, and things had unraveled since then. The remaining members wanted to get rid of the property as quickly as possible. It had taken three months of negotiation, but they were anxious to jump on Sal's offer of two million dollars for the whole operation, including the pair of heavy-duty JLTVs and the fully operational lab that had been built in the property.

The fact that it was right up against Wall Two and about an hour's drive away from the Staging Area was probably why the price was that low, Sal realized as he inspected their new complex.

Well, it would help with Kennedy's drinking problem, he mused. A decent tradeoff.

On top of a warehouse which had space to park both vehicles, there were three offices and five personal apartments, one of which was penthouse quality with three bedrooms. There was also an industrial kitchen much like the one at the Staging Area's mess hall, as well as an enclosed area to grow fresh vegetables.

Sal's attention was diverted when Kennedy pushed one of their new JLTVs faster than it was intended to go. He gritted his teeth when he heard her redline the engine across the road and skid as she entered the path that led to their new complex.

She screeched to a halt some ten meters from where he stood and engulfed him in a cloud of yellow dust. He coughed and waved his hand to dispel the sand as best he could.

"Sorry!" Kennedy called as she cut the engine. "I've had so much fun in our new vehicles. 'Our new vehicles.' Fuck, that has a nice ring to it, doesn't it?"

"Damn straight," he said with a grin. "Did you get all the papers signed?"

"Oh, yeah," she said and handed him the ownership papers. "That includes all the different stuff that comes with it. The vehicles, lab equipment...the works. Of course, they insisted on the whole payment up front."

Sal nodded. "It makes sense, considering the line of work we're in. So, that plus closing our contracts for living in the Staging Area, as well as signing on for a decent satellite connection out here... The company's bank account looks a lot lighter than before."

"It's worth it for a halfway decent internet connection," Kennedy said with a chuckle. "I'm sick and tired of having to rely on the Staging Area's fucking database connection."

"True story," he agreed. "Even so, five point two million goes so damned fast."

She smirked and nodded as she moved beside him to look at their new complex.

"Ask me for anything but time," he lamented and squeezed her shoulder. "Come on, we have a lot of work to do."

# AUTHOR NOTES - MICHAEL ANDERLE

## DECEMBER 26, 2018

THANK YOU for not only reading this story but these *Author Notes* as well.

(I think I've been good with always opening with "thank you." If not, I need to edit the other *Author Notes*!)

RANDOM (*sometimes*) THOUGHTS?

Wow, Christmas is finished and all through the house,

Practically no one is stirring...

*Not even my spouse.*

Until a few minutes from now, when we are going to go see Mortal Engines. :-)

I'm excited to see the movie not because of the story, but because of the visuals. The special effects look damned cool and I wonder how they are going to pull some of it off. I think it looks like a version of pirates on land, personally.

I've never read the books (I'm assuming the story came from a book series, but that might just be my bias that all stories come from books.)

I hope that YOU are having a peaceful holiday season (if you are reading this on release day, welcome to 2019!)

Or maybe, you are reading this with a hangover. If that is the case, I suggest lots of water and two ibuprofen. I'm told this is good for hangovers.

I wouldn't personally know, I have headaches from weather changes (yes, I'm that kind of person) not from drinking too much.

## HOW TO MARKET FOR BOOKS YOU LOVE

We are able to support our efforts with you reading our books, and we appreciate you doing this!

If you enjoyed this or ANY book by any author, especially Indie-published, we always appreciate if you make the time to review a book, since it lets other readers who might be on the fence to take a chance on it as well.

## AROUND THE WORLD IN 80 DAYS

One of the interesting (at least to me) aspects of my life is the ability to work from anywhere and at any time. In the future, I hope to re-read my own *Author Notes* and remember my life as a diary entry.

### La Puente, California

This city is about 30 minutes outside of LA on a good day. An hour in traffic (or more) on a bad day. For the first time in my life, I've had rye grass put down on the lawn and it looks damned good.

I come from Texas, and we use a lot of carpet grass there. So, winter is often a very brown lawn. To have a green lawn in December is just damned odd to me.

Very odd.

However, I like it! It took about a month of growing, but the little blades are about 2.5-3" tall already and the big patches of dead grass (my lawn looked like a case of mange had hit it) are all hidden for a few months, now.

The weather is cool but not cold, so not ridiculous tonight and I am looking forward to going out after a few business calls and some minor publishing jobs (like writing these author notes.)

We were successful publishing six (6) ZOO books in December, and have seven (7) lined up for January.

I've been told that the JIT readers (*thank you all for helping!*) enjoyed this story, so that was fun. Especially after the sex scene caught a few by surprise in the last book.

*Oops?*

The pen name for this book is Michael Todd. The reasons for choosing Michael Todd are many, but one of the main ones has to do with the sexual content of the stories. In a Michael Anderle book, if we have any sex scenes it fades to black.

*(Kind of like if a restaurant sells Pepsi instead of Coke in a Kurtherian Gambit. book, it fades to black...)*

With Michael Todd books, there is a tendency to be a bit more graphic with the jokes and the ... um.... Horizontal Olympics.

Coming (no pun intended) in book 03 next month we have a situation occur which challenges Salinger and the new team, causing us to lose a contact and of course, it's a blender of blood out in the ZOO...

So you know that some people are going to die.

FAN PRICING

If you would like to find out what LMBPN is doing and the books we will be publishing, just sign up at http://lmbpn.com/email/. When you sign up, we notify you of books coming out for the week, any new posts of interest in the books and pop culture arena, and the fan pricing on Saturday.

Ad Aeternitatem,

Michael Anderle

# CONNECT WITH MICHAEL TODD

Want more?

Find us On Facebook

https://www.facebook.com/Protected-by-the-Damned-193345908061855/

# OTHER BOOKS BY MICHAEL TODD

**PROTECTED BY THE DAMNED UNIVERSE**

PROTECTED BY THE DAMNED*

8 Book series

WAR OF THE DAMNED*

8 Book series

DAMIAN'S CHRONICLES*

4 Book series

WAR OF THE ANGELS*

8 Book series

**ZOO UNIVERSE**

BIRTH OF HEAVY METAL*

10 Book series

APOCALYPSE PAUSED*

12 Book series

SOLDIER OF FAME AND FORTUNE*

12 Book series

TEAM SAVAGE *

3 Book series

Dungeon Core TV*
6 Book series

Dungeon Rails*
3 Book series

Hellspawned Chronicles*
3 Book series

The Sheva Chronicles*
6 Book series

Unlikely Bountyhunters*
6 Book series

House Drakonnen

The Accord

The Anchor's Inheritance Saga

* DENOTES COMPLETED SERIES